Praise for *Red House*

A *Washington Pos*

"Ken Wishnia is a te
frank, fresh, funny, an   written."
—Barbara D'Amato, author of *Other Eyes*

"Ken Wishnia is a ventriloquist and a magician. *Red House* is
wry, dry, and seriously funny, a stellar addition to a highly
regarded series." —John Westermann, author of *Exit Wounds*

"Ken Wishnia's detective is smart, funny, offbeat,
and angry. This is a book for your inner bitch."
—Elaine Viets, author of the Dead-End Job series

"Smart dialogue, a realistic and gritty depiction of New
York, and the sensitive exploration of environmental,
racial, and economic issues make this another
great read in an energetic series." —*Booklist*

"An engaging character with [a] wry sense
of humor. The jam-packed plot makes for
an exciting story." —*Publishers Weekly*

"[Wishnia's] word play is as sharp as his social conscience,
and he has created a wonderfully intelligent and human
voice for his protagonist. She can move from angry to
funny to obscene in a handful of sentences, then climb
back out of the gutter to take on the big boys again
without hesitation. If only Buscarsela were real, the
world would be a better place." —*Washington Post*

RED HOUSE

Kenneth Wishnia

Red House
© 2014 Kenneth Wishnia
This edition © 2014 PM Press

ISBN: 978–1–60486–402–1
Library of Congress Control Number: 2013911530

Cover: John Yates / www.stealworks.com
Interior design by briandesign

10 9 8 7 6 5 4 3 2 1

PM Press
PO Box 23912
Oakland, CA 94623
www.pmpress.org

Printed in the USA, by the Employee Owners of Thomson-Shore
in Dexter, Michigan.
www.thomsonshore.com

To my parents
who will raise a fuss if I don't
dedicate at least one more book to them

INTRODUCTION

In detective fiction, there's an accepted set of rules: The dead body on the first page; the single-minded PI who puts everything aside in pursuit of that one case; the clean, simple story arc, the escalating body count; the ending that explains all, leaves nothing hanging, and gives everyone what they deserve.

As a longtime reader and writer of detective novels, I'm fine with the rules. I've read many a great book that follows them to the letter and have had no complaints. That said, there's nothing more impressive to me than a writer who can successfully break them—and Ken Wishnia proves himself to be exactly that with the fourth book in his wonderful Filomena Buscarsela series, *Red House*.

Forget about the dead body on the first page. We don't see one here until quite a bit further into the novel. But rest assured, there's lots to occupy us in the pages before. In this gritty, chaotic, and refreshingly real-feeling work of crime fiction, there are guns drawn and drugs consumed. There are sleazy lawyers and racist cops and shifty bootleggers and innumerable sticky and legally ambiguous situations navigated by our plucky heroine "Fil" so that, by the time the stiff makes its appearance, the reader feels a part of *Red House*'s world.

A wildly unpredictable world it is, too, with the first-person, present-tense narrative heightening the feeling that at any given time, anything can happen.

Early in the book, Fil finds herself at an affordable housing rally with her twelve-year-old daughter Antonia. It seems business as usual, Fil chatting with her daughter and making sharp observations on the goings-on, as well as introducing a new character (and the rally's star) Manny Morales, "an iron-pumping, hell-raising housing advocate." The reader is lulled into thinking it's a scene about Manny and the rally until a man in the crowd—the previously mild-mannered Sonny Tesoro—apparently angered by frequent police harassment, pulls a gun on the cops. And the tone changes fast.

Urged by Sonny's wife, Filomena sets out to find the real reason for his violent outburst. That search—which leads her through a maze of corruption involving a building occupied by squatters—could have easily served as the only plot thread in the book. But actually, it's part of an elaborate and fascinating tapestry, the Tesoro case one of many tackled by Fil as she apprentices at Davis and Brown Investigations in the hopes of getting her PI license. Blood leads to more blood, corruption begets corruption, and by the time all is revealed, we find several disparate cases held together by a strong yet surprising thread. "So that's it," Fil says late in the book. "With God's help, I have survived one more trip through the labyrinth." As have we all.

A detective with a realistically full docket is something rarely seen on the page. But the biggest rule Wishnia breaks may be the character of Fil herself—the polar opposite of the classic lone wolf PI. Placing her in a bustling firm loaded with colorful characters and surrounding her with people who need her for one reason or another, Wishnia also gives his heroine a real life with real concerns and responsibilities. Though she can match any iconic detective wisecrack-for-wisecrack, the Ecuadorian immigrant is also multidimensional and flawed. She sweats, she worries, she sometimes blurts out the wrong thing at the wrong time. She has a boyfriend she rarely gets to see and a daughter who is her entire world. In short, Fil feels not so much a classic fictional detective as a friend—someone you'd be more likely to spend time with in life than on the written page. In fact, Ken told me that several women have come up to him after reading *Red House* and said, effectively, "This is my life. How did you know this?" (His answer was, "Because it's my life, too.")

It's Fil who makes it possible for Wishnia to break as many rules as he does. She's a singular character, and that *almost* makes us expect a singular plot structure . . . almost. Down to its nontraditional ending (no spoilers!) *Red House*, like Fil, thrives on the unexpected.

It's a trip though the labyrinth. I can't recommend it enough.

Alison Gaylin
Woodstock, NY

CHAPTER ONE

**Discontent is the first step in the
progress of a man or a nation.**
—Anonymous Fortune Cookie

SOMETIMES I FEEL like my work is never done. Like
the two weeks of madness that started when the elder Mrs.
María Muñoz walked into the office one November morning,
plunked herself in front of me and said,

"*No sabemos de Pablito.*"

"Excuse me, do you have an appointment?" asks Katwona.

"I'll handle this," I tell her, and switch into Spanish. "*¿Qué
estaba diciendo?*"

The other trainees look up, because it's always a sign
of something. Trouble, usually, and no money. Somehow,
none of the cases with Spanish-speaking clients ever lead
to money.

Well, I'm here to change that.

Supposedly.

"Pablito is missing," says Mrs. Muñoz, her earthy round-
ness supporting an old, gray cardigan.

"For how long?"

"Three days."

I close the file I was reading and open a pale green steno
pad to a clean sheet.

"Where'd you last see him?"

1

"He was working in West Cove, on Long Island? There's a train station near there—"

"I know where it is."

There's a faint tremor below her blotchy skin as Mrs. Muñoz reacts to the slight harshness in my voice.

I don't want to go out to LI. It costs too much, and it's a pain in the ass. And I hate how working for money forces you to be ruthless.

"Sorry," I say. Wednesday of a rough week. Dead-end cases dragging me down into the cold, black heart of next Monday's performance review.

"But you know that I don't have the time or the authority to do it for free, and I doubt that you have the money to pay us," I explain in Spanish, as politely as possible. "Did you try calling the police?"

"No police," she says. "He doesn't have papers."

Of course not. So she's scared to call the police. Scared the Suffolk County cops will kick his ass instead of asking if he's getting enough hot meals. Scared the money will dry up and there won't be enough blankets to get through the long winter—gray, endless, and cruel to a family that once embraced the rich girdle of sunny, volcanic soil that carries the Savior's name. Scared the unforgiving, icy Nordic sky will fall on her head. And that the West Cove cops don't have the manpower to investigate a simple disappearance without evidence of a crime—like, say, a body.

"I'm not my own boss," I say. "I can't get to it for a couple of days, and I can't do it for free."

Eventually she accepts. "How much?"

Try seventy-five dollars an hour.

"A hundred dollars a day," I say. "Two days for a hundred and fifty."

"Oh. So much."

"It's the best I can do."

And the boss'll skin me for cutting his price by ninety percent.

I get the details, sign the contracts and lead *Señora* María

Muñoz to the door. She grips my arms, confirming the bond between my flesh and hers, and thanks me for my offer of help, to which I am now committed. Now I've got to tell the man in the corner office.

"Davis and Brown, please hold," says Katwona three times in rapid succession, patching each caller in with quick flicks of her two-inch, bright green nails dancing with abstract black squiggles that, when observed closely from the correct angle, represent ten different sexual positions.

"Ms. Brown is on another line, would you like to leave a message with her voicemail?"

Flick.

"Yes, sir. We are located at 147–02 Hillside Avenue and Sutphin Boulevard in Jamaica. Our office hours are 8:00 A.M. to 6:00 P.M., Mondays through Fridays, and 9:00 A.M. to 5:00 P.M. on Saturdays. No, you don't need an appointment, but it would probably go quicker if you made one." To me: "What precinct are we?"

"One-oh-seven," I say.

Katwona relays the info.

Flick.

"This is Miss Williams. One moment, I'll see if he's available." Flick. "Chip, Bobby Kane on line one."

"Put him through," says the boss.

Flick.

"We're on the dividing line between the One-oh-three to the south and the One-oh-seven to the north," I tell Katwona.

"'Kay." Flick. "Davis and Brown Investigations. One moment, please." No intercom this time: "Karen, got a Mrs. DiNapoli asking for you."

"Send it over," says Karen.

"Please hold while I transfer you to Ms. Ricci."

Len Hrabowski looks up from his screen. "What? No phone calls for me or Filomena?"

He says it with a long "e." Fil-o-meen-a. Wrong.

"Hey, I get your name right, Mr. Hrabowski. It's Fil-o-*men*-a. *Men*. Got it? Tell me what's so hard about 'men'?"

I regret *that* as soon as it's out.

"Well, let me tell you—" He begins half-rising out of his seat like he's about to strip down and strut around with the big hand on his Viagra-fueled clock pointing to 11:35. Possibly 11:40.

"It's a short 'e,' like in de*men*ted," I say directly into his leering eyes.

"Oh, I get it. Filo*men*a. Short 'e,' like in se*men*."

"Right, Len. Like in semen."

"So what was all that Spanish about?"

I look over to see if Chip Davis is off the phone yet. Len gets the hint—another charity case—and sits back down, shaking his head, and continues cruising the infobanks.

"*Don't* undersell, Filomena! It pisses off the competition," Chip admonishes me, hanging up the phone.

"What competition? There's only a dozen Spanish-speaking PIs in the whole borough."

"That's because the *latino* cases don't make any money."

"They will. Cases like this buy a lot of good will."

"You ever try to put 'good will' between two slices of bread? It tastes like bread."

"I'm building rapport with the community," I say. "Give me the rest of today and tomorrow afternoon off. I'll hit the biggest *latino* businesses in the area and give 'em my best pitch. If I don't bring back a solid-gold case within two weeks you can go ahead and can me."

That changes the energy. Chip leans back in his high-backed leather chair, glides his thumbs under his suspenders and stretches them into a nice pair of Vs away from his chest. I think this actually increases the blood flow to his brain.

"Look, Fil, you know I ain't gonna can you. You were collaring mopes before Morgan Stanley had their own Web site."

"Thanks for reminding me."

"I mean you've got street smarts," he says, pointing a finger at me while his thumbs stay hooked under the suspender straps. "You've hunted 'em down the old-fashioned way, plus you know your way around a database."

He snaps the straps back and sits up facing me. "But we're supposed to be charging six hundred dollars a day, not fifteen dollars an hour."

"The last defense attorney you tossed at me only paid twenty an hour."

"We'll get more next time. Lawyers have money. And big mouths. That means repeat business, Fil, with clients *who actually pay money*."

I glance past his shoulder out the window at the dirty, light-blue diesels and the gleaming metal elevated trains pulling into Jamaica station above the block-long piss-filled underpass. Two worlds of darkness and light, of crime and money, with a dreary stairway running between them. It's my job to know the face of every janitor who sweeps those stairs.

"I need time away from this case, anyway," I say.

"What case? It's just a background check."

"Yeah, but the guy's coming up clean, and I've got a feeling he's dirty."

"A feeling? How the fuck do we bill the client for a feeling?"

I lean in closer. "You better learn to start trusting my instincts."

Not the way a first-year trainee usually talks to the top half of Davis & Brown, Private Investigations, but I've got fifteen years of back street bloodhounding to his three under a civil investigator at a white shoe and powder-puff law firm.

"I've reread the reports several times, and I need to come at them from a fresh angle."

"Okay," he says, checking his watch. "Give me an hour of courthouse duty and I'll think about it. Fair?"

"Fair enough."

Ms. Abigail Brown calls to me as I walk past her door. "Filomena? Are you going to the courthouse?"

"Yes."

I lean in. Abby's a trained professional with two decades of experience as a black woman who has to dress sharply at all times or else she'll be followed by store security on suspicion of shoplifting. Abby does forensic accounting and she's good on the phone, and she doesn't know the street stuff from a tub of Shinola.

"Could you take this over to Tim Gallagher for me?" she says, holding up a thick manila envelope.

"Sure. Tell him to meet me on the steps."

She looks at me a moment, then acknowledges my request.

When going to the courthouse to troll for business, one tries to look professional. I pull one of the in-house trench coats off the hook, so *I* won't get followed by security.

Karen stops me with her arm. "Fil, my client has some underwear that she wants tested for DNA and, uh, I guess you'd call it 'substance ID.'"

Len makes a face and says, "Eeeww."

"So send it to a freaking lab. How much does she want to spend?"

"Oh. I'll check."

"You do that."

"I knew that dame was trouble the minute she walked in," says Len, giving his tight-lipped imitation of a doomed B-movie detective.

Enough of this. I step out too soon into the cool, bright air of a brisk November day and cross the street while buttoning up the trench coat. Halloween came and went, but I really didn't have much stomach for it this year.

No TV crews outside the courthouse today, just the usual convoy of lawyers casting their driftnets upon the waters, dredging for human silt. One guy's got a live one, face to the wind in his crisp blue suit and attaché case hauling in a whopper in a tan vinyl jacket and a green-and-white New York Jets cap who's saying:

"—sue them for false advertising. I wrote to the company to complain and demand my money back because my toothpaste *did not* come out red, white and green and then magically mix together with sparkles like in their ad, and my carton of laundry detergent *did not* cause trees and flowers to sprout in my laundry room *as shown in their advertisement on TV.*"

"I think we got a case here—"

I walk up the steps and spend ten minutes losing body heat in my extremities before Tim Gallagher comes barreling out the door, looking around for me. Big, burly guy with a pasty but genial face, curly thinning hair, and the don't-make-me-hurt-you body of a former Gaelic football player.

"Oh man, if this jury gets any dumber," he begins. "We're arguing that the defendant acted with 'a depraved indifference to human life,' and they keep sending out notes asking, 'What does "depraved" mean again?'"

"People—"

"—are idiots. So whadaya got for me?"

I give him the envelope. He flips through it, nodding and naying and uh-ohing and generally tuning me out.

"What?" I ask.

"Huh? Oh, another sucky case. Cracked fire extinguisher at PS 112 blows up two weeks after it was inspected. The federal ID stamp leads to Henderson Fire Equipment over in Hollis, who say they never did PS 112, and the principal of the school corroborates by showing us contracts and invoices from some place called Armor Point Fire Equipment in Glendale, who we find out don't even have proper inspection equipment—although they claim they had it at the time they made the tests. The paperwork suggests Armor Point faked a couple hundred inspections, mostly in public schools—"

"Scumbags."

"—but there's no proof. So we got over a hundred clients who want us to get their money back and we can't find the guy who actually went around to the schools. Armor Point says he quit three months ago."

"And you can't find him?"

"Three freakin' weeks we've been trying to dig him up."

"I'll find him for you."

"Say what?"

"You heard me."

He gives me that what's-it-gonna-cost-me look.

"Two hundred dollars."

"That's eight hours at my rate."

"Right."

"Okay," he says, handing me the papers. "You got a name, Freddy Lopez, a three-month-old address, and a bogus social security number. Good luck."

Back inside, I kick Len off the computer, dive bomb into Macrohard's Plexus™ database. Needless to say, there's no "Freddy Lopez," but there's fourteen Freds, seventy-eight Fredericks and fifteen hundred and twelve Fredericos. Screw that. I narrow my search to "Fred [not whole word] Lopez" matches with anything in Queens, and get three guys who I could have found in two seconds by opening up the phone book. Not the right profiles, either. Hmm.

"You want some coffee?" asks Len.

"No, thanks. Too much coffee makes me crazy."

"Me, too. That's why I drink it."

I try the rarer variant, "Federico," and get a hit, a very palpable hit, which proves that he was born, anyway. Did he get married in New York State? No. Does he vote? No. Bastard. Does he drive? *Yes*. Full name, address, and social security number. The address is dead but the number looks good, starting with a "9," which means it's not an SSN, but an ITIN, an individual taxpayer identification number issued to a resident alien who plans to work here *and pay taxes*, which means he just might be the honest type who would quit a place like Armor Point to avoid trouble and maybe even take the stand to testify against them, especially if it bought him some relief. Gallagher's going to like this, if I can close it for him. A guy who left a job and skipped on two months' back rent could lie low for about forty years without being pinched in this town, but he has to eat, and if he's a resident alien with a valid ITIN, he could have applied for food stamps and job placement assistance. And he'd have to use his real name *somewhere*.

It takes me an hour. Abby's happy. Davis?

"Damn it, Buscarsela, Gallagher only pays twenty-five dollars an hour! Plexus charges forty! That's a net loss!"

"Yes, but it was quicker and I need the spare time. Bill it to the client."

"Thanks, I'll do that. Spare time for what?"

"I need to pick up my daughter from school because there's no one at home to meet her today."

If you can call it "home": $500 a month for a six-by-nine-foot room in an overcrowded apartment because I wanted to be near my job.

"Charge him for two hours. Repeat business," I say.

"How about four? Can't make it look too easy now, can we?"

"Fine."

"All right, Fil. I've decided to let you go and do Friday and Saturday on Long Island. And when you come back you bring me a goddamn *paying* case."

"Yes, sir."

"Fil, call me Chip."

"Just a reflex, I guess."

"Okay. Now get out of here."

"Chip."

"Yeah?"

"I'm going to need a company car."

"That's just great. And happy fucking holidays to you, too."

Don't ask me how some of the private eyes you read about got their licenses, which seem to have just dropped from the sky. Maybe they all come from one of those states like Idaho or Mississippi where the only requirements are a $20 bill and a pen to fill out the application form. In New York, you need three years minimum investigative experience—and my five years as a beat cop *doesn't count*—and a $10,000 surety bond. You don't just rent a two-bit office and print up a bunch of business cards. Oh, I could set up as an unlicensed PI in my new *barrio* and get plenty of business, but I'm tired of doing it that way and I'm going to need that license.

Always the hard way. I came here from Ecuador ages ago right after I left school, got my papers and joined the NYPD, fucked up royally, then struck out on my own and I've been stringing it together ever since on the unofficial market. It's time to go legit and start saving for my daughter's college costs, because the once-free City University now tops $28,000 for four years of books and courses. That's still money in my neighborhood.

So I was a police detective for exactly one day (it's a long and colorful story), but thanks to some consideration and a fantastic bureaucratic glitch I got credit for one year, and now I'm six months into a two-year stint with Davis & Brown. Welcome to the lowest rung. But at least I'm on the ladder.

The hard part is going back to being an apprentice alongside a couple of kids and working for trainee wages when I've got a twelve-year-old kid of my own to support. It's really sobering to think that when Jesus Christ was my age he had already saved humanity and come back from the dead (twice). Maybe I can just stay forty forever, like some of those fictional detectives.

I cross the street and stand next to the Q44 bus stop, catching a little afternoon sun. There's a psycho-slasher movie poster on the Plexiglas wall showcasing a nubile female abdomen in low-slung panties alongside an erect blood-drenched knife that has gathered three levels of scholastic commentary. Some enraged gal has scrawled in thick black magic marker: THIS POSTER IS OFFENSIVE TO WOMEN. Under that, in thinner marker, someone else has written: THIS POSTER IS OFFENSIVE TO PSYCHOPATHS. And finally, in silver-paint marker: THIS POSTER IS OFFENSIVE TO PARANOID PEOPLE WHO GET OFFENDED BY EVERYTHING.

Well, I guess that covers everyone.

"Hey, Fil Buscarella, that you?"

I turn. Lonnie Ambush, sauntering towards me from the bluish shadows on the north side of the courthouse. *Not now.* If the regular lawyers are on tramp steamers casting their nets upon the waters, this guy's a barnacle stuck to their slimy white underbellies. A ten on my sleaze-o-meter, and as my friend Brenda Midnight says, lower than a snake's belly in a wheel rut.

It's a midwestern metaphor: You won't find any wheel ruts in New York City.

But you will find snakes.

"What's with the trench coat, Fil?"

Trench coat? Oh. Yeah. I was in such a rush I forgot to change out of it.

"Hi, Lonnie."

"You should cinch it in at the waist more—" He reaches for my umbilical region.

"Touch me there and I'll break your freakin' arm."

He tries to look cute about it.

"What do you want?" I ask.

"Now, now, Fil, be nice to me. I've got some business for your boss, Mr. Davis."

"So talk to him."

"Well, I thought I'd—"

"Try it out on me first."

"There, you see? We think alike—"

I give a sharp nod past his shoulder. He turns and sees the Q40 approaching.

"That your bus?"

"No." Damn it.

"So we got a minute. Let me ask you something: What is one of the biggest untapped sources of income in this business?"

"I don't know. Counterfeit white-out?"

"Criminal defense investigations."

And the Pope remains Catholic.

"Think about it, Fil. Three hundred thousand arrests in the city every year."

"And three-quarters of them use a Legal Aid Society lawyer."

"At the hearing, not the trial. Common denominator: None of them want to do the time. If we can prove that hiring us will make the difference between going free or being locked up, they *will* find the money to pay us."

Oh, yeah. From where? Little old ladies?

"You sound awfully sure of yourself," I say.

"Hey: Nobody buys cheap when you're talking about their freedom."

"You mean they're desperate and we can take advantage of them."

"Listen, five years ago there were only six thousand pot busts a year in this town, but thanks to Mayor Pazzerello's zero tolerance policy we got *forty-five thousand* pot busts a year now, and a bunch of them are high-bracket yuppie liberals who'll dig deep to keep out of the freaking State Pen."

Okay, not little old ladies. Little old IRAs and CDs. Lonnie sometimes brings in money for Davis & Brown, so I nod. "Sounds like a good idea," I lie.

"It's the wave of the future."

"You want me to take it to the boss?"

"Just grease the wheels for me so I don't have to go and cold call him on it."

"Sure thing, Lonnie." *Grease* is right.

"Thanks, Fil. I'll see you get a piece of this, too."

"I'd appreciate that."

Finally my bus comes. Lonnie seals our deal with a handshake and a pat on the back, then jogs across 88th Avenue to coil in wait for another victim.

One of these days, that snake's going to bite me.

There are seats in the back of the bus, and I slump down, tired. And it's only Wednesday. I think the week should go: Monday-Tuesday-Friday-Saturday-Friday-Saturday-Sunday. That way, you get two Fridays and two Saturdays every week, and today would be the first Friday. But no.

We turn onto Hillside Avenue and I stare out the window at the people and the stores, then scan the bus ads. There's one for maxi-pads that demonstrates how they work using a light-blue liquid. I don't know about you, but my menstrual blood is *not* light blue. Maybe it's an ad for Klingon women.

But the text is in English, Captain. How do these foolish Earthlings expect to reach their target market?

I settle in for the long ride north to Flushing, open up the paper, and get a page one sample of that special brand of Long Island weirdness I'm trying to avoid: A man was arrested for sending radium in tubes of toothpaste to Nassau County Republican Party leaders in a bizarre plot to kill them because he believed that they were lying about their contacts with space aliens.

Which explains why the ad is in English. It's all connected, man . . .

Elsewhere, in a secret memo revealed today, President Bush called for the armed forces to bump off every Arab in the Middle East, but to be careful to "make it look like an accident"; a seventy-nine-year-old man was caught robbing a hardware store and tried to dismiss it as a "youthful indiscretion"; and a prominent Eastern European Cardinal denied that his anti-Semitic remarks were inflammatory. "I've got nothing against Jews," he says. Sure. Some of my best lampshades are Jewish.

Downtown Flushing. I transfer to the Q48 and take Roosevelt Avenue across the park to Corona. My boyfriend Dr. Stanislaus Wrennchowski wanted me to move in with him in Glen Oaks on the Nassau County border, where he's in his first year on the staff at Long Island Jewish Hospital, but I said not yet. So Corona is a compromise, which is why I've got an appointment to see an affordable apartment in the neighborhood, and so Antonia can stay in the same school from September to June. She's made friends there, and I'm not in a hurry to move her.

I flip to the sports page. Another fistfight in the NBA. A lot of people complain about the spectacle of watching two multi-millionaires slug it out, but I for one would *love* to see Michael Milken take a beating from Rupert Murdoch, or watch Bill Gates kick the crap out of Donald Trump.

I'd even pay.

The place is big, white, and clean, with polished wood floors and large bay windows letting in the autumn light. Every wall is spotless (I can still smell the paint), in three rooms without a sliver of furniture to fill the emptiness. I can't believe we can afford this.

The last apartment I checked out was dusty, as dank as an underground torture cell (yes, I've been), and genuinely smelled like a dog kennel. The guy showing it to me looked like he slept in a refrigerator box himself, and the poster of nihilistic glam-Gothic rocker Jayne Mansfield Dahmer on the wall was the one bright spot in the room. I remember shutting the door with my hip. No reason to leave any latent fingerprints there.

The kid with the key to this place has straight, slick black hair and a pale, sharp face that needs a shave, but his white T-shirt, black jacket, and jeans are clean enough. No messing up this floor.

I check the closets, freshly painted. Pick up the phone, disconnected. Examine the bathroom, old fixtures but pretty well taken care of. It's a dream apartment. And yet, something is tickling me. Too-good-to-be-true paranoia? The illogical voice of intuition?

Listen to your instincts, girl.

"How much are utilities?" I ask.

"Depends on how much gas and electric you use."

Well, yeah. "Average."

"Hey, what's 'average'?"

Norm—ah, forget it. "You must have a lot of people looking at this place."

"Oh yeah, a lot."

"So how come you haven't rented it yet?"

"Yeah, well, we had a renter lined up, but the deal fell through at the last minute."

Renter? Deal?

"You mean you had a tenant lined up, but the lease fell through?"

"Yeah."

"How so?"

"You wanna see the kitchen?"

"Sure. How come the lease fell through?"

"Oh, you don't have to worry about that happening to you."

"Why not?"

"'Cause we got it all taken care of now."

"How'd you do that?"

"Ain't that nice new tile on the countertops?"

"Yeah, it's nice. How'd you take care of the lease?"

"You don't have to worry about the lease, believe me. It's been fully approved, certified, and endorsed by the National Association of Landlords."

"There is no National Association of Landlords."

"What?"

"You called me. You know my current address and phone number. And you know I'm not home right now, don't you? *You stay right there.*"

And there we are in the glowing kitchen, my trench coat flapping open as I point the two-inch barrel of a Colt .38 Special Lady at his waxen face, find the agency-issued cell phone with my left and dial 911 and tell them to "dispatch a squad car immediately to 40–18 Junction Boulevard, possible burglary in progress, third-floor rear apartment."

The voice asks: "What do you mean by 'possible burglary,' ma'am?"

My adrenaline doesn't have time for this. I tell her something like, "Just dispatch the fucking car and send another one to 97–05 Christie Avenue *right now* or somebody's going to get their fucking head blown off."

I hate the "Special Lady" name. It reminds me of Nancy Reagan and her "teeny-weeny gun," but the five-round cylinder of some of the other women's guns really messed me up. Muscle memory and all that. I need six rounds. Not seven .32s or eight .22s in the same cylinder size. Fuck that. If you're in a situation where six shots won't do it, seven or eight won't do it, either, my friend. Besides, a stainless snub-nosed .38 was the closest to the old police special I could get without it being a "cop's" gun. It ain't some classy semiautomatic, but it's reliable, and if I treat it right, it will never, *ever* jam on me.

"Listen, lady, I know about some really big crimes in this 'hood—"

"Save it."

The cops arrive and confirm that I've prevented a felony, so the gun is okay with them. But they want me to go with them right now to lodge a complaint against the "landlord" and his two accomplices, who they nabbed going through every room in my cash-only boarding-house.

"I don't have time now, I've got to pick up my kid. Put him on ice and I'll come by later."

"What are we supposed to do with him in the meantime?" asks Officer O'Brien.

I wait until his partner, Officer Chen, stuffs the guy into the patrol car and slams the door tight. I fold my arms, look up into his eyes, and say: "Flatter him."

No reaction.

"It's a pretty ballsy scam, keeping a pristine apartment like that as a decoy. Tell him how smart he is, ten to one he gives up the other two guys just to prove how much smarter he is."

"Oh yeah," he agrees. "We were going to do that. 'Course most of what he says won't be worth shit," he agrees. "But we'll have a good time holding that against him later."

"Uh-huh. Could you do me one other favor?"

I just nailed three perps and cleared maybe a dozen warrants for his precinct.

"Okay, shoot."

"Tell the lady on the phone I'm sorry I yelled at her."

The doorknobs at JHS 319 are beautiful intricately sculpted elliptical brass masterpieces, with "Board of Education" spelled out in ornate, curlicued Gibson-girl era raised-metal lettering. The rest of the place is held together with Elmer's glue and masking tape. Antonia's in one of the permanent "temporary" classrooms taking up half the asphalt play-ground, a loose confederation of Quonset huts made from army-surplus materials, and from the sound of the discipline being meted out inside some of the huts, it seems like the army threw in a few surplus drill sergeants as well.

I pass a handwritten poster warning the children, "Don't Give in to Pear Pressure." I suppose that's when fruit tries to get you to do bad things.

And there's a pile of pamphlets issuing dire threats that "the first sample is free, then they hook you, then they keep raising the price."

I'm all for drug-free schools. Twelve-year-olds shouldn't be smoking pot before their 8:00 A.M. classes. But that bull-shit's straight out of the hysterical 1950s anti-drug comic books. I mean, anyone who's ever watched a street dealer work knows that in reality, all they have to do is stand there and *people come to them*. Lines form, and dealers don't have to work overtime trying to "hook" newcomers.

I talk to my daughter all the time, but I tell her the more complex truth, that some drugs are worse than others, that many people mess up their lives but others don't, that sniff-ing legal stuff like rug-cleaning fluid is far deadlier than pot brownies, that she should *never* trust a boy handing her an open drink and that nobody under eighteen should be screw-ing with their delicate brain chemistry, anyway.

That's an adult's job.

She's only in seventh grade, but some of her girlfriends have already learned the trick of wearing a shirt two sizes too small so it looks like their busts are about to pop the buttons off the thing. Jeezus.

She proudly shows me her science project, a scale drawing of an Allosaurus skeleton, fully documented and labeled.

"Pretty impressive beast, huh?" she says.

"Ah, it had a brain the size of a walnut."

"Who needs brains when you've got a six-foot jaw?"

Gee, I wonder where she got that smartass mouth from.

But something is bothering her. It takes a while to excavate it. Turns out she's been getting crap about her "twiggy legs" and the traces of dark Spanish lip hair she's beginning to show. Her twelve-year-old body is not feminine enough for some, it seems.

I tell her I saw a woman two days ago at the public swimming pool who didn't have a left leg below the knee.

"Right, Mom. I'm thankful I'm not a gimp. Meanwhile, kids'll still make fun of me."

"We can bleach the hair if you want."

"Yes."

"But just because the world sucks doesn't mean we have to become assholes to get by. That's what Christ says. I'm paraphrasing."

"I figured."

We walk on. Andean bamboo flute music flows from a dented van on the south side of the avenue, so out-of-place beneath the stroboscopic skyline and the rapid crescendo of rattling under the elevated tracks of the Number 7 train, yet so fittingly transferred to this new culture, where they fly the Ecuadorian flag from row houses, advertise *La Cholita* foods and *cerveza Pilsener* imported from the mother country, and even paint the garbage pails red, blue, and yellow, same as the flag.

Amplified speeches reverberate off the el's cavernous pillars. We move closer, and spot a couple of squad cars from the 110th Precinct parked near the perimeter of a well-planned rally for affordable housing. I warn a sidewalk vendor offering "Cotten Shirts $3.00" to keep an eye out.

"You're peddling without a license *and* you spelled 'cotton' wrong, too."

Turns out I know some of the cops, who look like a delegation from the General Assembly of the United Nations. There's Police Officer Rajif Siddiqi, a new kid who's got about twenty minutes on the street; Officer Carl Thompson, a smooth-talking Brooklyn-born African-American; Officer Sally-Ann MacKenzie, a rarity with nearly eighteen years in uniform (you don't see too many older *women* cops); and Officer Vanessa Cordero, who just last week responded to an accident scene at a major intersection, grabbed a six-year-old girl who was bleeding to death in the crosswalk and wrapped her in a blanket and sped her to Elmhurst Hospital while her partner alerted the trauma unit to stand by and radioed other units to clear a route to the hospital.

"How'd you know about all that?" she asks.

"From the precinct's Web site."

"Oh." She studies a chewing gum wrapper on the ground near her left shoe.

They're here for the usual crowd control duties associated with legal demonstrations, but they won't tell me what all the undercovers sporting sunglasses and earphones are doing near the stage.

Antonia and I edge in closer, past a line of men wearing authentic Ecuadorian *paja toquilla* hats (mistakenly called Panama hats by Teddy Roosevelt and every other American since then), towards the stage where Elisha Kalinin, the local representative of the Met Council, is introducing Manuel "Manny" Morales, an iron-pumping, hell-raising housing advocate who works full-time at a group home doing behavioral therapy with autistic teenagers.

Manny gives a fiery speech attacking Mayor Ugolfo Pazzerello for signing a bill that relieved landlords of their obligation to clean up the toxic lead paint in old apartments:

"He says at least he's getting things done! Well I say it's easy to get things done when you don't stop to listen to anybody! It's easy to be razor-sharp when you're narrow-minded! Mayor Pazzerello's policies go through so quickly because he doesn't bother with details like community dialogue, cultural differences, compromise, or even democracy! Why slow down when you're unburdened by compassion of any kind!"

He switches into Spanish to say: "*¡Lo único que hace rápido por aquí es llevarse el dinero!*" The only thing he does fast around here is take away your money!

A cascade of applause issues from the crowd. To the right of the stage, a group of five young white women wearing leather jackets with metal piercings and look-alike blond crewcuts are holding up a banner and chanting, "You go, Ugo! You go, Ugo!" I can't tell from here if they're for him or against him. On the opposite sidewalk a couple of gang members greet each other with their left hands while their right ones stay deep in their jacket pockets. Maybe I should warn the cops. I start back towards the avenue as Manny introduces the keynote speaker, City Council Member Margarita Sánchez, who tells the crowd to organize for tenant unity and eviction protection, and to fight against tenant harassment and the privatization of public housing.

She's reminding the people that harassing tenants is illegal as Antonia and I work our way back towards the radio cars, and the pungent smell of pot smoke wafts over from a group near the corner just as the cops spot the activity and move in to stop it. Mayor Pazzerello's zero tolerance policy in action.

I recognize a couple of the smokers: Juan José Flores and Armando "Sonny" Tesoro, who throws the joint away when he sees the cops coming.

Mistake.

Officer Cordero seizes the smoldering roach as the other officers bust the four men. They're spread out, patted down and about to be cuffed when Sonny goes, "Aw, fuck this!" and pulls out a .22-caliber pistol, which they obviously missed.

Jesus. I grab Antonia and bring her down hard, flattening myself on top of her in the middle of the street while two tough, white male cops I've never seen before grab Sonny's gun and wrench it away from him. But Sonny is not subdued yet. People run for cover, legs twisting into Xs in front of me, blocking my view, stepping on me, there's a quick *whack!* and Sonny's on the ground covering his head with his arms and bleeding on the sidewalk.

What just happened? Busted for simple possession on Wednesday means you're out on Thursday, and since they missed the gun the first time around he might have tried to run, ditch it, or else face the lesser charge of carrying a concealed weapon. But Sonny just seemed to go *nuts*, and after pulling a gun on the cops, he'll be lucky if he can still eat solid food by this time tomorrow.

And I've crushed Antonia's poster. I promise I'll smooth it out at home.

Then I've got to go spend a couple of hours with the police.

CHAPTER TWO

**If trouble was money, everybody in
Harlem would be a millionaire.**
—Chester Himes

SOMETIMES all it takes is a word.

In this case, the word was "Massachusetts," staring up at me this fine Thursday morning from Mr. Willie Rogers's most obstinately resistant background check.

"Len, how far back did you go on this case?"

"What case? *Rogers*? You still on that one?"

"How far back did you go?"

"I did a complete statewide criminal history. I tell you, he's clean."

This is why you do the research yourself.

"Len, Massachusetts criminal records only go back two years. If he's a convicted felon who got out three years ago, it wouldn't show up."

"Staff meeting at ten-thirty, people!" Katwona announces.

"What?" says Len. "That's ridiculous."

"Don't look at me. You're the ones who came up with the idea of different laws for every state."

Vermont has a sex offender registry, but they won't let anyone look at it, Maine hasn't computerized theirs yet, and Connecticut isn't even sure *what* their policy is.

"We've got *provinces* in Ecuador, not these ridiculous separate sovereign entities like you do."

"Tenth Amendment, right?"

"This one's a do-over, Len. We've got to check the criminal court records in every town, city, and county where Rogers has lived for the past twenty years. And don't give me that look. I could throw you to Davis right now for turning in a crappy report."

That cows him. We split the list in half and spend fifteen minutes on two computers, Len accessing the screens more swiftly than I do, before he gets the hit:

"There it is," says Len, relieved. "Bristol County, December, 1991. Phone card scam. Two years' probation."

"There's *one*. Keep searching."

Len gives me the please-don't-do-this-to-me look of a teenager who's got a hot date all lined up but whose mom insists that he clean up his room and take out the trash first, but he goes back to his job while I follow-up with a phone call to the Bristol County courthouse.

Pretty soon we've got a pattern: Six arrests for numerous phone scams wherein he got the victims to reveal their credit card numbers and then he ran wild with them until the companies got suspicious and stopped things.

"That's enough, our job's done," says Len, flexing his hands backwards and cracking his finger joints.

"No, it isn't. He lives in Richmond Hill, and he's a creature of habit. Let's get his phone records."

"Can't get that without a court order. Or without hacking. Oh, no—"

I drop in deep. The guy who owns Macrohard Computers is worth more than the combined wealth of forty percent of the U.S. population. So fuck him. Someone once said I'm too intelligent to be this poor, though I'll never understand why so many of you Americans insist on equating salary with brainpower. We've got priests and engineers and tribal leaders in Ecuador whose combined annual salaries wouldn't buy a fifty-pound sack of soybeans at your local health-food store who are a lot smarter than those CEOs who make so much money they don't even earn salaries, they get "compensation," but who can't seem to figure out why there are 100,000 people on an eight-year waiting list to get into the city's public housing when the economy's doing *so well*.

I think financial solvency's overrated, anyway.

Alarm.

"Shit!"

"Break off, break off!" says Len.

"What's going on out there?" Abby calls from her office.

"Nothing!" Karen calls back. I didn't realize she was watching me.

Len takes over. "Here, let me show you."

I watch him closely. It's a different world from the days when I used to hammer out reports on the 34th Precinct's hand-cranked typewriters. It would also help if I hadn't been awakened at 2:00 A.M. this morning with the walls shaking from the fistfight one floor below, after spending three hours at the 110th Precinct lodging a complaint against the consumer-conscious thieves who not only stole TVs, VCRs, and stereos, but also took *the warranties and instruction manuals*. Between the three of them they had a total of nineteen felony warrants out for their arrest, thirty-eight prior arrests, sixteen social security numbers, twenty-two aliases, and were wanted in Albany, Newark, Philadelphia, and Trenton.

And Officers O'Brien and Chen owe me a big, fat favor.

"Nothing, Fil," says Len, pointing at the screen.

"Five calls a week," says Karen. "Can't be much of a phone scam artist."

I pinch the skin between my eyes, massage my eyebrows. Take your time, girl. Think. You've been in this spot before. All you need is a fresh angle.

"Okay," I say. "Forget who he called. Find out who called him."

They both look at me like I've finally snapped, one more casualty of the Industrial Age unable to adapt her fossilized mind to the Information Age.

But Len does it. More than eight hundred names and numbers scroll down like the seventh seal's been broken, all for the month of September.

"My, my, he's been busy."

"And most of the calls are coming from Queens."

"I don't see a pattern," says Karen.

"There's got to be a pattern," I say, trying to sound convincing. "Even if he's just going through the phone book one name at a time."

"But they're all calling *him*."

I call the first few numbers and get answering machines, gruff retirees, immigrant women whose children are the only ones in the house who speak English, college students at home studying. But the students have a story to tell. I call twenty more victims and find out that every number involves someone attending Queens College.

That's what I call a pattern.

I make some more calls and piece it together in time for the meeting.

"Filomena, we're waiting!"

Katwona programs all the phones over to the answering machine and we scurry into Abby's office, where everyone is sitting around, clipboards and coffee cups at the ready.

"You guys all just sitting here interdigitating?" I say, looking at Chip and Len, who are both in the exact same pose, hands folded over their groins.

"What'd you say?" asks Chip.

"Relax, it means interlocking your fingers."

Chip and Len look down and uncross their hands while the women chuckle. It's always good to start off these meetings with a joke. The next forty-five minutes is a slow-going update on the active cases, then it's my turn to shine. Abby announces that Tim Gallagher was quite pleased with our speedy location of Freddy Lopez.

"Anything else?" asks Davis.

"Yes," I say. "There's been a breakthrough on the Willie Rogers background check."

"Breakthrough?" Davis turns to Len. "I thought you said he was—"

"A very clever operator," I say. "In late August, two file drawers were taken from the Financial Aid Office at Queens College. There were no signs of forced entry, and the office personnel, thinking that it was some kind of bureaucratic snafu, did not report it as a theft.

"Now, it's pretty easy to copy the typeface of the college's billing statements and envelopes, and they've got the student ID numbers from the forms they stole. So they send out nearly a thousand bogus bills for a hundred, two hundred dollars each. Not enough to send up any flares, but that's a lot of money to these kids, so they freak out and *call the number on the bill*, and get our friend, Willie Rogers, who says in a serious voice, 'Hold on, I've got to ask you some questions for security purposes.' The old confidence reversal, right? So he asks them to give him their full name and student ID number, home address, phone, date of birth. He's got it so *they're* the ones being grilled, and nervous about what Mom and Dad are going to do when they find out what this is going to cost them.

"Then a sympathetic voice comes on, probably Willie's latest babe, and says, 'Yes, there's been a mistake. You only owe *thirty* dollars. We're terribly sorry. I can take care of this right now over the phone if you wish.' Now obviously there's some variation, but generally the students are so relieved that they just give out their credit card numbers, expiration dates, and the name 'as it appears on the card,' and Willie and Willbabe party for anywhere from three days to a month depending on how vigilant the credit card companies are, 'cause we all know how college students spend the plastic."

"He got *them* to call *him*," Abby says, relaying her understanding of the set-up.

"And the scam's plausible," says Len. "Everyone knows the City University screws up all the time ever since the Mayor's Office slashed their budget in half."

Abby nods.

"Do you know what it would mean if we could get CUNY as a client?" asks Davis, wide-eyed and unable to hide it.

"Well, first we call the cops and report Rogers," I say. "Then Len should take the case to Queens College and find out if they've got any other unreported thefts they want us to look into."

"Terrific idea, Fil. Len?"

"Fine with me."

"You two work pretty well together," Abby comments.

Embarrassing pause. Then it's on to new business.

"One of our marketing consultants has recommended that we get personalized pens to hand out and advertise our business," says Davis.

"I've got a better idea. Save your money and change your name to Bic MetalPoint and just hand *those* out—they're only six dollars for a box of twelve," I suggest.

"Any other ideas?"

And we go on for ten minutes, brainstorming about eye-catching marketing ploys that stop just short of having Karen serve subpoenas wearing a peek-a-boo nightie and high-heeled patent leather boots.

"Karen's got shift on courthouse duty today," says Davis, standing up, stretching. "So if there's nothing else—"

As the meeting ends, I tell Davis I've hooked another prospect, and he wants to hear more about it in his office. I describe Lonnie Ambush's defending-yuppie-potsmokers idea and he basically says to *go for it*. So I call Lonnie and set up a meeting for later, then I call the 110th Precinct and get ahold of Officer MacKenzie, remind her who I am and ask, "Can you tell me what happened yesterday with Sonny Tesoro?"

"That hairbag? The one who pulled a loaded gun on us?"

"It was loaded?"

"What the fuck is that supposed to mean? Yeah, it was loaded."

"I just mean it doesn't make sense."

"You expect some drugged-out hairbag to make sense?"

"Officer MacKenzie, I have seen Mr. Tesoro around the

neighborhood with his wife and child. He has a steady job, he helps out around the house, and after the kid is fed and changed and put to bed, he goes down to the street to split a joint with his friends."

"So that makes him an ideal parent?"

"It's not burnt-out druggie behavior."

"Yeah, well you didn't see him yesterday. Took five of us to subdue the son-of-a-B."

I decide not to tell her that I *did* see him yesterday.

"So when's the arraignment?"

"Can't fit him in 'til Monday."

"That's a long wait."

"So write your freakin' congressman."

End of conversation.

And I forgot to give her crap about how the five of them patted Sonny down and still missed the goddamn gun.

I grab a clean steno pad from the supply cabinet and head out to interview Camille Tesoro. One point for private enterprise over state-run business: You don't have to fill out a three-ply requisition form and wait six weeks to get a lousy green steno pad.

From the newspaper left on the bus seat I learn that the Long Island *loco* with the radium has been allowed to plead that he was not responsible by reason of mental incompetence, and it's pretty easy to see why: Turns out the guy wanted to kill Republican Party leaders and replace them with *Conservative* Party politicians.

Uh-huh.

I pull open the private investigator test preparation guide and take the second half of another practice exam, wherein I answer correctly that questioning a suspect for many hours under glaring lights without food or sleep is a procedural no-no that constitutes duress and thus invalidates a confession, and that the interrogator *must* refrain from threats, violence or the promise of reward.

Right.

Then there's a bunch of questions designed to find out

if I know what "introverted" and "surreptitious" mean. Also "exonerated," "redundant," "insolvent," "covert." Like, sure, I wanted to be a Navy SEAL, but I failed the vocabulary test.

But it's better than the dusty gray training manual I got from the library that was so out-of-date it actually advised investigators not to ask female witnesses how old they are, and warned them about collusion between a husband and wife, arranging for one of them to be "caught" having an affair so that the other could sue for divorce on the grounds of adultery, a gag I don't think anybody's had to pull since the late 1950s.

I've got twenty years' experience on both sides of the law and I can't wait 'til I have my own practice so I can take the cases I want, though I'll always have to work for money, I guess, green bananas *still* being considered an unacceptable form of payment by most utilities. Maybe even get a decent place to live. Right now, all I've got is an appointment to see another apartment this Sunday, second floor of a row house a long fly ball's flight from Shea Stadium.

Two blocks south on 108th Street I spot Manny Morales leaving the Isaiah School for the developmentally disabled with a muscular teen on his arm who turns out not to be a teen at all but an *enormous* twelve-year-old.

"That's why we're being real nice to him, 'cause he's only going to get bigger," says Manny.

The big kid puts my hand against his cheek and flaps his arm with excitement.

"He likes you," says Manny. "He's very affectionate. To Jerry, a stranger is merely a friend who hasn't fed him yet." That's good, because he's got one helluva grip.

"Is he a picky eater?"

"Oh, yes. The food has to be in front of him."

"Do-*dah*," says Jerry.

"We had to talk about food," says Manny.

"Do-*dah*."

"Say it better."

"I wan do-*dah*."

"Nut."

"Dah."

"Tuh."

"Tuh."

"Nu-*t*."

"Nu-*tuh*."

"I want donu-*t*."

"I wan do-*dah*."

"That's as close as he gets," says Manny. "All right, we'll go have a donut."

"So-*dah*."

"No, no, too much sugar, buddy. You know we don't drink that garbage."

They step off the curb, but Jerry stops on the sewer grating, looks down and starts bouncing on his toes a little, enjoying the weird sensation of seemingly standing on nothing.

"Get your mind out of the gutter, young man," I say.

Manny smiles. "Oh, he's much better now. You should have seen him a couple of years ago when he got mad at us because we wouldn't let him jump into New London Harbor."

Jerry giggles, perhaps at the memory.

"Sounds like he's trying to keep you off balance."

"No, he doesn't have to try. He's got a natural gift. If only we could exploit it, we'd solve all our money worries. Jerry could crack a safe if you put a chocolate donut inside it."

"So all you have to do is wait 'til that big merger between Chase Manhattan and Dunkin' Donuts goes through."

"Do-*dah*."

"Oops. We reminded him. We better get going."

I walk with Manny and ask him what he knows about Sonny Tesoro.

"Yeah, that was weird, wasn't it?" he says. "Sonny's a do-er. It's not like him to trade punches with the pigs. When they renovated the old Universal Lighting plant, Sonny put in most of the dry-wall."

"I know."

"Place was abandoned for fifteen years. Now that it's

worth something, the landlord wants them out so he can subdivide and charge *mucha plata* for the space."

"Can they get together and buy the building?"

"Not at today's asking price."

"But the place was *worthless* until they moved in and fixed it up. The landlord should compromise with a fair-market rent."

"Yeah, well, unfortunately we live in the borough of Queens, not the People's Republic of Queens, and our beloved mayor's the kind of guy who'd try to evict the Brooklyn Museum for showing a painting of the Virgin Mary holding a bloody coat hanger."

"There's always the stable."

"Yeah, but her husband's only a carpenter. Who's going to put in the plumbing? The insulation? The wiring?"

Time to move on. Manny leads Jerry by the hand into the donut shop. I cross at the corner and head towards the disputed building with my mind on other things when from twenty yards back spews forth the aggressive bellow of the steroid-enhanced male predator:

"Fuckin' faggots!" they yell.

I turn around. Manny is in the middle of the block, holding Jerry's arm and waiting to cross the street while three white guys in a black Camaro shout out the windows at them.

"Fuck you, ya fuckin' faggots—!"

"Yeah, ya fuckin' faggots!"

But they keep driving, and seize the opportunity to blow wet kisses at me.

I keep watching until the light changes and Manny crosses the street. Jerry doesn't seem to have noticed. He's too happy with his donut.

Camille Tesoro is bent down mopping the floor near the baby's crib, although the curling linoleum wouldn't polish to a shine if she scrubbed it with an industrial turbowaxer for the next fifty hours.

But looks aren't everything.

"*Mi Armando siempre ha sido un buen hombre*," she tells me. My Armando has always been a good man. "He worked hard, always brought the money home to me. No other women. No drugs."

She straightens up, looking at me with her young face and old eyes.

"He built most of this apartment, with Lucas and Georgio helping with the toilet and the lights. But the pressure, working unpaid overtime for that American boss, every day fighting the city because they say we can't live here anymore," her arm sweeps the room, "and he'd lie awake all night, and his head would hurt all the next day, and he'd get angry so easily he nearly got fired."

"How'd that happen?"

A little air comes out of her. She leans on the mop and thinks about what she's going to tell me.

"He got a call one day, the boss telling him to go work for a subcontractor in Jackson Heights. You know, cheap Spanish labor. They promised him four hundred dollars for three days' work and then paid one-fifty. My man Sonny didn't like that, and when they wouldn't give him the other two hundred and fifty dollars, he took his hammer and swung it at the wall he had just put up and put five holes in it and said, 'There: It'll cost you about two hundred and fifty dollars to fix that.'"

Gee, what does he have to do to get fired?

"How long ago was that?"

"A couple of months ago."

"When did he start getting so irritable?"

"A little before that."

"Has it gotten worse?"

"No."

No?

The room grows still enough for me to hear the baby breathing, to see the soft yellow blanket rising and falling like a leaf drifting on the faintest breeze.

I wait. A minute slips by like a drop of honey falling into a bowl of milk.

"He started smoking pot," she confesses. "I was worried, of course, but you know something? It helped. It helped his headaches, it helped him sleep at night. *Pot calmed him down, Señorita Buscarsela.*"

"Please, call me Filomena."

"In my land it grows wild in the fields under the blazing sun. Here you buy it in expensive little plastic bags from nasty people."

Yeah, the local drug dealers don't exactly belong to the Better Business Bureau.

"So my Armando built a place to grow the plants."

"Where?"

She eyes me without trust.

"Look, I'm here to help you. In four days, the cops are going to tell a criminal courts judge that your Armando threatened them with a loaded gun. He could get ten to fifteen years, and his bail is going to be—"

"Going to be what?"

Pretty damn high.

"I don't know. Twenty-five thousand. Maybe even fifty."

"Oh my God."

And I can actually see the shadowy physical weight of these troubles draping down to crush her, pressing her shoulders forward until she crumples. I help her to the hard, comfortless couch and she cries and tells me that she had only been worrying about the temporary loss of income, not really thinking about the cost of freeing her husband, beating herself up for not knowing more about how the system works here.

I don't tell her that anyone who points a loaded gun at a cop will most likely get the genuine crap kicked out of them in custody, and that unless we can get it lowered to menacing, the charge will probably be attempted murder, a Class B Felony and a fifteen-year-to-life sentence.

I tell her to take it easy, she's had a shock, she needs time to recover and that's why I'm here to help her.

"Can you help me get food? Can you help me pay the bills?"

"Sure, you can get emergency food stamps and cash grants from the government."

"I went. I filled out twenty pages of applications and they told me I wasn't eligible."

"You're not eligible for food stamps?"

"They said I wasn't even allowed to apply."

"Did they put that in writing?"

"What?"

"Did they give you a written notice of denial and inform you of your right to appeal the decision?"

"No."

Damn. This woman has more troubles than I've got fingers and toes. And I can't afford to take a day to walk her through the system.

"Go back," I tell her. "You have every right to temporary assistance, and if they try to tell you that you don't, you insist that you do. Threaten to sue if you have to. Show them this—" I give her Lonnie Ambush's card. "They will question you, they will fingerprint you, they will tell you to try your local church or food pantry or the Salvation Army, they will say you must be looking for work to be eligible and they will send you to an employment office. They will tell you if you're late for your appointment you have to come back next week. They can do all these things but *they can't deny you the right to apply*. But it will take time."

"And what do I do in the meantime? What do I do right now?"

"How much cash do you have on hand?"

She gets up and goes into the bedroom, shutting the door behind her, but it drifts open a couple of inches and I can see her reaching inside her mattress. My inner Groucho can't help thinking, Now *that's* what I call a padded expense account, waggle-waggle, but I silence him.

She comes back. "Seventy-five dollars."

"Can you get by on that 'til Monday?"

"I guess so. Then what?"

Then you pray the city comes through by Tuesday. Not bloody likely.

"I'm trying to figure things here. Why don't you show me where Sonny's grow room was."

She hesitates. I let the silence settle around us like dust on a grave. Gradually she inches over to a painted white door opposite the bathroom and shows me the empty closet. I get up to take a closer look. The inside is all painted white, no dirt on the floor, broom clean, not even a trace of the skunky smell of home-grown weed.

"What happened?" I ask.

"It was three weeks ago. The police came to the door. They had a search warrant."

"Signed by a judge? With your complete name and address on it and a description of what they were looking for?"

She casts her eyes down. "I didn't look that closely at it."

"No. You wouldn't. And they knew that."

"They checked the closet first. It was only three little plants, but they took everything, the lights, the electrical wires, the soil. Everything."

"They had a warrant," I say, mostly to myself, looking towards the window to see if anybody in the world outside has a clear view of the closet. I'd say probably not.

"Who knew about this?" I ask.

"Just his closest friends. They'd never report him to the police."

But they might tell someone who would.

"How about a neighbor? The gas man?"

"Sonny had just started growing them. They were tiny little plants. He got a year's probation."

He was *on probation* when he stood twenty-five feet away from Pazzerello's shock troops and smoked a blunt with a .22-caliber pistol under his arm?

Camille seems to read my very thoughts.

"After the bust, he . . . he changed," she explains. "He

stopped talking about a lot of things, he'd get mad when I asked him about it."

"Were drug tests a condition of his probation?"

"Yes."

"And did he comply?"

"Oh, yes."

"So he got worse again when he *stopped* smoking pot."

She realizes the truth of my words. "Yes."

"But he was smoking it when I saw him. So where is it?"

She looks up at me with the big, sad eyes of a strangled sheep.

"You want my help or don't you?"

She looks from me to her baby then back to me, and resigns herself to it.

Sonny put these walls up himself. High up behind the bathroom door, there's a little panel that slides open. Camille's too short. I stretch, grab ahold of a wire and pull about an ounce of double-bagged lumps from a space between the walls. I unwrap the wire, open the bags, and examine the contents. Sticky green buds, shot through with resinous red hairs. Pretty good stuff at market rate.

Enough for her to make it through next week all right.

I tell her, "I can take this to someone and get you a couple of hundred bucks for it."

What does she say to my felonious offer?

"Thank you, thank you, thank you."

CHAPTER THREE

1624: First Dutch settlement in New York.
1625: First Dutch settler mugged in New York.
—Little Known Fact

"**MAN**, when he had bad nights, he couldn't even hit a nail straight," says Georgio, scratching a mark at eye-level on the bare wallboard with a chipped yellow pencil. "He'd be easy to piss off, a real pain to work with."

Georgio places the bit over the mark, shakes the dreadlocks out of his eyes, drills a small hole through the wallboard into a stud.

"I swear, he made more sense *after* he took a few hits of the kind, you know what I mean?"

"Yeah, I've been hearing that," I say. "And I've been trying to figure it out."

"Ain't nothin' to figure out. He liked to unwind after a tough day, let off some steam. Ease the stress."

"What kind of stress?"

Georgio's down on one knee, measuring the plywood backing on a homemade bookshelf.

"The stress of being a man with dark skin, honey." He marks the plywood. "Camille tell you about the time he was beaten up on his way to work by five or six cops because he 'fit the profile' of a suspect they were after?"

Obviously not. Georgio nods at me as he picks up the

drill. "Know what their profile was? Get this: Dark-skinned male in T-shirt and jeans."

He drills through the plywood.

"Is that when he started carrying a gun?"

"Help me with this, will you?"

I help him lift the bookshelf and slide it against the wall. The holes don't line up.

"Damn!" he says. "Guess the floor ain't as straight as it should be."

He asks me to get down on the floor, then tilts up the shelf unit so I can shove a couple of quarter-inch wood chips under it.

"That's better," he says, eyeing our work. The shelf unit's a little wobbly, so he slips a washer over a two-inch wood screw, taps it into the hole and tightens it with a screwdriver. My wrists hurt from just watching him.

Georgio finishes, tests the unit, no more wobbling. Satisfied, he dusts off his hands.

"Is that when he started carrying a gun? After being harassed by the cops?"

"He wasn't gunning for the cops, if that's what you want me to say."

"Georgio, I don't *want* you to say anything. I'm trying to find out what was going on in Sonny's life, see if there's some way of defending him."

"What kind of defense you got for pulling a gun on six cops?"

"If there's a pattern of harassment, if he was being affected by the chemicals on the job—"

"Pattern of harassment? That profile fits every person of color in the borough."

This is going in circles.

"Listen, I'm not talking about the national war of white folks on black. First the cops beat him up while he was walking to work. Then they raided his apartment with a warrant, apparently, which means they either had probable cause, or they have targeted his ass for a very specific reason. Now, can you think of a *specific reason* for the cops to target *him*? As opposed to anyone else?"

He looks at me, takes a moment, then admits it. "No. Not really." He scratches his nose. "Except maybe taking us out one at a time."

Now we're getting somewhere.

"Tell me about it," I recommend, sitting down on a bare stool.

"City's been trying to get us out of here any way they can. They sent the fire marshal, but thanks to me and Sonny the place is up to code, we got illuminated exit signs and everything. They send lawyers, process servers, paste up notices. Nothing. But you see, a man used to be able to relax on the stoop and roll a blunt, you know what I'm saying? Same way the suits get to have themselves a couple double martinis at the end of the day. Cops were too busy chasing murderers to bother with folks like us. But that was Dinkins time, this is Pazzerello time. So the mayor starts cracking down on pot smoking in public, a few of us get arrest records and suddenly we're all criminals and no judge in the universe is going to let us stay in this building."

Doesn't seem like the mayor's style, using the cops to go after individual tenants. Too slow. When he wants to take back a building, Pazzerello tends to favor barricades, helicopters, riot police, and a special police tank equipped with a battering ram. But you never know.

·

The hallway is unfinished, water-stained wallboard, exposed conduit, the floor made out of 3/4-inch plywood crudely nailed together with great gaps between them for the north wind to whistle through.

I knock on the battered steel door of apartment 6-E.
"*Entra*."
Come in? The door's open?

Sure enough, it pushes in, offering me a view of a faded green couch and a man seated at a brick-and-plywood table, adjusting the calibrations on a triple-beam balance.

"*Hola.*"

"*Hola. ¿Usted es Señor Lucas?*"

"*No.*"

Oh. Uh . . .

"*No soy 'usted.' Solo los de plata son 'usted.' Yo soy 'tú.' Y tampoco soy Señor Lucas, soy compañero Lucas.*"

What's going on is I used the polite form *usted* and he wants me to use the familiar *tú* because, according to him, only people with money—literally, silver—are called "sir."

"Okay. So you're not a man with silver?"

"No," he says, "I'm a man of fine gold."

He gestures me over, I lean in and see this altar-to-the-great-god-of-plywood workbench overflowing with dirty rags and papers and designs and tiny curly metal shavings and some of the fine tools of the jeweler's trade.

I say, "Sorry, just whenever I see a triple-beam balance the first thing I think of is *not* jewelry."

"Sure, sure," he laughs.

I walk in carefully, since the man ran out of plywood and the unfinished floor leaves you staring right through naked crossbeams and pipes to the floor below. That must thrill the folks downstairs.

He finishes calibrating the balance, and tests it for accuracy with a collection of small metal weights. Then he opens a felt pouch, weighs out several pairs of gold wedding bands, selects a set and carries them over to his workbench. I talk to him while he hammers, heats, pinches, buffs, and polishes the inlaid leaf and filigree and cloisonné. I get much the same story that I got from Georgio.

"Sonny was never a quick-tempered guy," he says. "The only time I ever saw him get violent was when he got stiffed $400 for a week's work."

"Yes, I've heard about his particular method of debt collection."

"It just snuck up on him, you know? He'd be cool and relaxed and mellow and okay-how-are-you-my-man, then five minutes later he'd have *azogue en las venas*,"—it means quicksilver in the blood—"fidgeting and staring right past you. And nasty as a sunburnt bear. Not himself, you know?"

"Why'd the cops bust him instead of, say, you?" I ask, tilting the bronze-colored metal ashtray he lifted from The Starlite Lounge so all the roaches pile up together at the bottom. Three, four, five.

"Don't know. Guess he was the only one with a grow room."

"And they knew right where to look for it."

"You know cops. First thing they do is check behind every door to make sure you ain't got some friend with an M-16 hiding in the closet."

He's right. "But they knew it was there, which means somebody must have told them."

"Why would anybody do that? He was a good guy."

"You can get a few hundred bucks from Crimestoppers for leading the cops to a felony conviction."

"Man, nobody'd turn in Sonny-boy for a handful of dead prezzes! He was our best carpenter!"

"Who lives next door to you?"

"Six-B? Ted Hocks. But the girls all call him Teddy, 'cause he's just a big ol' Teddy bear."

I wonder if his floor looks through to the Tesoros' apartment.

It's a low-rent day care center, with a big black-and-white TV blaring mindless cartoons while three little blond kids take turns bouncing on a mini-trampoline and beating the last ounce of life from a busted down street-sale couch. Ted Hocks is frolicking with the kids, jumping on the furniture and delighting them by doing a handstand and then walking across the floor on his hands with a toddler hanging deliriously from his inverted waist.

I sit down at the wobbly Formica table and the

dirty-blond-haired woman who let me in explains that two of the kids are hers and one is her friend Cynthia's, and that Ted is just the best thing that ever happened to them because he's so good with kids and he only charges two dollars an hour per child, which is so cheap the women can afford to work in the neighborhood and spend even more time with their kids. I say it sounds like a great deal.

"How many children does he look after?"

"Not too many," she says. "He's a little choosy. Besides me and Cynthia, he only takes care of three other moms— Monika, Lisa, and Liz." I'm writing this down.

"They have last names?"

She gives them to me.

"Oh, and sometimes Gerta Wolf's newborn. By the way, my name's Genny."

"Mine's Filomena."

"Filo-what?"

"Fil-o-men-a."

"What's it mean?"

"Actually, it means 'beloved' in ancient Greek."

"Oh, you Greek?"

"I suppose if you go back far enough."

"Say something in Greek."

"*Andra moi ennepe, mousa, polutropon, hos mala polla.*"

"Wow. What's it mean?"

"It means I want to talk to Ted."

"Well, you just wait a minute."

Sure enough, Ted drops back to his feet and announces, "Snack time!" and the three kids come running to the table. I give up my seat, since there are only five chairs, as Ted takes out bowls and spoons, pours out four heaping servings of super-sugary children's cereal and sits himself down to gobble up some Lucky Charms alongside them while Genny gazes at him with much more affection than a baby-sitter usually gets.

Okay . . .

Except for his stringy blond mustache and a few wisps of chin hair, he looks like a big kid in blue denim bib overalls, his straw-colored hair tied back with a classic-hippie red paisley bandana.

And there are no gaping holes in the floor. Just a few cracks, since I can hear Camille humming a lullaby in the apartment below.

"Nice floor. Anybody help you with it?" I ask.

"No, ma'am," says Ted. "I built this place myself."

More adoring looks from Genny-the-mom.

I ask about Sonny, and Ted says, "Man, I knew that guy was heading for trouble—*chomp chomp*—You could see it coming—*gulp*—Didn't have the right attitude, you know? And the drugs—*slurp*—Drugs messed up his head, man. It's his own fault if he got—*chomp*—nailed for it."

Genny says, "Slow down, honey." Turns to me: "Teddy doesn't even smoke cigarettes."

Yeah, but he eats like a tiger shark on speed.

Belch!

She looks like she's about to say, "Isn't that sweet?" But it comes out, "And he doesn't eat meat."

"Animals are our friends," the kids say.

"That's right, little buddies," says Ted, drinking the last bit of pink-colored sugar milk straight out of the bowl. "Now who's up for a game of Twister?"

"Forget this guy, Fil," Lonnie Ambush says, picking up a menu. "He's not a sympathetic case. We want—"

"You want a fifty-year-old white woman who's been working on Wall Street and giving twenty percent of her income to charity and paying the rent on time for the past thirty years until her life-long partner brought home the AIDS virus and now she needs medical marijuana to keep herself from wasting away before the girls' soccer team she coaches wins the national championship. You don't want a resident alien with limited income and poor English who smokes pot to keep himself from swinging a hammer at his boss's head."

"Uh—yeah." He peers out the window at the action on

the courthouse steps, memorizing faces for the future. Back to me: "What's good here?"

"It's all good." I order a Greek salad. Lonnie looks up at the bright poster of the smiling blond model with perfect teeth proffering a gyro, and orders one, as if anyone could possibly stay so neat and manicured as the woman in the ad while eating something as unwieldy as a gyro, complete with onions, lettuce, and dressing, all wrapped up in a flat round bread. Next time, I resolve to take Lonnie to a place where the food must be eaten with a fork, in small bites.

"Unless you think they planted the gun," says Lonnie.

"They didn't flake him. I saw it."

"*You're* a witness to him pulling a fucking gun on the cops? What if they ask you that at the trial?"

"They won't ask it if I'm working for you solely as a private investigator. They can't subpoena me."

"But they can subpoena *me*."

"So? You're not a witness."

"Fil, why are you doing this?"

"Because there's a story behind it."

He prunes his face up in that "Yeah, right" way, about to dismiss me, then hesitates. Maybe he heard about me pulling in the City University as a client using the same methods.

"The guy's got no money, right?" he says.

"No."

His eyebrows float up, mirroring his expectations.

"Does it lead to money?"

"Probably." Not good enough. "Very likely."

"Hmm." He's pondering if I'm worth a 4-to-1 shot.

Our food comes, and I have to sit by and watch this man disembowel the struggling, squirming gyro that never hurt anybody in its short, sweet life and listen to him tear screaming pieces of it apart with his pitiless incisors.

My salad's good, too, but I'm going to have to brush and gargle the Spanish onions away. Another bad meal choice. I should just have plain yogurt and Wonder bread before meeting prospective clients, but I need the mental agility that only feta cheese and red onions can provide. You understand.

"How do you stay so trim?" he asks me.

"I come from a country without Ben and Jerry's ice cream."

"And you know exercising doesn't help me any. I think it's because of the family genes."

And I think it's because of the family *refrigerator*.

In a surprise move, Lonnie actually picks up the check, and we cross the street together, talking about the squatters' dens I visited today.

"I can't pay you for that kind of spadework," he says. "But if you can dig up something in this Tesoro guy's defense that's worth paying for, bring it in and we'll talk it over."

"Right." As long as it's not over lunch.

He slaps me on the back and climbs the courthouse steps like a steelhead trout struggling upstream to reach strange spawning grounds. Following the smell of money.

I've always thought that freshly printed money smells faintly like vomit. What's that about?

Money. I just worked a case a couple of weeks ago where I helped bring in enough evidence to free a man who spent twenty months in jail because he couldn't make $5,000 bail. He turned down two plea offers, and ended up doing more time than he would have under either offer, because he was innocent. Lack of money kept him in jail. It's that simple. You want justice, go turn on *Perry Mason*.

And I don't know why I should trust Lonnie, a guy whose word is almost as reliable as a two-dollar streetcorner watch. I'd like to help the Tesoros, but right now I've got to fulfill my promise to drum up some high-paying *latino* business for Davis & Brown.

As I turn away, two women walk past me on their way from the courthouse.

"My son got ten years, but he's getting three off for good behavior," says one.

"Gee, I wish I had a son like that," says the other.

What a day! I visit the Yago Foods factory, where all they say is, "Yes, we have thefts, but we don't need a PI for that, just more security cameras"; a snooty Cuban-American law firm that dismisses me on sight; a local bank that says they have their own security; a car dealership full of Yugos—which, for some deep and mysterious reason, come in a wide variety of styles and colors—where they also have their own security; and a Dominican-owned law firm that is interested in my services but doesn't have the money to pay me. I even stop into a funeral home because the sign in the back of their hearse caught my eye: WE PUT THE "FUN" BACK IN FUNERAL.

I'm *not* kidding.

They also have a neon sign in the window that says: MONUMENTS: GUARANTEED.

Guaranteed? Against what? Do the gravestones come with a thirty-year warranty for parts, ninety days for labor?

Good thing the housemates are home for Antonia. I call anyway to make sure she's all right, and she asks me to bring home this poster of the NGC 2997 galaxy (whatever that is) that she's been wanting for weeks. Well, it's only been about ten days, but it seems like weeks to her, and I don't want to discourage this newfound interest in science. I promise her we'll go get it this weekend.

The Club El Mocambo on the Horace Harding Expressway is the last stop on my list. I push open the door and step into the air lock–like vestibule that serves as an intermediary chamber between places of unequal light so that one may gradually grow accustomed to it and enter the thick, chocolaty darkness inside without getting the bends or some similar permanent physical damage to the optic nerve. There are already a few early boozers here, huddling in the dark recesses under the cavernous arches, but the real fun doesn't start 'til around eleven o'clock at night. A couple of techies are still bolting the stage together.

I grab a bar stool and order a beer. I've been nursing it

a few minutes when *Señor* Gonzalo Mendieta approaches from the back room, his image doubled in the mirror behind the bottles.

Another portly, well-fed guy. At least business is good for somebody, but I wouldn't want to be his liver.

"Hello, tall, dark, and foxy," he says, slapping a sweaty paw on my arm.

"Hello, cool, wet, and slippery," I answer.

"What is this? A beer? Pfff! Ricky, get *Señorita* Buscarsela an amaretto, a champagne cocktail, a sea breeze, *something* befitting a woman of her class."

Translation: I own a pair of X chromosomes. He likes that in a woman.

"Is she not something special, Ricky?"

"Oh, yeah," Ricky says to him. "If I wasn't married I'd tell her how cute she is myself."

"I believe the correct grammatical form is the subjunctive, 'If I *weren't* married,'" I explain. Gonzalo of course is under no such self-restriction.

"Do you mind?" he says, pulling out a thick, dark cigar.

"Smoke all you want, just don't blow it in my face."

He lights it up and blows it in my face.

"Now, what'd you want to see me about?" he asks.

"I wanted to talk to you about your club, see if you've got a problem we could help you with." I hand him a Davis & Brown business card. I don't have my own yet, not 'til I pass the six-month review. "We handle employee background checks, building security, injury lawsuit investigations, or maybe there's a rival club that's just trying to make life difficult for you. Give us your hardest nut and we'll crack it for you."

The hammering stops, and a solid young woman with bright skin and dark eyes wearing a sleeveless black T-shirt slides out from under the stage platforms, speed wrench in her hands, all covered with dust. She slaps the dirt off, flashing a couple of abstract tattoos on her upper arms.

"As a matter of fact, there is something," says Gonzalo. "Photos of me . . . with another woman."

"Is tough break, Gonzo," says the dark-haired woman, approaching the bar. Russian accent. Ricky hands her a glass of water without asking. "You screw woman, she screws you. That is capitalist system, yes?"

She gulps down the water.

"You've got to help me," says Gonzalo.

"Wait a minute," I say. I introduce myself.

"Sherry Aksakalova," she says, seizing my hand with a vise-like grip and shaking vigorously.

I get the story from Gonzo. His ex-mistress wants ten grand for the prints and naturally he doesn't want the cops involved. Discretion is our middle name, though there are a few other names I could think of calling it right now. Gonzo's willing to pay, but he wants to be sure that all copies of the photos and negatives are destroyed. I tell him that's impossible to verify, and that the best option is to set up the exchange, videotape the whole thing, and then threaten to have the ex-mistress arrested for blackmail. Then she'll either bargain—she gets to keep the money, but if the photos ever surface, the videotape goes to the police—or she won't, it goes to trial, the photos come out, and he has a lot of explaining to do.

"What do I do then?" he asks.

"Confess to your wife, Gonzalo," I say. "She'll either forgive you or dump you. Either way, it'll be quick and it's better than spending the rest of your life in the shadow of fear."

He thinks about it. "And if I want to—?"

"If you want to hire us, it's seven hundred and fifty a day."

That hurts him.

"But we work long hours." I write Chip's name on the card. "Why don't you come in and talk to my boss, Chip Davis? He'll give you a man's perspective on this."

Gonzalo nods, then pours himself a straight-up shot of Jamaican rum.

"You want problems, I tell you where to go," says Sherry.

I slide over to the stool next to her. She exudes the strong, sweet scent of a working woman. I learn that she's a hardcore rock musician, straight out of the rubble of the new Russia since the mid-nineties, who kicks it out at Sintonizando, a sixteen-track set-up on Broadway and Whitney Avenue, right near the LIRR tracks, the perfect location for a recording studio, right?

"You like industrial thrash?" she asks.

"Can't get enough of it."

"Then you will like to hear my group, Divided Urge, next time we play Roosevelt Avenue bar."

"Sure. Do you sing in English or Russian?"

"Both."

"You getting a lot of gigs?"

"Not enough. Let me tell you how music business works," she says. "You can have a really bad deal or a really *really* bad deal. We sell four thousand CD singles, but still get no money. I ask boss to renegotiate subrights and royalties, he says, 'No way. Rights and royalties are heart and soul of contract.'"

"The words 'heart and soul' and 'contract' should never be used in the same sentence."

"He smokes lots of pot, but still is asshole."

"I know the type."

"Is producing video movie of Ibsen's *Doll House* where Nora gets naked and axes everybody in house to death."

"What was that babe's name again?" says Gonzalo, butting in.

Jesus, where do you go for privacy in this place? What's the cover of darkness for?

"He has big money worries," says Sherry.

"What's his name?"

"Vladimir Dvurushnik."

"You won't find him at Sintonizando, *Señorita* Buscarsela," says Gonzalo. "May I suggest that you try the Krepki Factory on 43rd Avenue?"

Damn. There goes my high-paying *latino* business. But a lead's a lead. One more stop before I head home.

The Krepki Factory is two stories of frozen ugliness, a concrete shoebox made of cinder blocks and grimy glass window slits. It actually won an award in 1946 for the best use of war-surplus materials. Reason enough to avoid the next war. There's a big shiny red steel door in the middle of the block, with a bell and a handwritten sign above it that says, "DO NOT RING BELL."

Obviously a test of my logistical skills.

I knock, but my feminine knuckles were not meant to rattle steel like thunder. After a few silent moments I turn around and use the round part of my rubber heel to pound on the door. I half-expect a guy with an emerald ring and a walrus mustache to pop out and say, "Who rang that bell?" but when the door opens, it's a donut jockey in a blue rent-a-uniform, who says,

"Quit pounding, will ya? Why don't ya ring the bell?"

"Your sign says not to ring the bell."

"That's just for messengers."

Oh.

He does a quick pass with a hand-held metal detector, front and back, then pats me under the arms down to the waist and sends me upstairs.

"Private investigator, eh?" says Dvurushnik, the company president, tossing my card on the desk between us. "And what services do you offer me?"

"Security risk assessment, for one. I could've brought in a howitzer past that candy-ass body search. He didn't go near my ankles, where, in fact, I'm carrying a .38-caliber revolver."

That raises his bushy black eyebrows. He cranes his neck slightly, peering over the edge of his desk. I lift my pants cuff just enough to reveal a well-stocked ankle holster. Not where I usually pack it, but you've got to keep them guessing.

He's impressed, but not enough. "We currently contract with Glendale Loss Prevention Services," he says, placing a rate card on the desk where I can read it. "As you can see, they charge fifty dollars to provide us with name that goes with unidentified phone number."

"That's pretty expensive. I can usually get that info in a minute for about a buck-and-a-half."

"You promise a lot, Miss—Miss Buscarsela—but can you really do anything for me?"

What is this, a test?

"Okay," I say, tapping the ad with a hardened fingernail. "This company offers pulse-tone conversions, where you provide a recording of someone dialing a number and they decode it for you, at seventy-five bucks a pop. Pick up the phone. Fine. Now give me the receiver." I turn and face the wall. "Dial a number."

Boop-beep-boop-bip-bip-ba-deep.

I turn back to him. "Two-eight-two-three-three-five-nine. Whose number is that?"

"Never mind," he says, putting the receiver down. "How are you with computers?"

"We've got some real whizzes at the agency—"

"I didn't ask how good is agency. I ask how good are *you*."

The fabled Russian directness.

"I'm not a whiz," I admit. "I can't hack into the Pentagon's security files or anything, but I can set up a motion-sensitive microchip camera and operational software inside a PC without the user knowing about it, should that ever become legal in this state."

He strokes his thick black mustache.

"I believe I can help you, Mr. Dvurushnik. Why don't you tell me what the problem is?"

He contemplates the dull, gray cinder blocks behind me as if he expects their molecules to suddenly rearrange and spell out the secret of eternal youth in bright orange letters at any moment, then nods once, sharply. He holds up a box of Internet software and says, "This."

He puts two copies of the package side by side on the desk. The color on the first one's a little faded, not as bright as the original.

I tell him, "Pirated software is the FBI's jurisdiction. Try calling the National Computer Crime Squad."

"Is not just software, is everything. Videos, CDs. Listen to this—"

He presses a button on a portable CD-player and hits me with music that probably left four out of five test subjects covering their heads with a pillow and writhing in agony. I wait for him to tell me what this is.

"Is terrible copy, yes?"

I nod. "Videos, too?"

"Videos, too. Maybe is electronic eavesdropping?"

I shake my head. "You don't need a debugging expert." Which is a good thing, because it's not my field. "It is possible to send digitally encoded information through the phone lines, but it's a lot easier just to sneak out copies of the masters."

"All workers are inspected when they leave."

"You mean like I was inspected?"

"We also run very tight inventory check."

"And who checks their work?"

He rubs his thick black beard stubble. "Then maybe it's somebody in inventory."

"It could be a million things. It's our job to narrow it down for you."

"How?"

"Well, we start with the payroll records, look for somebody who's spending beyond their means and doesn't have a rich uncle. We get a short list of suspects, then you've got two options, surveillance or undercover. Meaning you follow the suspects around until they make a drop, or you plant someone inside the factory, on the shop floor, and try to find out what's going on. But it usually takes several weeks for a suspect to initiate contact with the plant. In your case, I recommend surveillance first."

He fiddles with my business card, then taps it firmly on the desk, picks up the phone, and dials. After a moment:

"Put Mr. Davis on," he commands.

"By the way, pirated products are a police matter."

"I don't trust your police."

CHAPTER FOUR

Everyone has a good reason for not wanting to die.
—*Paths of Glory*

THE MESSAGE DANCES before my eyes at sixty-eight miles per hour:

Praise God		Meet God
←		→

The choice is mine. I choose to praise Him, signaling left to cut around the eighteen-wheel diesel colossus blocking the center lane on the Long Island Expressway.

Paaarrp!

Jesus! A Chevy Suburban defies me with superior mass and acceleration. Thing was seventy feet back when I checked the side-view mirror about two seconds ago. SOB must be doing about ninety. Used to be people saw a car as messed up as the one I'm riding in, they kept their distance, knowing that here was a driver with nothing to lose. But not when they can commandeer a domestic tank so damn big they ought to be paying real estate tax on the thing. Think of it: $42,000 for a hunk of metal that burns gas. I expect a car to run on dilithium crystals for that kind of money.

I try the move again, and the guy in the Lexus behind me tries the same thing, angrily leaning on his horn. Man! How many dickheads are behind the wheels of cars in this country? Answer: Take the number of cars and subtract 2.

I push the company klunker to the terminal velocity of seventy-two, and it starts to vibrate like I'm trying to outrun the Red Baron on a bullet-riddled doghouse as I pull alongside the truck's long freight compartment with "Daniel's Supermarket" painted on it in lime green letters. I edge past the front end, signal, shift back into the center lane, and the Lexus driver gives me the finger as he roars past.

Too bad my gun's in a lock-box in the trunk, empty, in full compliance with the law. Fuck that. First stop, it goes into my holster, with the bullets in another pocket. Only break one law at a time, that's my motto.

The Lexus pulls away, displaying a red-white-and-blue bumper sticker that says: VOTE FOR GRANGER: PROTECT FREEDOM.

Freedom? What the hell does this white yuppie *gringo* know about threats to his freedom? I'd like to stuff him in a box and pack him off to a place where the government is *really* out to get you: maybe put him in a time machine and send him back to Chile in September of 1973; or make him a Hutu in Tutsi territory, a headstrong woman in Taliban territory, or absolutely anyone of the natives of Chechnya, Guatemala, or South Central Los Angeles.

Gee, highway driving brings out the best in me, all these creative tortures I never knew I had inside. Maybe some after-hours sex last night would have helped, but Stan had to drop out of our planned evening together with another emergency over at the hospital. Well, there's always tomorrow night or Sunday. Here's hoping.

I'm heading for Pablito Muñoz's last known address, Scarzello Farms, 486 Blueberry Ridge Road, South Cove Neck, Long Island, with a torn black-and-white three-inch photo of him and not much else besides his mother's prayers. At least that's where I should be heading, but the map and the road don't conform for an instant and I find myself passing through the center of town, which I was trying to avoid. There's a traffic cop in a pressed uniform in the middle of the main street, snapping his arms at motorists with such military precision you'd think he was guarding the border against marauding bands of French Canadians pissed-off about that whole acid rain thing.

Hey, if you're going to subscribe to a conspiracy theory, you might as well go all the way.

It takes me fifteen minutes to retrace my steps and find the turn-off for Blueberry Ridge Road. North to Scarzello Farms, a flat stretch of dust and dried corn stalks edged in by trees with a few sparse yellow and brown leaves still clinging to their bare, pre-winter branches. I kick up some dirt and breathe in the take-me-back-to-the-country down-home smell of a working barnyard. I'm a long way from Queens.

I watch the high clouds recoiling from an advancing cold front as if they, too, were seeking some warmer place to go. A southeasterly wind, the first real taste of the Arctic winds to come down from Hudson Bay, straight out of Canada, all part of that French Canadian plot, don't you know, to—

"Why so many bumper stickers?" asks the middle-aged farmer, squinting his bright eyes at me.

"Don't laugh, they're holding the car together."

I introduce myself, give him a card.

"Buscarsela," he says, giving it the proper Mediterranean lilt. "Maybe you a cousin of the Scarzellos, eh?"

"Could be." Distant cousins.

"My niece, she look a little like you," he says. "So what business you have at my place?"

"I'm looking for this man," I say, holding up the photo. He studies it with shaky hands while I tell him some of the story.

"It's no good, that picture. Mr. Pablito was much thinner. I remember he was with me two months."

"Do you know where is he now?"

"No. The work here dries up in mid-October. I only got three men left, then we start again in the spring."

"Can I talk to them?"

"Sure." He points me towards a shack on the south side of the barn. I start to walk away.

"What's he done?"

"Nothing. He's disappeared."

"*Che infamia.*"

The shack is heated, with a propane stove, a working sink and toilet and nine bunk beds, enough to house fifteen to twenty men in reasonable comfort during the height of the harvest season.

"*El patrón es buen hombre.*"

"*Sí, es hombre decente.*"

The boss is a decent man.

"We get coffee and donuts."

"Rice, corn, and beans."

"And Sundays off."

"*Señor* Scarzello is not like the other *patrones.*"

"He doesn't treat us like some cheap machine parts imported from Mexico, *entiendes*?"

"*Sí, entiendo,*" I say. Mr. Scarzello is a rare breed on any continent. "About Pablito—"

"He was with the last batch that was let go on the fifteenth." Nineteen days ago.

"You know where he went?" I ask.

"No."

"Try the job bank," says the other one.

"The what?"

"It's at the end of the train station."

"They stand around all day waiting for people to drive up and offer them work."

"What kind of work can they get in the winter?" I ask.

"Mostly home building."

"There's a lot of development out here."

"Tell me something," I ask. "Did Pablito seem particularly angry or upset when he left?"

"No more than anyone else who's just lost his job and his bed for the night."

"He knew it was coming."

"They all knew it was coming," says the other guy.

"That's how it is."

And how it will be, forever and ever.

"One more thing," I ask. "Where is this blueberry ridge?"

"Oh, they leveled it to build Blueberry Ridge Road."

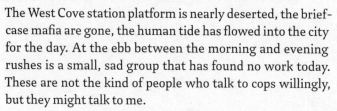

The West Cove station platform is nearly deserted, the brief-case mafia are gone, the human tide has flowed into the city for the day. At the ebb between the morning and evening rushes is a small, sad group that has found no work today. These are not the kind of people who talk to cops willingly, but they might talk to me.

Angry tones dissipate as I approach. They turn silently towards me, mouths dripping bits of bitterness. I feel so tall next to the Salvadorans.

I try not to sound too official: "You guys know Pablito Muñoz? His mother María is worried that she hasn't heard from him in a few days."

"And who are you?" asks the big talker in Spanish.

"I'm a friend of *Señora* Muñoz."

"Why doesn't she come herself?"

"She's too old and weak, and she wouldn't know how to do all this."

"And you do?"

"Sure."

"So she hired you?"

"Yes, she hired me to find her son. Have you seen him?" I take out the photo, show it around.

The older man says, "He was staying at a farm."

"Until two-and-a-half weeks ago," I say.

He considers this. "Maybe the yellow house on Hudson Street?"

"No, it's too crowded," says the big talker.

"It's better than sleeping in a drainpipe."

"I haven't seen him there," says one of the others.

"How about—?"

"Any money in telling you where he is?" interrupts Big Talker.

"Sure. How about twenty bucks?"

"Make it fifty."

"It's his mother's money."

"What do I care?"

"What a nice attitude. Since this is our first contact, it's twenty or nothing."

The older guy says, "I'll tell you for twenty-five dollars."

"You were going to tell me for nothing a moment ago."

"The price went up."

Aw, Jesus. "Okay," I say, digging out a couple of bills. "Here."

"He's working for East Cove Landscaping."

"No he isn't," say the others. "He's—"

Nothing.

"He's where?" I ask.

Hands come up, twitching for money.

"Oh, fuck the fucking bunch of you." I start to walk away. Diplomacy in action.

"Hey! Hey! Okay, forget it," say the voices. I keep going.

"Fifty dollars for the five of us," says the talker.

I stop. This is how it goes sometimes.

"Okay with you?" I say to the older man. He'd rather not, but he nods. Three more bills distribute evenly, then they tell me Pablito's working two jobs at Daniel's Supermarket downtown *and* at East Cove Landscaping.

"No hard feelings," says Big Talker. "We're just trying to provide for our families."

Right.

I log a fifty-dollar "cash payment to informants" in the Muñoz notebook, and head for the supermarket and its sprawling parking lot. I walk through the bright glass doors and stand for a moment in stunned city dweller's admiration of the Astrodome-sized interior, the wide aisles brimming with the bright reds and yellows and blues of name-brand packages, the miraculous fruits and vegetables section that would bring gasps of amazement from the narrow confines of Corona, the shopping carts loaded with groceries ready for stowage aboard sporty suburban supply ships.

"Can I help you, ma'am?" the security guard asks curtly.

"Oh, yes, I'd like to see the manager."

"About what, ma'am?" This is not a friendly encounter.

"It's a private matter."

"Well, why don't you start by telling me about it?"

Then it wouldn't be private, would it, asshole?

"I'm afraid I can't do that. Lawyer-client privilege."

He looks at me as if to say, *You ain't a lawyer*. Okay, maybe I'm not wearing my Lady Vice President's outfit, since I was heading to a farm and probably some dirtier places, but I still thought the trench-coat-and-red-nail-polish look was professional enough. It's not like I have to shampoo my hair because the lice are complaining that they haven't had a bath for weeks.

The assistant manager listens until I say a Spanish name, then quickly tells me to go try in back. Sergeant Slaughter stays on me the whole time, keeping an eye on my nimble fingers as I push through the big rubber-rimmed doors to the cold room and the loading bay, where I find the guy with the clipboard.

"What do you want?" he says.

"This guy work for you?"

"Who the fuck is this?"

"His name is Pablito Muñoz. Does he work here?"

"No," he says, not looking.

"You're sure? You've never seen him before?"

"Ronnie, get her the fuck out of here."

"Yes, Mr. Palladino."

And Ronnie actually grabs my belt and collar and carries me over to the big black doors and pushes me out through them, then grips my arm and walks me all the way out to the sidewalk and stands there elbows out with his fists balled-up on his shiny patent leather belt, waiting.

I wait, too, my chest pressing up against the .38 in my

shoulder holster with each heavy, purging breath. Some people just don't know how lucky they are to be alive.

"Stay out of this store," he warns me.

And it's over.

I've got a pretty big rage-suppression headache right now. But it's better than having to shoot my way to the Mexican border.

I guess.

The supermarket guys were either hiding something or they were just being complete assholes. Right now, my money's on them being assholes, but I'll have someone else check it out for me later, if there's any reason to think the whole thing wasn't a twenty-five-dollar sucker bet. I hope the landscaper gig isn't more of the same.

I go to the address scribbled in my notebook, where the dispatcher tells me, "I don't know anything about day hires. Talk to the foreman."

"Where's he?"

He gives me a list of seven addresses on the classy side of town.

"Could you narrow this down for me?"

He takes back the list, gruff but not nasty at least, crosses off a few entries from this morning, hands it back.

Four possibilities.

"Watch out for dogs," he advises.

It's pretty obvious where they've been. At the first two places the lawns look like they've been hot-combed and shellacked. The third actually has a stray leaf or two and a few blades of grass that don't all face the same direction. I pull over to check the map, and keep watching my rear-view mirror as a cop in a patrol car follows me all the way to the fourth address. This is heading straight past irritating into the absurd.

I park behind a pickup truck and trailer full of lawn gear while a crew of seven manicures the terrain into submission with relentless precision. Two guys are raking out the shrubs, two more work the leaf blowers, one operates an industrial-sized lawnmower and another works the edge-trimmer while a seventh, the foreman, plots the team's next move on a color-coded topographic map.

I get out and lean on my car door facing the police officer and enjoy watching him have a hell of a time trying to look like he's got some business being there instead of just watching me.

I finally take pity on him and turn my attention to the foreman.

"Yeah, he did a few days' work with us last week," says the foreman, handing back Pablito's photo. "But I haven't seen him since Saturday. If you find him, tell him we got at least a couple more weeks' work for him."

"Did he owe you any money?"

"I don't let that happen."

"You owe him?"

"Every worker is paid in cash at the end of the day."

"How much did Muñoz get?"

"Fifty."

That's not much to disappear on.

I spend some time talking to the other workers. Muñoz seemed like an okay fellow to them, did his work without major complaints, regularly sent money home to his mother, stayed in one of those illegal overcrowded subdivided attic apartments near the tracks for a few days, they think, but they can't or won't tell me which one, and it doesn't matter now because he is definitely gone and they've got other things to worry about.

The two guys deflect their leaf blowers in gentlemanly fashion, allowing me to pass through as I walk down the weather-sealed driveway to the street. Back at the car, I check in with Katwona and tell her that my investigation is definitely going to carry over into tomorrow. She informs me that the business will still remain operative despite my two-day absence.

On a lark, I decide to go up to the cop and give him my card.

"My name's Filomena, and I'm feeling kind of hungry so I'm going into town to get a bite to eat. Anyplace you recommend?"

"Sure, you can get good *tortillas* at Yanmei Wei's place on Front Street." He smiles at me. I'm not sure how to read that.

"Thanks, Officer Eastmann," I say, checking his nametag. "Listen, I'm out here on an assignment. I'm trying to locate this man."

I show him the photo, and he listens to the particulars. Nothing registers, but he promises to keep an eye out. Guard dogs sniff Spanish blood and start barking at me as I pull away down the street.

Yanmei Wei's is a small Chinese take-out place near the economic borderline dividing the community. An unlikely place to get *tortillas*, but as I order at the counter, pay in cash, get a receipt and sit down at a greasy Formica table to eat, dozens of soil-spattered hard-muscled men six inches shorter than me come in and order *pupusa* and other dishes, speaking in halting Spanish-English with Ms. Wei, who apparently lets them run a tab, something no other restaurant in the county would do for them. Actually, nobody would give them credit back home in Ecuador, either.

But if she knows her customers that well . . .

I walk up to the counter.

"Everything okay?" says Ms. Wei.

"It's delicious."

We talk while she's packing quart-sized portions of shrimp lo mein into pint-sized boxes. I show her the photo. Instant recognition.

"Sure, he came in a few times and asked if I needed kitchen help. I told him to try the diner on Church Street."

"What's the name of that place?"

"The Church Street Diner."

I should have known.

"They hire many Spanish people with no papers to do the dirty work," she says.

"And they all come here to eat," I say, looking around at the crowded tables. "When did you start putting Central American dishes on the menu?"

"Last year. They like it, but the landlord says I'm attracting a bad crowd and he won't extend my lease."

"How long you been here?"

"Five years."

"You could file a civil rights suit accusing him of discrimination."

"In this town? The landlords and judges have a foursome every Tuesday at the Cove Neck Country Club. They're all buddies."

"Don't file it in town court. File it in federal court."

"How do I do that?"

"Got a pen?" I write down a number. There are only so many causes I can take up. "Call them. They'll help you."

Then I talk to the customers about Pablito.

"There's so many of us, who remembers—?"

"I saw him a couple of weeks ago—" says one.

"Up at the farm—"

"He was working—"

Another one interrupts:

"—he was working at that diner. I saw him there."

"You did? When?" I ask.

"A couple of days ago."

"You saw him two days ago?"

"Maybe it was three."

I head for the Church Street Diner. It's a big-windowed chrome-plated soda shop with a pink-and-black jukebox by the door. There's a group of teenage metalheads hanging out on the corner trying desperately to age themselves prematurely by means of cigarettes and crude language. Spray-painted on the wall behind them is a most peculiar graffito expressing a dislike for the people of a single West African country: NIGERS OUT, it says.

I wonder how they feel about people from Mali?

"You want a job washing dishes?" asks the manager.

"No, I don't want a job washing dishes. I'm looking for somebody. My client hired me to—"

He jerks a thumb in the direction of the kitchen.

Fine.

Everybody's too hot and hurried to talk to me, but when I mention a mother who can't find her son, a short woman with a round, Mayan face and the name "Aminta" sewn onto her shirt stops washing dishes and leads me out the back door.

"Why are we out here?" I ask in Spanish.

"Because the boss fired my friend Cecilia for speaking Spanish in front of the customers," she says, also in Spanish.

And you wonder why immigrants stay in their own enclaves.

"Pablito only started here last week, part-time in the evening," she says. "He didn't come in Wednesday, and they still owe him two days' pay."

He didn't collect on two days' pay? Now I know something's wrong.

"You haven't seen him since Tuesday?"

"That's right."

"What time Tuesday?"

"Ay, let me think. It was the end of the late shift. Maybe twelve or twelve-thirty at night?"

As far as I know, that makes her the last person to see him.

Does she know where he went? No. Did he seem upset, nervous, angry, scared, anything?

"*Señorita*, we wash three hundred plates an hour, fifty hours a week to make a few hundred dollars to pay the rent. Everyone in the place is upset, nervous, angry, and scared. Whenever *el latino* tries to organize and fight for something, the bosses fire all the undocumented workers. But when they want cheap labor, they can't hire enough of us. No American would take this job."

Thus confirming a theory of mine that the poor exist in order to keep the middle class so scared of ending up like them that they'll frantically keep working overtime for the rich.

"You're a smart woman, Aminta," I say. "You should learn English so you can get out of here and progress."

"*Ave María*, only my ten-year-old María Caridad knows English. She translates everything for me."

Same old story. Coming to the U.S. without English is like landing on the moon without a space helmet. It kind of handicaps your movements.

I thank Aminta and walk out past the group of aspiring burnouts, who hurl a couple of ethnic- and gender-based curses at me, practicing for the real thing, once they're old enough to vote.

They probably think they're rebelling, but I have seen enough heavy metal post-punk teenage nihilism to know that rather than being a challenge to the system, it usually ends up serving the system by creating resignation to an everything-is-crap-anyway-so-why-bother course of inaction. The unspoken paradox is that *nihilism sells*. Rebellion is drained of real meaning and channeled into the buying of one set of products instead of another set of products. Even the once-subversive promise of cyberspace has become just another place where they can sell you Coca-Cola. And thus we see the dangers of the post-Heideggerian rejection of history.

Everyone write that down.

The wind blows my hair into my face as I fish out my car keys, invisible icy wedges piercing my suddenly thin coat, a real taste of the coldness of space in the sun's wake.

Darkness falls.

I head for the *second* cheapest motel in town (Davis & Brown can cover the difference), and I'm about to make a left turn across oncoming traffic when someone behind me driving a late model assault vehicle with anti-aircraft beacons mounted on top nearly runs me off the road.

"Signaling *is* legal!" I yell at the receding shape of the black steel-clad behemoth. I wonder if the damn fool realizes that one of the greatest classical tragedies was precipitated by an angry young man named Oedipus killing his unrecognized father Laius in a prototypical example of road rage.

"Some damn fool nearly crushed me as I was turning in here," I complain to the plumpish white-haired woman at the registration desk.

"Well, whenever something like that happens to me, I just think to myself, What would Jesus do?" she says.

"Oh, really?" Whenever something like that happens to me, I think, What would Vlad the Impaler do?

"Would this be the same Jesus who kicked the merchants out of the temple and once drove a legion of devils into the sea where they all drowned?" I ask. You can tell which Gospel *I* read.

She makes me pay in advance.

So I pay cash and keep the receipts. That's how Davis & Brown wants it done.

First stop is the bathroom, where there's a wall phone next to the toilet. Do people actually—? Oh, never mind.

And I can't resist taking a look at the complimentary toiletries. Soap, shampoo, conditioner, and something called a shoe mitt. I don't know what it is, exactly, but you realize that the spoonerism of "shoe mitt" is "moose shit."

Most people *never* notice these things. Sorry. It's been a long day.

Time to call Antonia, make sure everything's okay. I talk to the housemates in Spanish and stay with Spanish to find out how my baby is doing. She's fine, but she misses me, which is a mighty nice thing to hear from a twelve-year-old who *could* be entering the my-mother-is-an-idiot stage that so many of her friends are going through. I tell her I should be home by tomorrow afternoon, early evening at the latest, and we'll do something special together.

Like be together.

I try calling Stan at home, then at work, then finally dial his pager. A few minutes later he calls me back and we make tentative plans for tomorrow night and I can't help switching into Spanish for some steamy love talk. *¡Ay, cara mía! ¡Mi querida!*

I'm undressing for a much-needed shower when an

authoritative knock rattles the door. Flashlights beam in through the blinds and pounding shakes the walls as the metallic voices of cheap megaphones surround me with shouts of "Police! Open up!"

I throw on the trench coat to cover myself and open the door. Two beefy county cops rush in, guns drawn.

"Don't you fucking *move*, bitch!"

"Turn and face the fucking wall!"

Guns in my face. Contradictory directions.

"*Now!*"

The cop on the left sinks a meat hook into my arm so he can spin me and throw me against the wall. I barely get my other arm up to prevent a broken nose, and he places his gun next to my face.

"I said get against the fucking wall, greaseball!"

"And don't fucking move!"

He holds me there, and another cop comes in and quickly checks the room for bodies while a fourth covers me from the doorway. I don't talk or move, my hands spread out maybe eighteen inches away from my body, absolutely still.

When they're convinced I'm alone, they come back to me.

"Okay, where's the stuff?" they ask.

Some idiots are still shining lights on me through the window.

"What stuff?" I say. Taking it slow.

"Don't fuck with us, you fucking bitch!"

"Where's the fucking stuff?"

Jeezus. How did *these* guys pass the vocabulary test?

"Fuck her. Keep looking."

They pull the drawers from the night table, flip the Bible over and fan the pages, dump my overnight bag out on the bed and sift most unreasonably through my papers and effects.

One of the flashlights outside finally goes off, followed by some movement away from the window. Moments later Officer Eastmann walks in past the guard at the door, his scraggly brown mustache curled up in an unmistakably friendly smile.

I guess he finally recognized me.

"Sorry to bother you," he says, the slightly wiseass tone of his voice mellowed by years of cigarettes.

It seems there has been a mistake. The local motel owners have agreed to report "suspicious" guests to the cops and state troopers, and I fit the profile of a drug courier because I paid with cash, made several phone calls and was overheard speaking Spanish. I also displayed an unbowed attitude.

You'd think there wouldn't be much left to say after that—besides "Sorry, ma'am" as they back out—but no, we have to spend an hour "verifying" my claims with phone calls, close study of my papers, especially close study of my pistol permit and empty revolver (no, it hasn't been fired recently), and me answering the same questions over and over as if I must be guilty of *something*, they just haven't figured out what it is yet. They almost try a body search. I've still got a few friends on the force, but I'm a long way from them. Otherwise I would definitely knock out a few teeth and claim that one of *them* "slipped and fell." Yeah, I can play that way, too.

Assholes.

They leave without saying a word. Except Officer Eastmann, who touches his hat and says, "Sleep tight."

I'd like to go ask the manager if she thinks Jesus would have called the cops on someone without a damn better reason than hearing her speak another language.

I pick my stuff up, try to straighten everything out as best I can, and get back to my lonely life in a cheap motel room miles from anywhere. I need to take my mind off what just happened, if possible. There was a rack of paperback bestsellers by the front desk. No. At this point, Stephen King should be paying *me* to read his books. You want horror, try what I just went through. I'm still wearing the trench coat over my frigging underwear, for God's sake.

Wind beats against the window, as if it has been listening to me. I stare out into the forbidding darkness, thinking about María Muñoz and her child, lost somewhere out there, far from those who love him, wondering if he's getting the basic necessities of food, clothing, shelter, hope, love, and respect.

Because so far all attempts to break people of the nasty habit of eating have ended in failure.

Necessities. Needs. Must-haves.

I flatten out the county map and lay it out on the table.

Pablito was doing okay. He was still sending money to his mother, still working, until three days ago.

After two months on the Scarzello farm, three miles north of here, the job ends, but he lands on his feet, working two jobs on the east side. But where was he staying? Not in the overcrowded illegal subdivisions, according to every one of his *compañeros*.

If I were him, where would I go?

Okay: I've got enough day work to stay fed, but I can't afford to live anywhere *and* send money home. I need some shelter, near the east side or a bus line that serves it.

All of a sudden there it is, as obvious as if someone had been declaring it to me in a language that I had forgotten until now. A bright green trapezoid between the east-side bypass and the highway: The woods. That's where a country boy like Pablito would go. He knew how to live off the land. Jesus Christ, part of it's even a nature preserve.

If he's there, I'll find him. I've just been thinking like a city dweller for too long.

And I'll take that shower now.

●

Breakfast is a bagel-shaped object that would get laughed out of any bakery on Queens Boulevard, tolerable coffee, and a local paper that supplies me with my cynical Quote for the Day: A kid got suspended for bringing *a loaded gun* to the high school and his father defends him by saying, "It's not like he was gonna set off a bomb or anything." Well, when you put it that way . . .

I sit in the car and study the map. The highway cuts

through the nature preserve but provides no access, which must have made sense to somebody. Two short, tiny lines leading off the bypass indicate a possible entrance, but when I drive over there it's blocked by a steel mesh gate, eight feet high, padlocked. I keep going and turn down a smaller road along the western edge until I come to a gravel path leading into the woods. I drive about a quarter-mile in, stop, and get out to take a look around.

The forest is very flat and open, sparsely dotted with mostly bare trees jutting up into the ice-blue sky, a few evergreens. No shelter around here. I study the layout on the map. I had some jungle fighting experience in Ecuador when I was younger, something you won't find on my PI trainee's resumé (or my citizenship application, for that matter), and I'm looking for where I'd seek shelter under the circumstances.

Considering how barren the place is, there's really only one likely stretch for a person to set up camp. A thin blue line on the map that I didn't pay much attention to before, but now that I'm here it makes all the sense in the world. A creek. Running water. And it passes right under the highway. That's where he'd be. Nearly a mile away. I'll have to drive around to that fake entrance, find a way in, and track him along the creek.

I'm about to get back in the company junker when I spot a black Mercedes sports car advancing slowly up the path from the main road. I lean against my door and wait for it to pass, but it slows down and the passenger window glides open. The driver's a sandy-haired, trim suntanned fellow in his mid-fifties, and his passenger's a thin blond woman in a short, tight dress, about fifteen years younger.

"Are you lost?" she asks.

"No," I answer.

The man leans over and says, "This is a private road," with such a piqued upper-class British tone of reprimand you'd think I had just broken in and tracked mud across his hand-woven Turkish carpeting.

"Sorry, the map doesn't indicate that," I say.

"There's a sign right up there," he says, pointing up the road. I don't see a thing.

"Well, I was just leaving," I say, getting into the car, and I have to do a seven-point K-turn to pull out because the idiots sit there blocking the narrow road, waiting to make sure I leave before they continue on to whatever private pleasure dome awaits them.

There's no prick like an upper-class English prick.

Now I'm pissed off enough to enter a more aggressive frame of mind. The hell with trying to find a break in the damn fence. I've wasted enough time and dignity on this gig as it is. I turn around and head for the highway, and midway through the forest there's a sudden drop-off and a brief glimpse of rocks. A creek bed. I pull over to the shoulder, carefully get out as cars whiz past at seventy-five miles per hour, step over the guardrail, and climb down the embankment past the twisted roots at the base of the trees.

The dank under-the-bridge smell beneath the overpass drifts up my nose, bringing a dark premonition with it. Cars sail by a few feet above, in another world, as I reach the flat silty bottom. Even as I approach, I try not to contaminate the footprints, at least three sets going to and from the shadowy area below the highway. The icy wind whips up a swirl of dead leaves around my feet.

There's a man lying face down in the creek.

Judging from what I can see, it's been a few days.

I don't touch anything. Three empty liquor bottles and a miserable burnt-out fire. A ratty blanket and some soggy lottery tickets at my feet. He was probably just trying to keep warm and drank too much. Fell and hit his head or something.

Anyway, it's a police matter now.

I take out my phone and dial 911.

CHAPTER FIVE

Sleep? Who can sleep in America?
—Leon Kobrin

"**YOU'RE HOME EARLY**," says Antonia. "Bad news?"

She knows. We've always shared this peculiar connection, some unfathomable place between us where the harsh, wet winds sweep down from the highlands of the soul.

I hug her to me.

"Bad enough." A distant signal ripples across the surface of a deep, dark sea. An echo from a bottomless ravine.

"Ah! Your hands are cold."

"Yo, Fil, you gotta call that *Señora* Muñoz!" yells Santina, taking her nineteen-year-old mouth off the telephone. "She keeps bugging us 'bout when you comin' back."

Meet my roommates. Luba, the thirty-four-year-old grandmother, and her daughters, Santina, Alejandra, Magdalena, and Adela, aged nineteen, eighteen, seventeen, and sixteen (get the pattern?), and the *seventeen*-year-old is the one with the baby. I don't care what it takes. Antonia and I are moving out of here before we go nuts.

Of course, we may have to go nuts.

I can't talk to María Muñoz yet. There's no point telling her anything without a positive ID.

I wait for the bathroom, and finally wash up. The ritual of cooking will do me good.

"How old is this?" I ask, pulling a plastic dish of rice from the refrigerator.

"I don't know, but I think there's an Egyptian curse on it," says Antonia.

"All right, we need rice. Where's the shopping list?"

Piles of junk mail and teen mags everywhere. I dig through them until I find a pad with too much writing on it.

"Antonia, please don't write phone messages on the shopping list."

"That's the shopping list?"

"Sure, unless we also got a call from Mr. Tilex Cleaner and Mrs. Garbanzo Beans."

"Keep it down, I'm on the phone!" Santina says.

"Yeah, and when you gonna get off—?" says sister number two.

"Leave me alone—!"

"—my turn—!"

"Mom—!"

"Knock it off!"

And we're out of there.

"You want me to make you something special?" I ask, as we wind our way down the stairs.

"*Patacones!*"

Great. There's nothing like multi-stage frying in hot oil in a kitchen with no counter space and full of bad teenage attitudes and other dangerous distractions. But I offered.

Antonia spent most of the afternoon in our room waiting for me to come home, reading the latest volume in the bestselling series Regina Wheelwright, Teenage Sorceress.

"What's this one about?" I ask, as we cross 104th Street.

"Well, she's invited to this costume ball, but she leaves her purse somewhere, and then, stuff happens, and then she finds it."

"'Stuff happens'?"

"Yeah."

"That's quite a plot summary." I'm going to have to remember that for my next report: Operatives tailed the suspect for five hours, during which time stuff happened. End of report. "Maybe some day the president will create a cabinet-level position for you, Secretary of Stuff."

"I don't want to be a secretary."

"That's not—"

Antonia jumps as we step off the curb. A wet leaf clings to her sneaker, then blows away.

"What?"

"I thought that was a rat," she says. She's actually fascinated by them, always leaning over the platform to observe them scampering along the streams of water from God knows where that dribble through so many subway tracks. "I'm not scared of them, except when they're right near me."

"That's natural. I'm not scared of roaches unless they jump off the shelf at me and try to crawl down my shirt."

"Or like seeing a shark at the aquarium isn't scary, but finding a shark in your bathtub is scary."

"Right. And *very* suspicious, I might add."

We fill up on authentic Ecuadorian groceries, then Antonia reminds me that the Twinkling Star is open until 6, leaving me just enough time to fulfill my pledge to buy her that poster this weekend. I forgot that they close on Sunday.

It's on display high up the wall behind the cash register: A full-color photograph of NGC 2997, spiral galaxy in Antlia, viewed from "overhead," that is, perpendicular to the galactic plane so the star-dust arms float in nearly perfect spirals around the brightly clustered globular center.

"We're all out of that one," says the bored, tattooed teenager, taking a break from fiddling with his tongue stud. "But we got plenty of the other one." He means a poster of another galaxy, an equally hospitable place, I'm sure, but not the one Antonia wants in her bedroom.

"I don't want that one," she says.

"It's the same galaxy, photographed from a different angle," the guy says, indifferently.

"Oh, really?" I say, unable to prevent the edge from creeping into my voice. "I'd like to meet the photographer who traveled *thirty million light-years* out of her way to get a shot of 'the same galaxy from a different angle.'"

It's been a rough day and I'm losing my patience with this my-generation-has-no-reason-to-care-about-anything stuff. Some of them say they actually wish they had a war to prove themselves at, as if you're not a real man until you've killed somebody; as if people didn't die fighting for the right to screw who they want, to organize where they want, to take a bathroom break on an assembly line. How about fighting for universal health care? Bunch of fucking whiners.

When my red-shifting vision normalizes, we are the proud owners of the display copy of NGC 2997, heading home to juggle the terrifying Kitchen Implements of Death, including the Gas Burner with a Mind of Its Own, the skin-searing Spattering Oil, and the heart-stopping Frying Pan with the Loose Handle. Yet there is no applause from the galleries when the finished dishes are brought to the table, only a twinkle in my daughter's eye and an appreciative crunch while the teenage phone-call madness swirls around our heads like jets stacked up over JFK during a winter storm.

"Fil! Phone! It's that Muñoz woman," says Magdalena.

I get up and take the phone from her.

"Keep it short," she orders.

I tell Mrs. Muñoz, "Nothing yet . . . By Monday . . . Yes, I'll call you."

I return the phone to its rightful owner. "Was that short enough?"

I don't even merit the effort of being sneered at.

Antonia helps with the dishes, then I shut the door to our room and make some private calls using the cell phone. It takes about ten minutes to locate him.

"You skipped, didn't you?" says Officer Eastmann, his smoky voice smooth and confident.

"Considering what I've just been through in your precinct, I decided not to be discovered with the body."

"You going to put that in your report?"

"I'm still waiting for you guys to ID him."

"Why? You could have done it yourself."

"That's what we have coroners for. How bad is it?"

"Guy looks like a bluefish. They're going to need dental records."

I shudder involuntarily.

"But it seems like your guy," he says.

"How soon will you be positive?"

"You know, your car was reported near the scene."

Oh. "You tell the county cops that?"

"It came from them."

Shit. If it's traced to the agency . . .

"I don't want to be dragged out there to answer questions."

"So what do you want me to do about it?"

"Tell them you chased it down, and it's nothing. Please."

"And what do I get out of this?"

"The full story and a chance to crack it yourself."

"You mean, so I can get out of this chickenshit backwater where the average home costs eight hundred grand and there's no violent crime?"

"You're forgetting about the other side of the train tracks, Officer Eastmann."

"Nobody gives a fuck about them." He says it without contempt. It's just the truth.

"As long as they stay on their side."

"You're the one who left the scene of the crime, sweetie."

"And spent the next forty-five minutes testing my gag reflexes. I called it in like a good citizen, and there's no crime in leaving the scene. Especially since he'd been dead for two or three days."

"How do you know that?"

"Are we talking here?"

He takes a moment. Then: "Yeah. We're talking here."

I tell him the whole story from my end, leaving in everything but the lousy bagels. Don't want to hurt his civic pride.

"So it could have been an accident," he says. "But if it wasn't, anybody could have done it, for any reason."

"Well, there's plenty of evidence at the scene."

"Like what?"

"Like three sets of footprints."

"Ha! They overran the place. Anything there was contaminated in minutes."

"Fucking county cops—"

"Careful what you wish for—"

"I know a couple of Feds who specialize in the forensic identification of footprints, Officer Eastmann."

"Call me John."

"Fine, John. Three months ago a woman on my block got whacked in the head with a two-by-four and robbed while leaving a deli. Her coffee cup hit the ground and splattered on the guy's pants, then he squished one of her jelly donuts while he was running away. It left a footprint. Everyone's looking at me like I'm nuts, but I go into the deli, get out a clean spatula, scrape up the donut, put it in a Baggie and take it to my friends. The cops had a few circumstantial leads, and two days later they nailed the son-of-a-bitch with a matching print. He hadn't thought of changing his shoes."

"No shit."

"You could look it up. The One-ten Precinct in Queens."

"So what are you saying?"

"I'm saying I found the guy. Who did it is your problem." What I mean is, Do your damn job.

"I'll call you back on Monday," he says.

I hang up and a minute later Stan calls.

"Jesus, Filomena, *both* phones have been busy for half-an-hour."

"Four teenagers and a possible murder."

"Oh." Nothing fazes a city doctor. "Listen, *babe-eleh,*

about tonight, I can't make it. Got a double shift, but I'll call you around three or four tomorrow, as soon as I wake up."

"Okay, honey. I miss you." Antonia makes a mocking face at me. "And I miss your warm, masculine embrace." Antonia pretends to retch.

Kissing sounds, and I'm asleep within minutes, Antonia's arm beneath my head.

But I wake up several times during the night, chasing away wisps of splintering doors, gun barrels aimed at my eyes, and the eternal chill of cold creek beds.

No coffee or tea! Or chocolate! No *wonder* it took them so long to get out of the Middle Ages! How lucky we are to live in such an enlightened time. I hot-wire my brain with a caffeine-bath and spend the rest of the morning forcibly ejecting the cobwebs from my brain and making my body strong and beautiful by hoisting dumbbells. No, I'm not hopelessly self-loving, the word "calisthenics" comes from Greek, meaning "strong and beautiful." So there.

My legs have been powerful since my childhood in the Ecuadorian Andes, but I've got to build up my upper body strength. Half the guys I go up against have spent several years in prison, most of it on the weight machines. Fortunately, the surprise of a semi-strong woman counts for a lot, but once the surprise wears off after about three seconds it's a hard job because most tough guys would rather die than surrender to a woman.

Antonia and I shower, then head over to 39th Avenue, a tree-lined street on the other side of Roosevelt, a couple of blocks into the 115th Precinct, to look at an apartment. It's a modest, well-kept row house owned by an aging couple, Nick and Sophia Kyriakis. They like the fact that I've only got one child, show a little worry when I say I have a boyfriend, but those clouds of concern dissipate when I tell them he works at Long Island Jewish. We go up the stairs and look around. Kitchen, bath, and something we've never had before: *Two* bedrooms. What a treat that will be.

The back door to the kitchen opens onto a tiny balcony

with a narrow staircase down to a fenced yard where Mr. Kyriakis has planted wine grapes. You can just see the edge of the upper tiers of Shea Stadium to the east, lying dormant under the dark blue blanket of winter. I stand there looking things over, then watch the sky as a plane takes off from nearby La Guardia Airport.

"One every sixty seconds," says Nick, coming up behind me. Hmm. Everything has its price, I guess.

They seem to like us. We sit down in their living room and talk a bit, thank them for showing us around, and get ready to leave. They tell us they've seen enough people and they're going to decide very soon.

We head up to 37th Avenue, turn left, and walk over to Our Lady of Sorrows on 104th Street in time for the noon Mass and the obligatory incomprehensible reading from the Old Testament. Am I the only one who gets the impression that the Hashmoneans were a rather wasted bunch of people? Then it's on to the New Testament, which clearly conjures up a crime scene to my deranged one-track mind, the Apostles offering contradictory testimony, as all witnesses do. But they agree on one thing: The door to the tomb's open and the body's missing. Their inevitable conclusion: He rose from the dead. Try putting *that* kind of reasoning in a report.

Probably the most influential trial and execution in history, and we're *still* not clear on who did what or why they did it, what the facts are and what they mean, or the mysterious disappearance and the ultimate mystery behind it all.

Maybe they're still filing the paperwork.

Sounds a little like my career at Davis & Brown, which is certainly not turning out the way I thought it would. I mean, I expected the low pay and the burdensome regulations, but I think I could do a much better job if I had fewer cases. But that's the job: A really heavy caseload and tons of paperwork. It's just that—well, I guess this isn't a big revelation, but life is not infinite. It is finite. I am becoming acutely aware of how finite it is. And every day something annihilates a portion of my time and energy forever. All these piddling cases that are slowly sucking the life out of me. Little by little, the stack of gold I started with is dwindling, dribbling away a pinch at a time. I'm not exactly counting the days, but several recent events have reminded me how precious every minute of life is, how rare and delicate.

And it hurts me to see my talents wasted, my time spent, my energy used, just to keep afloat. Where is the freedom? Where is the possibility? The so-called promise of America? Why are all my skills being ground up by this chickenshit job while I sit around waiting for The Big Case? And with Pablito dead—forgive me, Lord, but there goes my stake in that gig. There's no way *anybody's* going to pay me to do legwork the Suffolk County Police Department is supposed to be doing seventy-five miles east of here.

On our way home, I have to ask Antonia to repeat what she was just saying because my mind keeps slipping into the mire alongside the body in the creek, when suddenly the loud clang of galvanized garbage cans shakes me from my cyclical thinking. Manny Morales is lining up the trash cans outside his building, beneath hand-painted bedsheets that flutter majestically from the fire escapes and declare in red-and-black block letters that this is WEEK ONE OF THE RENT STRIKE in five languages.

"Taking the leap, huh?" I say.

"Just like a circus act, *hermana*," Manny agrees. "You know, those trapeze artists don't just jump onto the thing. They jump towards the spot where it's supposed to be, before the trapeze actually gets there."

"Sounds like my life. One big leap of faith."

"Working without a net."

We talk about what this one building's struggle represents for the hard-working people who can't afford to pay the rising rents and who are told, "That's the free market. If you don't like it, move." Which naturally leads to a discussion of the absurdity of seeing increasing numbers of soft, middle-aged men in crisp white shirts and wide Technicolor Looney Tunes ties driving troop transport–sized vehicles through the neighborhood to get to work.

"I'm lucky to live near my job," he says.

"How's that going?"

"It's rough. We're short on staff, so I end up spending half my time filling out paperwork for the state instead of working with the kids."

Man, that sure parallels my thoughts.

"We get new cases every week, but it's hard to find good therapists. Most people don't understand what autism is or how it works."

"Is that what Jerry has? Autism?"

"Yeah." Manny explains that autism is the third most prevalent childhood disability, with no known cause or cure, although it may possibly stem from a combination of neurochemical and environmental factors, and that four out of five autistic kids are boys, a condition that tends to produce both asocial behavior *and* large penises. I can't help wondering what the connection is there.

By the time we get back to our place, Stan is there waiting for us, looking well-rested in his Sunday casuals, loose-fitting blue jeans, and a National Yiddish Book Center sweatshirt. I get a hug and a kiss, Antonia permits him a squeeze.

"What was today's sermon about?" he asks, pretending to quiz Antonia.

"It was the one where Jesus is working in the chocolate factory, and the conveyor belt starts going too fast—"

"Oh yes, I've heard about that one."

"You have?"

"Well, sure, the New Testament is my second favorite testament."

We're trying to decide between the Hall of Science or a walk along Meadow Lake when the phone rings and it's actually for me. It's Nick Kyriakis, asking how soon we can move in.

"How about right now?"

Believe it or not, sometimes it happens like this. I enlist Stan's help, and it doesn't take long to throw our meager one-room belongings into three short taxi rides over to 38th Avenue, except for the dumbbells, which keep ripping through the bottom of several corrugated boxes. When Antonia scrapes her knee on the steps, I drop everything to wash the cut and swab it with alcohol. She squirms, until Stan explains, "If it stings you, imagine what it's doing to those germs." Antonia the microbiologist considers this, then stoically accepts the treatment. Smart kid.

By the time we get everything loaded in, it's time for a dinner break. No time to make anything fresh, or to soak beans for twenty-four hours, obviously. So I root around for a pan, some rice, and couple of cans of beans. It's not much, but nobody complains.

I overhear Stan in the bathroom joking with Antonia, "You know washing your hands before dinner? The Jews invented that."

We sit around the plain wooden table and give thanks for this meal and our newfound home.

"You know, the Air Force is complaining that everyone else gets a bean named after them and they don't," says Stan, contemplating a forkful. "They're lobbying Congress to earmark $17 billion for the development of an Air Force bean to go alongside the army and navy beans."

Antonia gives him a look that says, You can stop trying to win me over already. Just keep Mom happy.

We get a fair amount unpacked and set up before it's time for Antonia to stop decorating and start studying. I sit on the lumpy bed and comb and braid her hair while she reads through her social studies notes. I'm making what we used to call "pigtails," but the radical fringe of the hairdressing lobby declared that term to be offensive to women (and to pigs). The new, politically correct term is "bilateral hair interweavings."

"Okay, quiz me," she says.

"All right. What's 1423?"

"It's either the Albigensian Crusade or my gym locker combination."

I can see that moving has been a traumatic experience for her.

By the time she finishes studying for her vocabulary test and she asks me, "Why is 'abbreviation' such a *long* word?" I know it's time for bed.

"Not bad," I say, surveying our domain. "The place is halfway there already."

"Sure is," Stan agrees. "We must sacrifice a red heifer in honor of the occasion. Or at least run over a squirrel."

"We did a pretty good job," I say, hooking my arm through his. "Thanks, Stan."

He tries to say it's nothing, but I push that aside. I place my thanks on his lips, his tongue, the nerve endings of his soul. Finally. We slip quietly inside to inaugurate my new bedroom.

"Teach me some Yiddish, lover boy."

"Sure thing, *mayn sheyne kepele.*"

"I already know that one."

"Oh. Okay. Then: *Ikh bren un ikh bren un ikh ver nit farbrent.*"

"Sounds hot. What does it mean?"

"I burn and I burn and I am not consumed."

"Ohh . . ."

Something stirs within me. A profound and untouchable emptiness, suddenly swelled to filling.

And the shadows from the street form bars across our bodies.

I press my lips to the pulsing veins in his neck as our hearts beat so so fast and gradually start to slowwwwww to normal.

Some welcome sleep. Then jarred awake by the chirping of the company phone. Groping. Christ. The sun isn't even up yet.

"Bad news, Fil." Len's voice. "Lopez won't talk."

CHAPTER SIX

**In a time of universal deceit, telling the
truth is a revolutionary act.**
—George Orwell

"**WHO?**"

"Freddy Lopez. The bogus fire extinguisher guy. They've
got him in Gallagher's office, but he won't talk."

Right. The guy I traced five days ago for thirty-five bucks.

"You gotta convince him to testify, or Gallagher says he
won't pay," says Len.

"Can't someone else do it?" Silence. "Or am I the only
Spanish-speaking PI-in-training in the borough?"

He takes a moment, trying to phrase it right. "Mr. Davis
and Mr. Gallagher both think that Lopez might be more
willing to talk to a woman PI."

What the fuck time is it? Five A.M.? Jesus!

"You left out a 'mister,'" I say.

Now I've got to go in early and do some research.

By 9:30 I'm in the prosecutor's office, which is lined with
gray-haired men in long gray coats, looking through a wire-
reinforced window at Freddy Lopez sitting in a gray metal
chair in what is basically an 8 × 10-foot detention cell. Guess
what color the walls are.

"Oh, this is really comfortable," I say towards Gallagher,
opening the door. "Come on, Freddy, let's go."

"Wait a minute," Gallagher objects. "It took us three weeks to find him. If he runs—"

"He won't get far. You want me to talk to him, not interrogate him, right?"

You like that "us"? I continue:

"Don't worry, he's not going to jump me. Are you, Freddy?"

Freddy shakes his head dully. This man needs some serious coffee.

I take him to a Spanish coffee shop around the corner on Hillside Avenue that has twelve-inch plastic Salvadoran flags strung over the counter and fading posters of tropical beaches that fail to transform the climate on this rainy November morning. But the soothing rhythms of *salsa* music and the familiar smells of Central American delicacies soon put *Señor* Lopez a bit more at ease than he was in the holding pen.

"*¿Quieres tomar algo?*" I make the finances clear by laying out a few bills from Davis & Brown's petty cash.

He orders a beer. It's about eight hours too early for me, so I get a *café con leche*. I let him drink his beer with lime and order another while we talk about his new job installing fire alarms for local mom-and-pop stores, the repetitive, slightly sexist lyrics of a current *merengue* hit, and Mariano Rivera's latest truck-stopping World Series performance for *los Yanquis*, before I switch to the topic we've all been waiting for.

"What's in it for me?" he asks, real tough-ass.

No jail time, I'm thinking, but they probably hit him with that already without success, or I wouldn't be here. I try to explain the community's particularly harsh attitude towards falsified inspections of cracked fire extinguishers in public schools.

"*No pasa nada,*" he says, shrugging it off.

"Nothing's going to happen? What if something *does* happen?"

"*¿A qué me importa?*"

"What difference does it make? These are *children*."

"So what? They're *gringo* kids."

That does it. I'm sick of the tough guy act.

"All right, Mr. Federico Lopez, date of birth January twelfth, 1961, ITIN number 994–28–6698, height five feet nine-and-a-half inches, hair color black, driver's license number 939–331–895, currently residing at 65–04 Woodside Avenue, phone number 718–606–2917, current neighbors Humberto Robles, phone number 718–606–0842, Angel Peña, phone number 718–634–5789—" I flip a page in my notes "—and Margarita Velázquez, phone number 718–606–1789, bank account number 897–9323–4686, bank balance $718.23 as of 8:17 A.M. this morning: What if it were *your* daughter, Angelica Lopez Utrillo, date of birth July seventeenth, 1994, *cédula* number 314–159–26535, currently attending the *Nuestra Señora de la Gracia* elementary school in Quetzaltenango in the Sierra Madre, Guatemala, what if there were a fire in *her* school, and she were trapped inside because nobody ever bothered to put in emergency exits because no one thought anything would ever happen and even if it did, so what?—it's just some ignorant, backwoods *campesinos*, who cares about their stupid little kids?"

He looks at me like he's just remembered that God sees all.

Yeah.

"You planning on ever going back?" I ask.

Ten minutes later we've got a deal.

"Relax," I say. "Maybe we can even shake a few bucks out of them for your trouble."

He nods.

"Good. Now get in there and testify before I throw your punk ass in jail."

"Officer MacKenzie? It's me again."

"Yeah?"

"How soon can I see Sonny Tesoro?"

"Good luck. A mutt like that ain't gonna come up with two hundred thousand dollars bail anytime soon."

Two hundred thousand dollars?

"He's not a mutt."

"Whatever you say."

"Mr. Tesoro is my client. When can I speak with him?"

"Oh, jeez." I can almost hear the pencil scratching in the details in the blotter. "Tomorrow. Nine A.M. sharp." Click.

Time to call another cop, but Officer Eastmann is on assignment and can't be reached. Yeah. He's probably parked behind a row of evergreens waiting for somebody to drive by at thirty-one miles per hour.

"What an SOB," declares Karen.

I look over at her. She's been loitering in an online chat room for a couple of days, posing as a thirteen-year-old girl, and has just gotten a message from her suspicious client's husband offering to mail her a bus ticket and some cash so that she can come to the city and meet him. I'm not sure that's enough for us.

"Is there a specific solicitation of sex?" I ask.

Karen scrolls down to the rest of the message. I read it.

"What an SOB," is all I can say.

I start dialing Lonnie Ambush again when Chip Davis calls me into his office.

"Start a file on that Russian guy, Vladimir whatzisname, Dubchek?"

"Dvurushnik. Nobody started this on Friday?"

"He asked for *you*, and we want to keep our new client happy, okay?" I guess I should be flattered. "There a problem?"

"No, I've just got a crowded schedule right now."

"Well, clear it up. This Duvrushnik'll pay top dollar. But he wants *results*."

"It's not going to be that easy—"

"No, that's not the way it is, Fil. This is an assignment." Pause.

"You're ordering me to drop everything and talk to Dvurushnik, right now?"

A trace of doubt overshadows his features.

"You okay with that?" he asks.

So this is what getting a little respect from a superior feels like. I'll try not to abuse it.

"Sure, Chip. No problem."

All smiles again.

"And don't forget this afternoon's disability surveillance with Karen," he reminds me, needlessly.

Yeah, I'd like to be working another case, a *real* one, but I've got to do this first.

At least they gave Len the odoriferous Gonzo Mendieta screw-the-female-blackmailer case, claiming something about a single man's superior objectivity when dealing with a spurned mistress, just because I suggested that we let both women have at him with rusty meat hooks. What's not to object?

I call Comrade Dvurushnik and tell him to send me copies of his payroll and personnel records.

"That's going to cost money to copy," he objects. "Why can't you come here?"

"Because it's going to be pretty obvious what we're doing if you keep having someone come into your office to examine documents. Word of that will get around pretty quick."

"Yes. I see. I will send them by messenger right away."

I hang up and go over to the supply cabinet to get out some fresh steno pads and a few file folders. Someone left the empty box of folders on top, so I have to crouch down and pull a new, shrink-wrapped box from behind the battalions of pristine pencils and legal pads. Davis has shut the door to his office, but I can actually hear his muffled voice among the erasers due to some bizarre sound wave condensing effect.

"—Yeah, Fil's great. She's good *and* cheap. Got tons of experience and works for trainee wages." Silence, then laughter.

Nothing left to do but smile, smile, smile. But I'm going to remember this listening device.

My phone rings. I run over and grab it.

"Miss Buscarsela?" says Officer Eastmann.

"Yes?"

"It's him." He waits. "They've ID'd Muñoz."

"Damn." At least I don't have to tell his mother. That's Eastmann's job now. "And—?"

"There's no sign of trauma or struggle, nothing. But his blood-alcohol level was two-point-four."

Three times the legal limit.

I need a moment to take it in.

"So there's no case," he says.

"Hmm."

"What?"

"Well, I could see him getting drunk and passing out and freezing to death, but falling into the creek . . . ?"

"Probably got up to take a piss."

"And he didn't have the wherewithal to pull himself out? To save his own life? We've got an expression in Ecuador, *Ningún borracho come mierda*. It means nobody ever gets so drunk they'll eat shit."

"You ever been dead drunk?"

"If he was dead drunk, how did he get up and pee?"

"I admit it's a little weird, but it's not impossible, and there's no sign of a struggle."

How much of a struggle would it be to drown a man that drunk, I wonder?

He continues, "But the fact that you are known to have been looking for Muñoz could cause some trouble."

"What, am I a suspect?"

"There's nothing to suspect you of. It's been ruled an accident. But the fact that your car was reported—"

"I thought we discussed that."

"Well, those bumper stickers sure made it easy to spot, especially after half-a-dozen cops went over every inch of it back in the motel parking lot."

"Yeah, I haven't forgotten about that. And if anyone makes trouble for me over leaving the death scene I will sue the county for—"

"No one's going to make trouble."

"You mean, as long as I don't make trouble, either."

He lets out a breath. Answer: Yes. Change the subject, Fil. "What was the time of death?"

He perks right up: "Well, it's hard to tell with floaters, especially in ice water, but they figure sometime late Wednesday or early Thursday morning."

"I've got a hundred alibis."

"You would."

He lets out a breath. Answer: Yes. Change the subject,

"Fil, it's Abe Fleischwolf's office," Katwona announces emphatically. He's a big area landlord. "They want you to dredge up some dirt on this troublemaking tenant so he can be evicted."

"Tell them to fuck off," I say, not looking up from my keyboard.

"Uh, Ms. Buscarsela is unavailable right now, may I take a message?" says Katwona in the pleasantest voice.

It loses so much in the translation.

I'm finishing up the Muñoz report, which unfortunately leaves out some of the most colorful stuff, such as "Friday, 9:00 P.M.: Operative nearly busted for suspected drug smuggling when goofball county cops try to get the jump on the state troopers by raiding my motel room on the word of a right-wing Jesus freak who thinks Spanish is an international code for thieves." (Forgive me, Jesus.)

I file the report, and take a moment to collect my thoughts. So many little jobs, so many loose ends, if only I had one solid *paying* case I could sink my teeth into. I mean, there's helping Camille and Sonny Tesoro, but that one's strictly for the charity rolls. Like the man said about being vice president of the United States, sometimes I feel like my job here ain't worth a pitcher of warm spit.

Actually, a pitcher of warm spit is *more* useful than being vice president: You can always wash out the pitcher and re-use it.

This Russian video piracy business could produce some money if it goes right. The Motion Picture Association of America pays around $15,000 for information leading to the arrest and conviction of anyone making pirate videos of their films, and you can get another couple of thousand for busting the lab if it uses more than thirty VCRs to make copies of MPAA films. Of course the big money is in espionage. Blocking an international spy operation can get you $500,000 from the U.S. Attorney General's Office, and stopping an act of terrorism is worth *$4 million* from the State Department. So why am I screwing around with the local lawyers and their lousy twenty-five dollars an hour? Come on, terrorists, where are you? Or don't you have the balls to come to Queens?

I pick up the package Dvurushnik's messenger left with Katwona and scan the files for likely suspects. The names alone tell me nothing, but it's a short list—only thirty-two of them—so it doesn't take long to run a limited criminal background check that flags three names. That doesn't mean it's them, but it gives me a place to start. I search a little deeper, but so far they come up clean. Of course the piracy gig usually pays cash, precisely so it won't show up on this screen, but sometimes the street-level boosters are dumb enough to funnel it through their bank accounts. Still, I hoped this one would be easier.

I know a convicted ex-video pirate who works for the companies he used to scam, advising them how to prevent future losses with sophisticated anti-piracy technology that he developed, but he can wait until I run into a real roadblock.

I call up Dvurushnik.

"You have suspects yet?" he asks.

"Yes."

"Good. Give me their names. I want them arrested."

"You can't do that—"

"Why not?"

Because this is America, asshole.

"What if it isn't them?"

"So what? It will scare others."

"What if they sue for wrongful arrest?" New concept for him. Try again. "It will end up costing you money."

Ah, the international language.

"So what will you do for me now?" he asks.

"You got some new products this week?"

"Yes. Always new products."

"Tell me about them."

He's got a new CD by the Russian-emigré post-punk rockers the Savage Yeltsins, a two-CD collection of Andean folk music played on traditional instruments, a couple of porn flicks and three Hollywood blockbusters, *The Laminator* I, II, and III, dubbed into Russian, Spanish, Mandarin, Hindi, and Korean, coming out on video. That's the one to watch out for.

"Send me some copies of the original packaging. I'll need them as exemplars."

For once, he doesn't give me an argument.

I tell Abigail Brown that we need to free up all three operatives for surveillance at the Krepki Factory starting at 4:30 today and continuing for at least three days. I give her the details and show her the low-resolution digital copies of the three mug shots.

"Okay," she says. "But you need to cover that other surveillance with Karen first."

"Right."

As I'm leaving Abby's office, Katwona offers me an open box of circular pastries from the corner bakery.

"You want some sticky buns?" she asks.

"Sounds like something you'd get in a gay bathhouse," I answer.

And she looks at me like that is one of the sickest things she has ever heard.

"She needs to get out more."

"Yeah, there are some people who just seem to be wearing a sign that says 'push me,' says Karen.

"I was just messing with her," I say.

We're lying flat on our stomachs on the chilly tin-and-tar roof of a five-story brick apartment building with a back-yard view of a line of row houses. The fourth house from the corner belongs to a man who is suing the Fortune 500 company whose forklift mangled his right arm. Nobody's disputing the disability—his arm had to be amputated below the elbow—but he claims he can't even use the prosthetic devices, making him a near invalid, and he's suing for $7 million. So the company thought it was worth spending a few thousand on surveillance to see if we could cut the damages down to half-a-million or so, and I'm sorry to say that the odds are in their favor, what with two ace operatives like Karen and me watching his every move through high-powered binoculars and an SLR camera with an 80–300 zoom lens, and a video camera standing by.

"Of course, now that you've pointed it out," says Karen, not taking her eyes off the target, "the gooey white glaze on those sticky buns *does* look a lot like dry cum."

"That going to keep you from eating them?"

"On the contrary . . ."

I put down the camera for a second to rub my gloved hands together. At least the sun came out, so we're not *completely* freezing our asses off up here.

"I wonder what it's like when it's cooked," I say, picking the camera up. "Since raw sperm tastes like unripe Brie."

"And how would *you* know?"

I don't need to answer that.

"I think we got a novel cook book concept here," says Karen, checking her watch. "When the hell are his kids getting home from school? I'm freezing my goddamn buns off."

"Any minute now."

"Been waiting two-and-a-half goddamn hours for him to move."

"This whole gig's about waiting."

"If I were a fruit fly, ten percent of my life would be gone by now. You got him? I need a stretch."

"You're covered."

She puts down the binoculars, rubs her eyes, arches her back like a cat, and creeps over to the other end of the cold metal roof so she can stand up straight and walk some circulation back into her legs.

She comes back refreshed.

"I never thought I'd say this," she says, getting down on her elbows, "but I'd rather be serving subpoenas. Bottom-rung stuff, I know, but at least you're out and moving around. You hear about that *latina* PI who got past an all-male security force by dressing as a fan dancer with a naughty singing telegram and served the boss his papers?"

"I refuse to work that way."

"Yeah, well I believe Aristotle referred to it as *anagnorisis*, or 'making a goddamned living.'"

"We got movement, Karen."

She snaps into position, both of us peeping into the guy's kitchen via the rear window. School bags drop into chairs, refrigerator and pantry doors open and close, two glasses of milk and cookies are set out on the table.

"Yeah, that's some real criminal activity," I say.

"It's better than doing domestics," says Karen. "I hate domestics. Women crying, 'What does she have that I don't have?' Angry husbands coming after you with baseball bats."

"Just show them your gun."

"Naah, that just makes things worse. Here's my lethal weapon of choice," she says, picking up the video camera.

"Well, you kill him and I'll skin him," I say, snapping a few establishing shots as our subject comes out to the back yard. And we watch as he rakes the leaves into a pile so his kids can jump in, then he rolls around in the leaves with them. I shoot two rolls of photos, and Karen tapes the whole thing. Oh yeah, the mean ol' company's going to get their millions back, and this guy will be lucky to get a few hundred grand.

Man, I hate doing this. Who says domestics are any worse than hanging around on a freezing rooftop with a video camera and a telephoto lens waiting to prove that some guy's healthy enough to hug his kids?

"Come on," I tell her. "We've got another job in forty-five minutes."

"At least we're inside this time," says Karen, wiping the foggy window so we can see outside the Laundromat and across the twilit street to the Krepki Factory.

It's getting dark. We're not going to have much time.

"Let me know when the door opens," I say, turning back to another PI exam preparation guide. Every one of these damn things begins by "exploding the myths," telling me that being a PI is "not like it is in the movies or on TV," like I needed to hear that. This one has an interesting tip about charging extra for "hazardous duty pay" that I'll have to bring up at the next staff meeting, but otherwise it loses all credibility with me when it states that PIs cannot arrest anyone on suspicion alone, which is true, but only "after a felony" has been committed, which is dead wrong. It should say *during* a felony or in immediate flight therefrom. Bit of a difference. Wouldn't want to rely on this book to get me through a tough situation.

And remember, gals, you *can* shoot a rapist immediately afterwards. Just be sure to read him the fine print first.

"Yo, Fil. Feeding time at the zoo," says Len.

Time to leave the bright lights of the Laundromat and wait under the frayed awning outside the deli on the corner. Nothing much happens for a few minutes, then the workers start to come streaming out and we split up to follow our marks.

I came all prepared with layers of clothes, prop glasses, two different hats and an extra scarf so I could change my "look" from time to time. Nothing doing. It's cold and windy and the guy's heading straight home without looking back. So I keep a pretty close tail on him from across the street until he gets to Queens Boulevard and stands there at the Q60 bus stop, looking very much like a guy waiting for the Q60 bus, destination Sunnyside, which is where he lives.

I cross over to his side of the street and stand there keeping an eye on his reflection in a store window until the bus comes, then I climb aboard and stare blankly ahead, using my peripheral vision and the windows, bright as mirrors now that it's completely dark outside. I don't have to stay close. I figure he's getting off around Fortieth Street. And when he does, I'm there, twenty feet behind him. He makes one stop at a grocery store, buys beer, plain white cheese, and a couple of lottery tickets, then heads inside his apartment building. I wait a few minutes until a couple of kids come running out, clutching a few crumpled dollar bills and heading to the store to buy some essential missing ingredient for tonight's dinner. I catch the door before it shuts and step inside.

Now I decide to play it safe and reverse my coat, switch to a white beret and put on my flat-lens glasses. I trudge up three flights and knock on the door. I hear footsteps, the peephole blinks at me, then he opens the door.

"Yeah?"

"Mr. Murillo?"

"Yeah?"

"I want a divorce."

"Huh?"

"My husband is having an affair with this little *puttana* from his office and they are meeting in an apartment right across the street! I thought maybe I could see them from your window." I walk right past him and go over to the window and press my face up to it.

He comes up behind me. "Uh, which one is it?"

I point to a darkened pair of windows barely visible through the elevated train tracks.

"You're not gonna have much luck there," he says.

"I suppose not," I say, turning around and getting a good look at the apartment. It's pretty shabby.

"Listen, lady—"

I turn my face back towards the window. "Ooh, that little bitch! What does she have that I don't have?"

"It wasn't Murillo," I say.

Karen's got the same story.

Len reports, "Mr. Mendoza's got a kick-ass sound system, some fancy brass furniture, and mirrors out the wazoo."

"Okay, Karen, I'm taking you out of this one. You've got other assignments to cover," says Davis. "Fil and Len, I want both of you to tail this Mendoza guy for the next couple of days. Pick him up as soon as he leaves work."

"Right," we say in chorus.

We don't have to worry about watching the factory at lunchtime because Dvurushnik only gives them twenty minutes to eat and he won't let them out of the building. But in a concession to his employees, he recently removed the guard towers and the electrified barbed wire.

We're leaving Davis's office with that rare feeling of actually having accomplished something today and there, in the middle of this bright fluorescent office space, stands María Muñoz with her deep black shawl, black mood, and stony countenance seemingly sucking the light from the room, which darkens around her in shared mourning. My heart flutters for a moment upon seeing her, this painful shape with the unreadable, grim visage. Is she coming for comfort, or to curse me for cutting off my feelings and pushing this horrible reality down into a little box and trying to lose it somewhere in the dusty attic of my emotions? Did I really think I could escape this?

"*Filomena, he perdido mi hijo.*"

I rush over and help her to a chair. She wants sympathy. She deserves sympathy.

What do I deserve?

She thanks me. "*Gracias por todo, Filomena.* I know there was nothing else you could do by the time you found him."

But if I had gone looking for him as soon as she asked me to, he might still be alive.

"*¿Está cierto lo que dicen?*"

"Is what true?"

"That it was an accident."

"Yes, *señora*, I'm afraid so."

"Couldn't you investigate it for me?"

"The police have closed the case."

"But you have handled such 'cases' before, finding the true murderers long after the police have stopped looking."

"Yes, but my instinct on this is that it was an accident, a terribly sad one, but an accident all the same."

She draws herself up, and her eyes sharpen. "Maybe it is true that he was killed by nobody's hand, but he never should have died. The men who hire and fire him, the people who think he's good enough to be their worker but not good enough to be their neighbor, surely they killed him. The whole society killed him."

"You want me to prosecute American society?"

"Judgment will come, *mi hija*. With you or without you, judgment will come."

I take the long ride home, past the darkened shell of Shea Stadium in the off-season, and get caught on the Roosevelt Avenue bridge under the rumbling el, watching the frozen banks of red and white lights on the Grand Central Parkway below as people try to get the hell out of Queens as fast as they can. There's another distinct rumble as a jet takes off from La Guardia, creating a fourth layer to this strangely gridlocked crossroads. The glaring headline on the seat next to me cries out, MAYOR ORDERS HOMELESS ARRESTED, but I've got no mind left for the fine print as we inch along through unusually thick traffic.

No mind left for anything but endless rumination about how I *should* be taking the Muñoz case, and beating myself up for not helping the poor old woman, but what can I do? Besides sit here trying to convince myself that I'm too far away from what happened to be effective, when the fact is I'm physically capable of doing it. It's just not realistic or practical. I'd have to take a week's unpaid leave from work and abandon my daughter *again*—all very inconvenient to my present reality. And there's no guarantee I'd get results. But—yes, there's the remorseful bite of conscience—it's not as if it's impossible. I *could* make a difference. Justifiably or not, I am choosing not to get more involved, telling myself that it's a police matter and I'm overcommitted, all of which is true, but the question is, What if it were *my* child? I'd find a way to stir things up then, wouldn't I? Of course I would. So part of me wants to call out the flaming cavalry, but another part of me knows I can't abandon all my other responsibilities and chuck it all so easily, like the rich man who made the mistake of asking Jesus what he had to do to gain eternal life in the kingdom of Heaven, and Jesus answered, "Go and sell all your possessions, and give all the money away to the poor, then come and follow me." And the guy couldn't bring himself to do it, to give up *everything* for a cause, however just, prompting Jesus to say, "You're going to have one helluva tough time getting into Heaven with that attitude, pal."

Way to lay on the guilt, O Son of Man. As if I don't have enough trouble, working without a net, ladies and gentlemen. And such work is never done, it seems.

After far too many minutes sitting here soaking up exhaust fumes, I finally get up and ask the driver to let me off. It's only a couple of blocks further, and the way things are going I could out-walk this bus while dragging a four-hundred-pound boulder chained to my neck. But we're stuck on the narrow bridge and he insists that this isn't a regular bus stop. What a time to get sticky about the rules. But I've started something, and eventually enough people are demanding to be let off so that he concedes and opens the door. Half the bus empties out, and the driver stares at me like he's going to post fliers in the dispatch room warning all drivers on the route to beware of picking up this noncompliant female passenger. Banished from the Queens bus lines. I thought only Brooklyn could do that.

Drivers who took the wrong exit are trying desperately to read the dark green signs under the poorly lit el:

TO	25A	Northern Blvd	TO		Grand Central Pkwy East
↑	278	Triboro Br		495	L.I. Expwy
		Bklyn-Qns Expwy		678	Van Wyck Expwy
	678	Whitestone Expwy	→		
					Zoo
			↑		Hall of Science

all in about two seconds while everybody honks angrily at them. Fortunately, there's a transmission repair shop right across the street, and a storefront Church of the Kingdom of God flying a banner with a white dove on a red heart-shaped background and the words STOP SUFFERING in big block letters.

There are also people crowding the sidewalk and spilling out across 108th Street, blocking traffic. There is yelling, the rhythmic chanting of protest and sharp exclamations that are indecipherable from this distance, but their intent is clear enough.

As I draw closer, the Babel of voices resolves into laments, curses, calls to action, accusations, denunciations, and profanations.

Suddenly a sallow, greasy face looms in front of me. It's Lucas, the jeweler from the factory squat.

"Filomena! *Que pena, que cosa*."

"What is it?" I ask.

"Manny Morales was just found beaten to death."

CHAPTER SEVEN

Only those who still have hope can benefit from tears.
—Nathanael West

TUESDAY MORNING, 9:00 A.M. Eastern Standard Time, finds me waiting in a police cage that still smells of the cigars the detectives used to smoke here until the late 1980s. Ah yes, the days when you could smoke in the interrogation room. That takes me back to the Ice Age.

"Aren't you going to read me my rights?" says Sonny, sitting down with a rattle of metal. There's no privacy in the cage, but that's what they gave me since I'm not his lawyer.

"I'm not working for the police, Sonny. This isn't an interrogation."

He looks at the reinforced steel mesh that surrounds us. "Sure feels like it."

Why are we speaking English? I switch to Spanish so I can tell him how his lovely wife Camille is doing, in her own words. It's not some kind of secret code. A good-sized chunk of this squad room understands at least some Spanish, but it helps put him at ease. Eventually, I get to it:

"Tell me how you got the gun, and what happened last Wednesday."

I let him tell the whole story his way first. He says about two months ago the families occupying the old factory started getting harassed and threatened by a gang of leather-clad skinheads. Nasty messages were sprayed on doorways, pipes were broken, conduits slashed open and worst of all, in the middle of the night, six or seven different gang members would tramp through the hallways armed with metal chains and clubs, making as much noise as possible, banging on the heavy steel doors, waking everybody up, stealing the emergency lighting fixtures and setting off the fire alarms. The weird part was that some of them were women.

The city denied Sonny's application for a pistol permit, so he got a cheap seven-shot semiautomatic from a reputable dealer with offices under various train bridges in Dutch Kills, Long Island City and Hunters Point. He says he never fired it. He started carrying it to work, grocery shopping, pretty soon any time he left the building.

As for Wednesday, he was looking forward to relaxing with his *compañeros* and when that was interrupted, he just cracked.

"I still don't know why I did what I did," he says.

"You mean sparking a blunt fifteen feet from hizzoner's blueshirts with a loaded gun in your waistband?"

"Yeah, that was pretty stupid, wasn't it?"

Sounds pretty rational to me.

He goes on: "No, I mean, when the cops came at me, my first thought was to ditch the blunt. Like, I wasn't even *thinking* about the gun. Then, I don't know, I realized I should have tried to get rid of the gun, too, but when I reached for it they all jumped me, of course."

"You didn't just reach for it, Sonny. You pointed it at them."

"It's gotta point *some* way. I'm supposed to point it at myself? Or at you?"

"Pointing it at yourself might have been better."

"Yeah, well, I didn't have the time to think about the suicidal psycho angle, you know? I wasn't thinking straight."

"Why not?"

Half a syllable falls out of his mouth and rolls across the floor before he starts over and admits to me, "I don't know."

Still in Spanish:

"How much pot do you smoke?"

"Man, pot doesn't make you violent."

"It does to some people."

"Well, not to me, and not to you, either. Yeah, I heard about your past, sugar."

"It's all there," I say.

He looks around to see if any ears have pricked up after the use of the Spanish word *yerba*.

"I mean, so you know pot's not so bad. It's not poison."

"It's not exactly a health food, either."

"Compared to the crap I work with every day? We got lacquer thinner, toluene, Evaporane—"

"What's that?"

"This new kind of quick-drying glue. Contact cement for laminating with Formica. Man, I spent an afternoon putting in kitchen counters with that stuff, with the windows closed on account of the cold weather? I nearly fell down the frigging stairs afterwards. That stuff messes you up." He gestures around the cage. "The air's better in here."

"You feel better in jail?"

He shrugs. The obvious answer is No, but he admits, as if confessing to a priest, "My headache's gone."

We look at each other. The invisible fibers ensnaring us just got more complicated.

"Pretty weird, huh?" he says.

"Yeah. Most guys get worse in jail, especially if they're dealing with some serious emotional troubles."

"So . . . ?"

"So if it isn't emotional, maybe it's environmental. Could be good news for you."

His head jerks back skeptically. "You want to explain that?"

"If I can demonstrate that the chemicals you've been using at work can cause unstable behavior, maybe we can weaken the charges against you."

"But not dismiss them?"

Ha! In Pazzerello's New York?

"Let me make a few calls."

He smiles for the first time in days. A genuinely warm, sunny smile. "Thanks, Filomena. I thought I was screwed for sure."

I start getting ready to leave. "Sure. And next time you're in a crowd, remember, if it doesn't have your prints on it, there's no proof *you* dropped it."

He nods.

"But if you're all alone when the cops see you toss it, that's 'abandonment,' and it's not covered by the Fourth Amendment's protection against warrantless search and seizure. Got it?"

"Got it. *Gracias, hermana.*"

"Hey, what happened to 'sugar'?"

"You almost missed him," says Officer Sally-Ann MacKenzie. "He's taking the ten-thirty shuttle to Riker's."

"He didn't seem to know that."

"Why spoil his morning?"

How considerate.

"Anyway, his kind are better off in prison with a roof over their heads," she says.

"What do you mean, his kind?"

She looks at me, scanning the frizzy, dark hair and cinnamon-colored skin, but my hair is tied neatly back and my skin is cloaked with company-issued clothing and I speak English with very few errors.

"The kind who smokes a joint and tries to ice a cop. Half the guys we bust for petty crap like weed turn out to be wanted for assault, armed robbery, you name it."

"You got the statistics to back that up?"

"Sure. You can walk through the park without getting mugged."

"It's just that Sonny Tesoro's not a habitual criminal, and he's not a threat to the rest of us."

"Yeah. And Hitler was nice to dogs, I hear."

"You gave him a drug test when you brought him in, right?"

"Sure did."

"And he came up clean for cocaine and heroin?"

"Yeah—"

"The only two drugs that laboratory rats will keep taking until it kills them. Right?"

"Yeah, so?"

"But you didn't test him for other toxic substances, did you?"

"He was smoking a joint right in front of us—"

"Right. Only your manual's so out-of-date it says marijuana can be smoked, swallowed, or sniffed. Sniffed? When's the last time you busted someone for snorting ganja?"

"What the hell is your point?"

"My point is that clueless legislators sometimes pass harsh laws that produce almost as much crime as they prevent."

She tunes me out and turns back to her work.

I go on: "You've got fifteen years on your arm, Officer MacKenzie, so I think you know you can get twenty-five years for selling one vial of crack in this state. The day they started sentencing coke dealers to life in prison without parole for possession of four ounces of rock was the day the coke dealers started killing cops. It's the same deal for murder, so they figured it didn't make any difference."

"Wrong. You can get the death penalty for murder."

"Uh-huh. Chief Powell of the LAPD just told the Senate Judiciary Committee he supports the death penalty for casual pot smoking." She looks at me like I've finally penetrated some deep-down Catholic sense of mercy. "So how'd you like to bust a kid under those rules? Tell some mixed-up seventeen-year-old he just toked his life away, that firing up a blunt is a capital offense? And what about a hardened repeat felon? Think he wouldn't try to kill you to beat the set-up? What's to lose?"

She thinks about it. "You were a cop, right?"

"I only lasted five years."

"'Cause you sure seem to know how the criminal mind works."

"It's a gift."

"EPA."

"Gina, how are you?"

"Uh-oh. Politeness. That always spells trouble from you."

"We can cut right to it if you want."

"I'd appreciate that."

Ms. Gina Lucchese, just your typical tiny-but-tough-talking scientifically minded Italian babe from Brooklyn who works for the U.S. Environmental Protection Agency as a regional investigator, kicking the crap out of corporate polluters with deep pockets and shallow consciences.

"Okay, what do these symptoms sound like to you? Insomnia, weakness, memory loss, headaches, irritability, nervousness—"

"They sound like every commuter on the Manhattan-bound subway."

"Fever, rapid heart rate, muscle cramps, blurred vision, tremors, loss of appetite, personality changes—"

"Whoa whoa, slow down. Loss of appetite and personality changes? Any kidney damage, or blistering and peeling of the skin on the hands and feet?"

"I don't know. I can check. What is it?"

"Sounds like mercury poisoning."

"Mercury poisoning?"

"Why the surprise?"

"Because I'm looking at a skilled carpenter who's constantly being exposed to adhesives, cleaning fluids, and solvents. I don't know where the mercury comes in."

"Maybe he's moonlighting as a gold miner."

"Tell me about it."

"Fil, I don't really have time right now—"

"Just give me the two-second version."

"Okay, okay. Elemental mercury vapor is quickly absorbed through breathing and accumulates in the brain tissue and the kidneys. I don't have the complete neuropsychological toxicology in front of me, but the nonspecific psychosomatic symptoms of mercury poisoning could easily be misdiagnosed as mental illness."

"Like when a responsible family-man pulls a gun on five cops."

"Oh. I'm beginning to see your problem."

"Yeah. If I can prove he was suffering from the effects of a degenerative nerve poison at the time—"

"Have they given him a blood test?"

"No. Just a urine test."

"A urine test? What for—? Oh. Man, you sure can pick 'em."

Yeah. Another gift.

"Well, have them give him a blood test," she advises. "As soon as possible. The motor system effects are reversible, but the cognitive deficits may be permanent. You know, they used to use it to block hats, driving all the hatters insane. Hence the expression. I can probably get an expert to testify for you. That it? I've got to go."

"What's the big rush?"

Gina takes a breath, then suddenly she's showering me with sparks of excitement.

"Did you see the Metro section of today's *Times*?"

"Uh—"

"With the front-page photo of Governor Fowler holding up a twenty-five-pound striped bass and declaring that he's going to consider reopening the Hudson River to commercial fishing for the first time since 1976?"

"Sure, I—oh my God, Gina. You snagged the Hudson River PCB case?"

"Head geologist and Site Project Manager for the highest-profile clean-up job in the whole freaking state."

"Damn, girl! I'm jealous."

"Well, you shouldn't be. It's the biggest political football in the tri-state region, a royal pain in the butt to spin to the public after years of industry propaganda, and it's deep freezing my love life."

"But you gotta love it. So can we eat the fish or not?"

"Oh, you can, but the stupid article doesn't say you still can't eat more than one a month, pregnant women and children shouldn't have *any* at all and anybody with half a brain agrees—"

"That's a quarter-brain more than President Bush has."

"—that it would be a big mistake to resume commercial fishing right now, and Fowler knows that."

"Sure, he'll probably retract it in a few days. But what are people going to remember? The full-color photo of him reeling in a twenty-five-pound striped bass."

"Yeah, they're pretty shameless. And it's nothing but the usual smoke and mirrors."

"What kind of mirrors are they using? Concave or convex?"

Gina laughs. "You know, that's just where you might come in. You got a few minutes?"

"To help a woman whose love life is in the deep freeze? Do I *ever*."

Gina checks the time. I hear her let out a breath.

"I've got to keep it short."

"Fine."

"The river's taken quite a beating over the years. Nearly half a billion gallons of raw sewage were dumped into it *every day* until the Clean Water Act passed in 1972. But to everyone's amazement it actually worked, the river has nearly recovered from all that. But the persistent problem is the one-point-three million pounds of PCBs Universal Lighting's two upstate plants discharged into the Hudson from the 1940s until 1977, when PCBs were banned, contaminating a two-hundred-mile stretch that provides the drinking water for the cities of Waterford, Poughkeepsie, Rhinebeck, and even New York during a drought."

"Doesn't sound like anything you can't handle. So what's the problem?"

"The problem is the Honorable Tom Sipperly, congressman from Universal Lighting. He's telling everyone who'll listen that *we* created the problem, that the river is flushing naturally and we're a bunch of arrogant Big Government bureaucrats blowing it all out of proportion in some kind of deranged effort to destroy the economy of the upper Hudson valley."

"Sipperly, huh? How much did he pay to have the 'l' moved?"

"I wish somebody would remove him altogether. You should hear him go on about us: 'This is a public process and should be an open process! This sham of a hearing process shows a critical lapse of judgment and complete disdain for the people! The Appropriations Committee is going to hear about this!'"

"I can see the attraction of working with rocks."

"Yeah. Rocks are orderly. They break along predictable fault lines, have fine crystalline shapes—"

"So, you want me to get something on this bastard?"

"Uh, that's not—"

"We both know the guy is bought and paid for, right? And you want me to find out who's holding the receipt."

"I can't do that."

"Sure you can. Well, you can't hire me to 'get something on this bastard,' but you can hire me to uncover relevant conflict-of-interest issues."

"Or to track down former Universal Lighting workers."

"That's the stuff."

Gina switches the phone to her other ear. I think she's scratching her head.

"I've got to go upstate tomorrow for a public meeting in Troy," she says. "Sipperly's going to be there, with his loyal army of industry-funded scientists and 'concerned citizens' who all seem to live at the same three addresses. Whenever we say the river needs to be dredged, they all say the PCBs are flushing away naturally so why spend the money? When we present the data demonstrating that eating PCB-laden fish from the north river poses an unacceptably high risk of cancer, they counter by saying there's no proof PCBs cause cancer. It can get pretty surreal, and it would sure be nice to have something extra up our sleeves. But it can't appear to come from me . . ."

"I can pass for a concerned citizen."

"Not in Rensselaer County, Fil. You, uh—"

"I'd fail the physical, huh?"

"Thanks for saying it for me."

"How far upstate are we talking about?"

"It's about a hundred and fifty miles."

"You know how spread out my family is."

I hear her chuckle. Then it's back to reality: "You really think you can get something on him?"

"Anyone who handles dirty money is going to leave plenty of fingerprints."

"Smart. You get that from a fortune cookie?"

"You have your research methods and I have mine."

"Okay, Fil. You're hired."

"Great, only you can't hire me directly. I'm still unlicensed. You have to hire the agency and ask my boss, Mr. Davis, to assign me to your case."

"Gee, is anything ever easy?"

"I wouldn't know."

Davis practically kisses me.

"The U.S. Environmental Protection Agency! Talk about your big-name clients!"

"The EPA has its own investigators. They just can't do what I do."

"That's why I love having you on board, Fil."

"I'm saying don't expect a lot of repeat business."

"Don't worry, we'll get it, and from other branches of government, too. You can't beat this referral, Fil. And that one from Queens College CUNY. I'd say you've passed your six-month review. Starting now, you get an extra three bucks an hour."

Raising me to ten.

"Thanks, Chip."

"Next stop, junior partner."

"Yeah, that'll widen our customer base."

He looks at me quizzically.

"Look at the company name: Davis and Brown. At least get an Abramovitz in there," I tell him. "That'll bring them in from Kew Gardens Hills. And it wouldn't hurt you to learn *a bisl* Yiddish, too."

"Yeah, and right after that we'll all learn Hindi and Chinese. Look, Fil, I keep telling you to go after the big fish. The small-time community business will trickle down from there."

I look out the window, through the driving rain, at the flashing yellow-and-red lights under the train bridge. Some poor rookie is getting soggy, cold feet because some jackass made an illegal left turn. Bad day to be a working cop.

"Anything else?" Chip asks.

"Yes, I think we should spring for a copy of the Phonesearch Power Locator system. It's a hundred and twenty-five million listings on six CD-ROMs with two-way address search capability, for a hundred-twenty dollars. Fifty more and they'll send us an update every six months. We're spending a lot of time right now pulling the stuff from expensive Web sources. It'll save money."

"A hundred-seventy dollars for the whole shebang, huh? Okay, sounds good."

"Fil, call on line three." Katwona throws her voice around the doorway.

It's Dvurushnik. "So what the hell are you doing? I am paying five hundred dollars a day—"

"And we've worked one day."

"Where are results?"

"We have a primary suspect at this time, Mr. Dvurushnik."

"You will call me Vladimir."

"Fine, Vladimir."

"Who is he? I want his—"

"Just let us handle it, okay?"

"I am making big fuss about new products. But where are results?"

"You want daily reports? That's an extra hundred dollars." Bit of an exaggeration there, but it shuts him up. "We agreed on twice weekly. You want them more often, it'll cost you."

"How about three times a week, same price?"

"You'll have to negotiate with my boss, Mr. Davis."

"Miss Buscarsela, that is not how you get ahead in this business. You must learn to make the deals yourself."

"I'll report anything to you as soon as it happens, okay?"

That seems to satisfy him. *Ay, chihuahua.*

I spend a couple of hours researching Gina's nemesis, the Honorable Tim Sipperly of Glens Falls, NY, and dredge up plenty of circumstantial evidence of campaign finance abuses, including large cash transfers from industry "lobbyists" to re-election funds that don't seem to hold liquid assets any better than a sieve, and one trump card that I've got to verify with my own eyes, or at least with a single-lens reflex. I square it with Chip, then I call Gina up and say, "Give me directions. I'll meet you at the press conference."

I hope it's only a day trip.

I'm getting ready to head across the street for a Cuban sandwich when the local police report catches my ear:

"—botched investigation into an ambitious scheme by organized crime to infiltrate Wall Street. The confidential ninety-seven-page memorandum outlining the government's prosecution strategy was mistakenly made public, revealing the names of potential witnesses against nineteen reputed members of the Genovese and Bonanno crime families, greatly imperiling the case."

"And the safety of the witnesses, asshole," I add, under my breath, while slipping on my coat.

"We go live now to the 110th Precinct in Elmhurst, Queens, for a statement from Police Captain Dan Mulroney on the death of special education instructor and community housing advocate Manuel Morales."

I freeze.

"Hey, Fil, you going out? Can you get me a—?"

"Shush!" I run over to the radio and turn up the volume. Unruly shouts punctuate the background. I think I recognize some of the voices.

"We regard the death of Mr. Morales as a felony homicide due to a mugging, and we are currently investigating every possible lead. We have no further statement at this time."

The community voices swell a little louder.

"So the police have just made a statement saying that there will be no statement," says Len, trying for levity.

I check my watch. I've got a couple of hours.

"Tell Davis I've got to check up on something. I'll be back in time for the Mad Russian's tail job."

Len and Karen spend the next few minutes watching me clean and reload my gun.

"I tried to call, but your phones are all out."

"The phone company cut the lines, even though we were all paid up," says Camille Tesoro, bending over a wet mop and scrubbing the floor near the baby's crib.

I was hoping to take off my raincoat and warm up, but it feels like the heat's off, too.

"I came to tell you something about Sonny."

She straightens up and glares at me like a songbird who's just heard a twig snap.

"They're going to give him a blood test." Her eyes show fear. "But it's hopeful. If the test shows that he's been exposed to psychotropic chemical fumes at work, we may be able to reduce the charges and lighten the sentence."

For a moment she seems like a visitor to the U.N., waiting for each word to be translated through a headset in her ears. Then the whites of her eyes begin to glisten, reflecting the cold gray light outside her window, and a tear drips down the right side of her face like a drop of calcite ending a thousand-year fall off a stalactite in an underground cavern.

Ever seen a statue of the Virgin cry? There's something miraculous about it.

We hug for a long time.

"How are you fixed for cash?" I ask.

"We can last the week, thanks to the extra money you got for us."

I'm waiting for the best moment to ask her about Manny's death, but the heavy thumping coming through the floor above gives me a better idea.

I promise to come back with better news, and climb the chilly boilerplate-steel steps to the sixth floor. After a couple of knocks the door flies open and Ted Hocks stands there in a plain black T-shirt with the word "PRIDE" spelled out across his chest in thick, white, machine-made letters. He was wearing all that loose clothing before, and I didn't realize he was so muscular.

"Aren't you cold?" I ask.

"Nah. Got to toughen up the old bod. The city's getting ready to throw us out of here one of these days and we've got to be ready to fight for what's ours."

"Yeah, that's the system. If you owe a hundred dollars, they take your car. If you owe a thousand, they take your house. If you owe a million, they work it out, because you're obviously too important to screw with."

"This isn't about owing. We don't *owe* anybody anything. When Benjamin Hitchcock and the original homesteaders settled here in 1870, they were trying to establish a worker's paradise, you know? With a big park and the borough's only zoo and all. Everything for the workers. So we're just carrying on the tradition, reclaiming the territory from the iron triangle of special interests. Did you know *corona* means 'crown' in Italian?"

"Yeah. In Spanish, too."

"Really. So where you staying now?"

"Oh, I'm renting a second-floor apartment from a couple named Kyriakis."

"Kyriakis? Don't know them. They nice?"

"Sure. Nice enough. And it's good to have someone around the house when my daughter comes home from school. No kids today?" I say, looking around.

"Short day. They went home twenty minutes ago."

I notice the TV is still on, playing black-and-white cartoons.

"The Greeks have a real sense of pride in their culture," he says, crossing over to a pot of homemade soup that's simmering on a hot plate. "What does 'Kyriakis' mean?"

"Well, *kyrie* means 'lord,' so I guess *kyriakis* means the Lord's Day, or Sunday. Like the name Domingo in Italian or Spanish."

"Lord's Day, huh? That's a pretty powerful name," he says, stirring the soup.

"What kind of name is Hocks?"

"It used to be Hochs, with that 'cch' sound, but my parents changed it during the war. Didn't want it looking 'too German,' you know?"

"Yeah, my name's been through a few changes, too."

"Those Mediterranean names can get pretty long." He tastes a spoonful of thick lentil soup, and seems satisfied. "Sure I can't tempt you? It's my mom's recipe."

"No, thanks, I—I've got to spend some time in close quarters after I leave here."

He smiles. "I get you. Actually, my mom always put a ham bone in it."

"None of that for you, huh?"

"No way. It's time to stop eating so much meat. I mean, meat is animal flesh. Meat is murder, except we give them a 'humane' stun-bolt first so they 'don't feel pain,' don't have to see their own blood spurting onto the ground. Like we're so superior, 'cause we know how to keep the blood contained."

"Plus they're full of chemicals," I say.

He's changed from the first time I met him, when he was bursting with energy like an overgrown kid. But there's still the same *intensity* to his emotions.

"Yeah," Ted agrees. "They're so vulnerable."

I can hear Camille singing to her baby on the floor below.

"Speaking of which, did you hear about Manny Morales?"

"Sure. Everybody's heard."

"What do you think?"

"What do you mean, what do I think?"

"I mean, the cops are saying he was mugged. You see it that way?"

"Hard to say. He didn't live on the best block, and he took a lot of risks."

"What kind of risks?"

"You know. He pissed a lot of people off."

"Like the rent strike."

"Yeah."

"Think he was killed over a rent strike?"

"I don't know about that. But you can bet it was about money. Isn't everything?"

"Sure is. Was he involved with the factory at all? In your struggle with the city?"

"He came to a few meetings. Tried to stir everyone to action. But you know those potheads, they kept saying crap like, 'Jah will provide, mon.' I been around long enough to know Jah don't provide no rent money, baby. And he don't stop the government from kicking down your freakin' door." For a second he looks like a kid who's been caught cursing in Sunday school class. "Sorry."

"That's okay."

"Why do you want to know?"

"Just wondering how many fights he was involved in."

"Probably quite a few, and some you don't know about, huh?"

"Probably."

I better get back to my day job. But I take the slow way around, keeping my ear to the ground for low-frequency grumblings about justice for Manny.

CHAPTER EIGHT

De noche todos los gatos son pardos.
All cats look the same in the dark.
—Ecuadorian Proverb

"**I LOVE** the old neighborhood. All the kinky dresses, and the outrageous jewelry and the exotic perfumes."

"Yeah, and the women look pretty good, too," says Len, taking a sip of coffee. We're in a company car with the heat up full, watching the exit to the Krepki Factory. "What time is it?"

"Four-thirty."

"It's getting dark already."

"Of all the days for him to work them overtime! How does he expect us to follow Mendoza if we can't even spot him?"

"I'll spot him," says Len. "Now ask me another question."

I lift the study guide from my lap and angle it towards the pink-and-blue neon sign offering Chinese take-out.

"Okay, here's a good one. 'An investigator has been assigned to tail a suspect who will be traveling by car at night in the city. The simplest way to carry out the surveillance would be to: a) mark the car ahead of time so it is recognizable at night; b) memorize the make, model, and color of the car; c) memorize the license plate; d) disable the car so it will be unusable.'"

"B and C."

117

"That's why I would have said. They want A."

"A? Mark the car ahead of time? How? Bust a taillight? Paint a big white X on the trunk?"

"I guess you have to know how to read the question. They want the *simplest* way."

"Simplest or stupidest? How much you pay for that thing?" He flips the study guide over and checks the cover price. "Thirty bucks? What a rip."

"It's a big-budget book."

"Yeah, they changed the ink cartridge *twice* when they were printing it out."

"You could always use the new auto tracking device endorsed by the National League of Women Investigators. They're only eighty-nine dollars each."

"What's the catch?"

"It takes half-an-hour to install."

"Pass."

I check the clock again. Exactly three minutes since the last time I checked. I open a section of the *Times* that's been folded into sixteenths and stuffed between the two front seats, and read a passage out loud about a major league sports figure who says he doesn't want to take the Number 7 train to Shea Stadium and "sit next to a junkie with an orange Mohawk, a welfare mom with eight kids, and some queer with AIDS."

"That's ridiculous!" says Len.

"Yeah, everyone knows they're all on the Number 1 train. Okay, you read. I'll watch," I say, stuffing the paper into Len's hands.

"Watch my coffee," he protests.

I stare at the factory gate while he flattens out the paper and scans the headlines. "Will you look at this," he says. "It says a politician used his influence to sell favors."

"Yeah, what are the odds of that happening?"

"You're cynical."

"You spend ten years in a pit full of manure, you get a little sensitive to the smell of shit."

He turns the page. "Speaking of which, looks like the

grave diggers are going to go on strike," he reports. "Talk about bad timing."

"You mean, with Thanksgiving just around the corner?"

"I mean a strike would have a lot more clout during the summer, when storage is a big-big problem, you know? So what are you doing for the holidays?"

"Surviving them."

"How about the annual office party? Got your costume ready?"

"Sure, I'm going as someone who *has* a life."

He must be thinking, That time of the month already? So I tell him, "My boyfriend just called to say he's off tonight and we can get together, but no, I've got to spend the evening sitting in the freezing rain waiting for Vlad the Mad's loyal workers to walk out the fucking door."

"You don't owe me any explanations," he says. "That guy's a doctor, right?"

"Yeah."

"So they're as bad as we are, always rushing around with their beepers and last-minute emergencies. Criminals keep odd hours, too, you know? I'd think he ought to be able to appreciate that."

"Oh, he does, he does. He's one in a million."

And the fact is, we get together whenever we want it. We just train ourselves not to want it too often.

Len opens up the sports page. "Knicks are taking it on the road tonight—"

"Lights out, Hrabowski. The gate's opening."

The papers and manuals fall to the floor. Len drains the cardboard cup and crushes it into a ball. No distractions here. In a few minutes, we spot Mendoza. I start to get out of the car, but Len grabs me.

"He hasn't seen me before," I say.

"He hasn't seen me, either."

"I thought we had this worked out—"

"He's got a real eye for the ladies, Fil. Dynamite babe like you on his tail, he'll make you in two minutes."

"Thanks, but—"

"I'll go."

"Okay, I guess."

He gets out while I climb over the parking brake and scrunch behind the wheel, temporarily dazzled by the words cast off from this young stud-muffin-in-training. Someone under thirty thinks I'm a "dynamite babe"?

Oh, yeah: Reality. I remember that. I slip the car into gear, let them get a head start, and slowly follow behind, keeping a close watch on everything, which is not easy in the rain.

Maybe he's just being chivalrous.

I keep about a block behind Len, who's maybe half-a-block behind Mendoza. This is a really screwy set-up. Both of us should be on foot, but we brought the car because of the weather, and to serve as a mobile base, and how far do you figure the guy is going without a raincoat, anyway? I should have thought this through better, but it's too late now. Welcome to *Surveillance on a Shoestring*, with your host, the shamefully clueless Filomena Buscarsela. A Girl Scout troop could have planned this better. But they're not working six other cases, nor could they have followed Mendoza into the dimly lit bar on the corner of Lamont Avenue and 94th Street, like we're about to do.

Len trots up to me as I'm parking. "Come on, we'll fit in better as a couple."

"How's your Spanish?" I say, already feeling the *salsa* music pulsating through the paint-flecked walls.

"I'll have to be your date, not your live-in lover."

"Oh, too bad," I joke, opening the door. The music's loud, but not too loud. The place is a hang-out for regulars who come here to chew over the day's events, and the TV is tuned to channel 47, which at this hour is showing a Venezuelan soap opera. On screen, the meddlesome uncle is trying to keep the rich girl and the poor boy apart, but without much conviction, as if he's read next week's script and he already knows how it's going to turn out.

Mendoza's chatting with the bartender. He gives us a quick glance as we come in, then turns back to reach for a slice of lime. We take a table near the door where we can see everything Mendoza's doing, which at the moment involves gazing deeply into space. A full day on the assembly line will do that to you.

If we were just keeping tabs on the guy I'd have stayed in the damn car, since letting him see us like this is going to burn us for any more close surveillance. But he doesn't seem like he's in any hurry to leave, and his coat looks awfully bulky. "I say the drop is here," I tell Len, staring into his dark brown eyes and chucking him under the chin like I've just told him the sweetest little nothing.

We order two glasses of watery draft beer and sit there occasionally holding hands and touching, speaking loudly in Spanish and softly in English and laughing every now and then at each other's jokes. We're discussing contemporary film clichés—if you shoot people at the beginning of the movie, you're the bad guys, if you shoot people at the end, you're the good guys—when a man walks in past us and takes a table near Mendoza. Mendoza picks his beer up and sits at the table across from the guy.

I study the newcomer thoroughly, so I can describe him to the police if I have to. He's wearing a heavy wool raincoat, light brown. He has a watermelon-shaped head with dark wavy hair thinning to a small bald patch in back, a long, slightly convex nose with downward sloping base, medium-thick lips half-hidden under a bushy downturned mustache, round fleshy cheeks, liver spot half-an-inch below the mustache on the left side, short protruding lower jaw, dark smoker's circles under brown, thick-lidded eyes, and long ears set a little high and close to the head. When I'm convinced I could pick him out of a crowd of several thousand people, I tell Len to get the check while I go to the bathroom.

I get up and walk past Mendoza and Mr. Fleshy Cheeks to find the ladies' room. Mendoza's hands are low. He might be counting money, but I can't tell using only peripheral vision.

On my way back, I allow myself a more direct look, and notice that Mendoza's coat is open and empty-looking while his companion's coat is buttoned and bulging. You're supposed to limit your assumptions in this business, but I sense that it's worth the risk in this instance.

I tell Len, "Let's get out of here. I want to leave before he does."

We sit in the car and wait, listening to the news reports about who killed who with which blunt instrument, who died in this apartment house fire in Glendale or that three-way collision on Utopia Parkway and all the other horror stories that seem designed to turn you away, making you think, Who needs more bad news? so you'll stop paying attention to all the *real* shit that's going on out there. In other words, I am forced to conclude that the actual purpose of most news reports is to distract you from finding out who's *really* running things and precisely how they steal from, poison, and imprison us.

But then, that's how a former revolutionary thinks sometimes.

The door opens and Mendoza comes out. I snap off the radio as he steps off the curb and crosses the street with a jaunty spring in his step, coming right towards us. Damn! We're a couple in a car. Why are we still here? I'm about to start yelling at Len and accuse him of flirting with my friend from work, switching to Spanish to punctuate the appearance of a lovers' quarrel, but that might attract too much attention and the next thing I know Len grabs me and—boom!—we just find each other's lips and the two of us press tightly into each other to avoid being looked at too closely. It's so dreary and windy and damp out there, and in here the feel and the smell of wet clothes make me shiver, and his touch is so warm. So warm. And I have to admit this feels good. It's . . . Jesus.

I stop.

It works. Mendoza walks sprightfully by us looking like a guy who's just made some easy money.

We sit there staring into silence for ten straight minutes.

We don't have to pretend how weird it is. We don't have to act like a couple whose relationship has just entered the Twilight Zone.

Finally Len says, "Damn, I should have gone to the men's room before, when I had the chance."

"You gotta pee, go ahead. I won't look."

I turn and face the passenger window, looking out at the dark, rainy avenue, while he gets the wide-mouthed plastic bottle out from under the seat. But I can't help hearing it. When the last drips sound, I say,

"I don't know how you guys all piss together at those cattle troughs, you know, those public restrooms with twenty urinals lined up with nothing between them."

"When I really have to go, it's no problem, but yeah, sometimes with all these guys staring at the back of my neck, I just freeze."

He twists the cap tight and stows the bottle back under the seat.

"You know, Len . . ."

He's leaning over, groaning under the Herculean strain of putting the jar away. "Yeah?" He won't look up.

"You made the right move before."

He sits up. Our eyes finally meet.

"You kept us from burning the tail. It was—thoroughly professional of you," I tell him. "Now we better take our eyes off each other and watch the freaking door before he gets away from us."

And we sit here and wait for old Cheeky to come out.

Ten minutes.

"You want to see the paper?" asks Len.

"Nah."

Fifteen minutes.

"Mind if I read?"

"Go ahead."

He pulls out a men's magazine and opens to a feature that I swear is called "Where to Buy It, Eat It and Fuck It in New York."

When it's time to switch, I ask, "Can I see that?"

He hands it over. I keep my gloves on.

I flip through the magazine. "Man, why do porno mags bother with page numbers?"

"There's no pornography in a clean mind."

"Who told you I had a clean mind?"

Then I get to the back pages with all the phone sex ads. Talk about subtle. There's a photo of a young woman dressed up as a high school girl with pigtails and a short plaid skirt flipped up to her waist, beckoning to the viewer with one crooked index finger and encircling her sex with the other. The number to call is 889-CUNT. Almost makes you nostalgic for the days when they used to sell this stuff in a plain brown wrapper and the vice cops thought *Ulysses* was a threat to public morality.

"Well, you gotta understand, Fil," Len explains, "men have different values. Like I think whoever invented the sports bra deserves the Nobel Prize."

"In which category? Physics or economics?"

"*There he goes*," says Len suddenly.

I have to squint into the darkness. All I see is a shape heading up 95th Street. "Are you sure?"

"Yes, yes, it's him."

"That's not his walk."

"*What?*"

"Damn it, it's too dark to tell now. All right, go ahead and follow him. I'll wait here. Set your beeper on vibrate."

And we separate. Just when I thought this gig couldn't get more miserable. At least there was someone to trade jokes and split the shift with. Now I'm alone, and I can't take my eyes off the door for a second. No talking, no reading, just watching and waiting, watching and waiting.

Trade jokes? What am I saying? Half-an-hour ago I was practically tongue-kissing the guy. And it felt good, too, goddamn it. What's going on here? Maybe it's because I'm always presenting such a hard-edged front at work, the momentary tenderness caught me unawares. Maybe it was just being alone with another warm body in this miserable weather. A moment of weakness, with the dampness seeping into my bones making me feel my age prematurely. Or maybe it's that special thrill associated with the tangy juice of a fresh, young sapling.

Oh yes, part of me is definitely tingling from just imagining the attractions of giving in, of yielding to the excitement of some hard ribs and firm thighs, of running my hands over a fresh set of round ass cheeks belonging to someone with a whole new set of baggage—but no, I will not be unfaithful, as God is my witness. No. Because I'm with Stan now. Although . . . if I'm feeling like this, maybe something's missing. Why am I with Stan? He's not Antonia's father. (Antonia's father was a fucking jerk.) I can't explain. But I made a choice, and the only course now is to honor it for as long as it lasts.

So where are Stan and I going? And why does Len present such an attraction? Is it just the perennial conflict between having a sensitive and supportive partner like Stan, and the thrill of the hunt, of catching a fresh scent and clawing the dirt like a pair of wild beasts who *don't* have to remember to wake up a half-hour early the next day because the whelp's got band practice on Friday mornings? Is it just some evolutionary process that made sense half-a-million years ago when producing live offspring required considerably less commitment, but is terribly out-of-place on Lamont Avenue and 94th Street on a Wednesday night at the dawn of the third millennium? Or am I just a horny old slut?

I guess I could opt for Bogie's classic evasive answer: It was a combination of all three.

Eventually the rain starts to let up a bit, and I figure it's time to buzz Len and find out if he's tailing the right guy or not.

I'm feeling around for the phone, keeping my eyes on the door, when it opens and Mendoza's contact steps out. It's definitely him, and there's no time to flag Len. I send him a three-letter code to "contact me," then I have to shut off my phone. I don't want it ringing when I'm sneaking around behind this guy.

This isn't exactly stalking a black marketer through the Vienna sewers. He's just a low-level chiseler trying to get out of the rain with a few crappy videotapes, not something that we have to fear falling into "the wrong hands." He heads east on the avenue, crosses Junction Boulevard, turns right on 102nd Street, where he picks up some cigarettes and a pack of gum in a cramped, Pakistani-American convenience store, then continues south and stops at a green-gray storefront just before the railroad tracks. Keys out, he looks around, notices me crossing the far side of the street a block behind, hat pulled down low against the drizzle, but it's just a reflexive New Yorker's let's-make-sure-there-are-no-ax-murderers-around look that doesn't really register me as a threat. He turns the keys and goes in. I suppose it would be too much to expect him to hold the door open for me.

It's a corner building, so there's a tiny window on the south side. I take a peek. The glass is smoky and the shades are drawn so I can't see a thing. But the light goes on and I know he's there. I take out the phone and call Len.

"Jesus, Filomena, where the hell are you?"

"Shh!" I stage whisper. "I'm at the northwest corner of 44th Avenue and 102nd Street. He's in there."

"Wait for me."

"Fat fucking chance."

"F—"

The phone's back in my pocket and I'm checking out the locks. There are some serious hardened cylinders and face plates and jimmy-proof braces, suggesting that my friend has a great deal of stock worth protecting inside, but most of this metal is meant for locking up for the night. Right now he's in there with only a Medeco and a rusty Yale between us.

Time to tickle the tumblers.

Of course it would be easier just to knock.

Hmm . . . Well, we wouldn't want him to flush the evidence, eh?

Sorry, Cheeky, but the Fourth Amendment only protects you against agents of the government sneaking in like this, a freelance loony like me can do it anytime and it's admissible. Of course it's like stepping in shit, legally, and it could bite back at me, but I think I can handle whatever this mercurial peddler of video knock-offs does to unexpected female intruders.

The door opens into a dark alcove that's been thrown together with quarter-inch veneer plywood and indoor-outdoor carpeting to serve as a brake between the noisy street and the long, low inner room stacked high with humming VCRs and furlongs of thick, black cable snaking across the floor towards overworked junction boxes.

He's sitting behind a desk at the far end of the room, toasting himself with a shot of barley-brew and watching the smoke from his cigarette curl up towards the dull yellow light hanging just above his head.

"Is this a private party?" I ask, slinking into view like a dame on a pulp novel cover.

He draws back, bringing his hands in line with his waistband.

"How did you get in?"

"You must have left the door open."

He scans me for blunt metal objects.

"You're trespassing."

"So ask me to leave."

He hesitates. "What do you want?"

"I could use a nip from that bottle. I'm chilled to the bone." I start forward.

"Stay right where you are." He's a fast draw for a big man. A lot of them are. It doesn't mean he can hit me at twenty feet with a cheap handgun that looks like it couldn't put two bullets within four-and-a-half inches of each other under NRA-approved test conditions.

Whatever happened to fists?

I'm not above whimpering if it gets me out of a mess alive. But I'm not about to whimper for *this* nobody, unless I absolutely have to.

Five seconds go by and he hasn't shot at me yet, so

statistically speaking the odds are in my favor, which is really comforting, let me tell you.

"I can come back later," I say, edging backwards.

"Hold it right there, honey," he says, standing up. Son-of-a-bitch is menacing me. "Remember: No witnesses."

"No witnesses works for me, too."

He's going to shoot.

I dodge. His first two shots go wide and I'm down in a stance pumping shots at him, one, two, and the third through his carpal flexor. His gun flies up and ricochets off the back wall and hangs there a moment—by far the weirdest part of this whole exchange—then falls to the floor with a heavy clatter, as I stride rapidly towards him with my Special Lady cradled in both hands. He's on the floor cupping his bloody forearm to his chest. He sees me coming and reaches for his gun.

"Oh, no. You try that again and I'll shoot you somewhere you'll *really* feel it." I'm standing over him, aiming the gun at his chest. I aim lower.

The phone on the desk rings. I take a slow step back and pick it up.

"That you, Cholly?" says a man with an authentic Queens accent.

"Charlie's under arrest right now. Who's this?"

Click.

I'm going to have to bill Mr. Dvurushnik for some of that "hazardous duty" pay.

When I get a moment, I count the VCRs. Twenty-seven. Just my luck.

"Why the hell couldn't you have three more?" I yell at my confused prisoner.

I go home.

I'm cold. Wet. Tired.

And breathing.

It's good to be alive.

CHAPTER NINE

When the enemy has no face, society will invent one.
—Susan Faludi

"**LIVING IN A** PCB-laden area is *not* dangerous," blares the tin-throated matron in a voice so shrill and strident it sounds like she would be at home ordering three hundred prisoners of war to dig their own graves. "The problem here is alarmist and ignorant *chemophobia*. You see, some people are just naturally scared of chemicals. But most of us have no trouble understanding the fact that in a couple of years *seventy-five percent* of the Hudson River fish will meet FDA standards. Now that's good for business, and it's good for all of us. Check with the Chamber of Commerce: The Erie Canal Cruise Line was booked solid all season!"

"But you can't eat the fish!" says a man in a worn corduroy jacket.

"What about the commercial fishing?" asks a local reporter.

"If the only danger is in eating the fish," snaps the Church Lady from Hell, "and no one is eating the fish, then *why are we here?*"

"Because it's a symptom of deeper environmental problems," Gina's boss Caryl Redman starts to say.

"What can you tell us about this natural recovery process?" says a woman holding a pocket tape recorder.

A suit on loan from Universal Lighting leans in to the mike. "A new computerized modeling study, the most powerful quantitative tool ever developed, shows that PCB levels in major species of fish have dropped ninety percent since 1977."

A groundswell of voices in the audience shows signs of being suitably impressed.

"Mr. Taylor, the summary of your company's report fails to mention that several of the PCB levels recorded came from samples taken *upstream* of Universal Lighting's electrical plants at Hudson Falls and Fort Edward, the largest single sources of PCBs entering the river," says Ms. Redman. "Nearly ninety percent—"

A man jumps to his feet. He's wearing faded blue bib overalls and a red plaid flannel shirt. "I question the legality of the EPA to intervene in the Hudson River crisis at all, since PCBs are not considered a pesticide or a food additive."

"Sir, I believe you're thinking of the FDA—"

"If PCBs were considered pesticides, I could see the intervention of the EPA, which seems to have a free hand here as an unelected and largely unaccountable bureaucracy!"

Another man with the same mud on his boots joins in. "You call yourselves the Environmental Protection Agency, but who protects us *from you*?"

"The PCBs are not magically disappearing, as Universal Lighting would have us believe," says Ms. Redman.

"Then how do you explain the *forty percent drop* in PCBs in the Thompson Island Pool over the last ten years?" asks the suit, pointedly. Voices in the crowd murmur along with him.

It's Gina's turn. I've never seen her look so nervous, but she's in a tight spot, and she has to stand on a cardboard box full of documents to appear the same height as the suit at the podium.

"Three-quarters of the PCBs lost from the Thompson Island Pool simply washed downstream to contaminate the rest of the river, and the remainder—"

"And the remainder are naturally dechlorinating," says the suit.

"Anaerobic dechlorination of tetrachlorobiphenyl removes less than ten percent of the mass," Gina replies.

It doesn't mean shit to the farmers. She tries again: "With very limited exception, dechlorination does *not* break down PCB molecules. It merely turns *tetra*chlorobiphenyl into *tri*chlorobiphenyl, or di- or monochlorobiphenyl. The end product is simply a PCB molecule containing fewer chlorine atoms. We even found some thirty-five-year-old sediments with little or no dechlorination at all."

I feel for Gina, armed with nothing but facts and logic, going up against the PR machine of a $7 billion company whose CEO makes $40 million a year for coming up with sound bites that can travel to 375 million TV and computer screens in 2.3 seconds while she's still pulling on her steel-toed boots. And if that isn't enough, the cardboard box is starting to crumple under her weight. She steadies herself with one hand on the podium as she points to the chart immediately behind her, a series of bar graphs comparing the Thompson Island Dam water column with pool sediments and porewater.

"The PCB load from the Thompson Island Pool has a readily identifiable homologue pattern that dominates the water column from the Thompson Island Dam to Kingston . . ."

I look around the room to see who else is tuning her out. Of course, my excuse is that I was up half the night opening boxes of video cassettes (damn things have so much packaging you'd think they were individually safety-sealed—I mean, it's not like I'm planning *to eat them* or anything) and making sure the cops got my version of the story, wherein I do *not* break any of the state and federal laws that would effectively end my quest for a PI's license. Then I spent some time recovering from the shock of nearly killing a man in a gun battle.

Too soon after that, I had to get up and spend all morning driving up here, another couple of hours sniffing around a sleepy little suburb of Glens Falls, taking pictures of a glorified mudhole and dashing around like mad to find a one-hour photo place one hundred miles north of the get-it-done-now zone, which only extends about fifty miles from New York City in each direction. But I got what I needed, and it's all here in a plain manila envelope.

I summon one of the EPA underlings, hand him the envelope, and tell him to deliver it to Gina *this instant*.

". . . so you see, the PCB load from the Thompson Island Pool originates from the sediments within the pool," Gina concludes.

"But the fish ingest PCBs from the top layers of sediment, not from the buried layers of sediment, so the risk declines with each passing year," says the suit.

"And now the EPA wants to stir it all up again by dredging the river!" says the Church Lady, who hasn't spoken up for a while.

The secret word must be "dredging," because the two politicians who've been lying dormant at the far-right table since I pushed my way in suddenly spring to life like a pair of mechanical musicians who brighten up and start playing when someone drops a quarter into the box. One of them is Town Supervisor Carl "Dutch" Lavender, who starts to say, "The PCB problem is being taken care of naturally—"

But a gesture from the other man humbles him into silence. This is Congressman Sipperly. He speaks with a measured, media-trained voice that is weighted down with *gravitas* and severity, lightly airbrushed with a dusting of Reaganesque fatherliness as well. "What you fail to address, *Ms. Lucchese*, is that there is no evidence that PCBs pose any health risk." He puts some extra spin on her last name as if trying to emphasize its foreignness.

"In fact," he goes on, "we now possess incontrovertible evidence that PCBs aren't even a health problem."

The Church Lady cues her audience with astonished gasps at this revelation.

"What do you think, we just invented it for job security?" says Ms. Redman, getting a few laughs.

But Congressman Sipperly goes on to cite a study of male and female capacitor workers at two "upstate New York" plants that found that mortality was "significantly below expected."

"This study, the largest and most statistically powerful study ever conducted on humans exposed to PCBs, concludes that there is *no link* between PCB exposure and cancer."

Church Lady directs the choir to gasp now, *tutti e fortissimo*.

But Gina jumps right in like an action-hero kickboxer in a warehouse full of hired goons. "I've read the report, Congressman. Why don't you tell the people that Universal Lighting paid for the study? And that it only examines mortality, so if you're merely dying of liver cancer, you don't figure in the story? And who decided what the 'expected' number of deaths was? Most of the workers examined didn't work with PCBs, and are too young to have died from cancer—yet—although they did report higher rates of melanoma and cancer of the liver, rectum, gastrointestinal tract, and brain."

You go, girl, but look at the envelope.

"I'm confused," says a man in a football jersey. He's got a beer gut, drooping sandy hair, and a mustache to match.

"You have the floor, Bill," says Sipperly. "What's on your mind?"

"Well, I just don't understand why nobody can figure the situation out here. We can't seem to get a straight answer, and every time one of you does a study, we get completely different results. So who do we listen to here? Universal Lighting make it sounds like PCBs are good for us. The EPA makes it sound like I might as well drink the water at Chernobyl. And if they've got nothing to hide, why won't they share their findings with Universal Lighting's scientists for a—what do they call it?—one of them 'peer review' things. I tell you, I just don't know who to trust."

"Thank you, Bill, for sharing that with us. I, too, feel that if the PCBs are being buried—"

"But the newly deposited sediments also contain PCBs," says Redman.

Gina, the envelope.

"Fifteen years ago the EPA said no to dredging the river," says Sipperly. "And I agreed. We all agreed that it would needlessly stir up the PCBs and bring them to the surface—"

"It's been my position for three terms that dredging is not needed," interjects "Dutch" Lavender.

Gina finally looks closely at the name on the envelope. Her eyes flit up, scan the audience and quickly catch my attention. I brighten and nod, trying to convey the message, "Yes, yes, open it up." She does, removing the contents and immersing herself in them, blocking out the white noise around her for a few fleeting seconds.

"Now they say dredging is needed. What has changed between fifteen years ago and today? If anything, the stuff is buried deeper than ever. I have always said that dredging is not needed, that it won't work, and I am very proud that these are positions I never veered from. I never changed."

"Congressman Sipperly," says Gina, cutting through this cloud of hogwash like a trumpet. "You say that dredging won't work."

"That is correct—"

"Then why did you spend the last four months convincing the county to dredge a PCB-contaminated pond one block from your house?"

The Colosseum in Rome never saw such mayhem, not with fire, swords, or hungry lions.

"Thanks, Fil. That was my ace-in-the-hole."

"Yeah. When are congressmen going to learn that it's perfectly okay to take money from an industry you're trying to deregulate, but you can't be seen as *personally* benefiting from the arrangement?"

"Yeah, one's just business, the other's just plain sloppy."

"You're supposed to wait until *after* you retire from Congress to become a full-time lobbyist for the electric industry, for God's sakes."

"A full year, by law," says Gina, sipping her half-decaf

mocha java. "But they get around it. Ex-senator DiCatania says he isn't a lobbyist for the banking industry, he's a 'strategic consultant.'"

"Sure, you can reshape reality in your image if you want, but it still has to be consistent with the physical laws of the universe. Sometimes, there's not much difference between these career politicians and the junkie who tried to convince me he was as innocent as the Lamb of God by telling me, 'I wasn't stealing, man, I was *comparing* the bills in the cash register to the ones in my wallet to see if they were printed in the same place.'"

"You didn't buy that, huh?"

"They could at least put a little effort into coming up with a better story. We once busted a guy who had kidnapped two different women and kept them chained in his basement for three-and-a-half weeks. Know what his defense was? He said they were already there when he moved in."

Gina nearly spills her mocha java. She puts it down and wipes the outside of the cup clean with a paper napkin.

"You want to stay for dinner? The EPA will pay for it."

"Gee, that's a tempting offer, but I've got to get back to the city and spend the night under the same roof with my daughter."

"That's right, keep flaunting that child in front of my face."

"Are there no men in the U.S. government?"

"Actually," she can't help grinning, "there's a new guy in our legal department who looks pretty good. Single, interesting background. Cute, too."

"A lawyer?"

"He's got a degree in geology, and he's studying to be an environmental lawyer."

A match made in Heaven.

"Sounds like you've been doing a little investigating of your own," I say.

The conspiratorial grin spreads further across her face.

"Why, Gina, you little predator."

"Speaking of which, what's your boss going to charge me?"

"I don't know. Should be about a thousand bucks, but he'll milk it for computer time, expenses, and travel. Say fifteen hundred."

"And how much do you see?"

"I'll get two hundred, if I'm lucky. Before taxes."

"Oh, Filomena, when are you going to get your license so I can hire you directly?"

Eighteen freaking months.

"Believe me, I'm working on it."

"That reminds me." She starts rummaging around in one of her briefcases. "I was so caught up in preparing for this public meeting . . . let me see . . . ah! Yes. Remember that guy I said sounded like he had mercury poisoning?"

"Sure I do."

"We thought it was his job, right? It's not. It's his home."

"What?"

She lays some documents on the round, white table.

"Forty-fourth Avenue and a Hundred and Eighth Street, Corona, New York," she says. "Six-story former industrial building converted to sixteen residential spaces. That it?"

"Yeah, that's it. They used to make electrical appliances there."

"No, they made light bulbs. And fluorescent lights, rectifiers, and mercury vapor lamps, for fifty years. I wouldn't be surprised if we found residual traces of mercury between the floorboards."

"The whole building's sick?"

"Probably. I'll have to check it out, and all the residents should be tested for fluid-mercury levels."

"Great, only who's going to get twenty paranoid anarchists to take a blood test?"

"Uh, it's not just a blood test."

"Even worse."

"I'm afraid so. But we won't share the results with any other government agencies."

"You try telling them that."

"Look, Fil, mercury vapor is a central nervous system

toxin. The poison accumulates in the kidneys and the brain. It can cause neurological disorders, spontaneous abortions, and severe brain damage to the unborn children of women exposed during pregnancy. We may have to take over the building, relocate the residents, tear the thing down brick-by-brick, monitor the drinking water, cart off the contaminated soil, and dump it in New Jersey."

"And plow salt into the ground?"

"Don't worry, something will grow there eventually, after we get through with it. Not like some of the ruined landscapes I've visited. You ever see what's left of a mountain after the rich veins of silver have been extracted with mercury and the rest of it strip-mined?"

"Yes, in Bolivia."

"Oh, right. Yeah, it's still used in small-scale mining and in underdeveloped countries, where it's slowly killing the miners and making idiots of their children."

And I just realized: Azogues. It means "mercury" in Spanish. But it's also the name of a town in the Ecuadorian mountains known for its metallurgy, where the residents have a reputation for being slow-witted and stupid. A whole town.

"Fil? Hello? Fil?"

"What? Oh, sorry, I was just—"

"Overwhelmed by the responsibility of knowing precisely which poisons are killing us and exactly how fast. Join the club."

"Well, I better go warn the anarchists."

"Good luck. And thanks again. You really came through for me."

"Yeah, I'm slowly working my way up to saving your life," I say.

"You don't have to do that."

"Sure I do."

To make it even.

The sign says: KEEP OUT OF BIN.

Right. Otherwise I might have been tempted. It looks like such fun, diving into a bin full of used mufflers.

The sky is a hard slab of flagstone, as I wander around the truck stop, taking a break from the state thruway and its long stretch of filthy ugliness. Or is it ugly filthiness? I can never get that straight.

I'm watching the tiny suburban women piloting their amphibious personnel carriers, thinking about how the luxury jeep is actually third world importation. The concept started there. European- and American-style luxury sedans are often impractical when the road to your second home in the country is impassable four months of the year due to heavy rains. Now everybody's got them.

I climb onto an abandoned picnic table and look out beyond the low-lying warehouses and wet tree skeletons to the cold, gray shore of the Hudson River, swirling past much as it did in the days when it marked the western frontier of colonial expansion. I'm turning around and I nearly fall on the slippery planks as a juice bottle comes sailing past me from a moving car and shatters like a bomb against the cement pillar of a water fountain. Jesus. I'm too worried about breaking my wrist against the splintery edge of the table to ID the vehicle, allowing my shoulder to whack the dark wood instead. By the time I look up the car is long gone.

I absolutely cannot understand the male mindset that craves this sort of anonymous violence. I mean, I understand serial killers better: A serial killer's a sick SOB who hates the world. *These* guys are "normal." It's normal for boys to hurt things weaker than themselves, to hurt people they don't even know and to have fun doing it. You tell me which is sicker.

And now my shoulder hurts. I'm wiping off the dark, wet picnic-table residue when I hear the distinct, polyrhythmic piercing tone of a language whose lamentations usually resonate through the mountains of south central Ecuador.

"*Ari, caypimi cani.*" Well, here I am.

I turn around and look at the polished red pickup truck that just pulled in with more than a dozen rain-soaked men crammed into the cargo bay. The men are wearing American-made work clothes, but I can tell by their faces and their straight, black hair that they're Cañari Indians, probably all from the same village.

"*Cay isma allcucuna.*"

Those shitty dogs. Who's being shitty to them?

Nobody but an Ecuadorian would even know where to find workers like this, much less bring them to the U.S. I go up to them, introduce myself and ask what's going on. They're not the least bit surprised to meet someone up here who speaks their language. I doubt they know exactly how far from home they really are. As I suspected, a middle-class Ecuadorian couple brought them here, along with their wives and children, and they all live together in a big barn with no heat, being moved from place to place, wherever there's work, never venturing away from the safety of the group, kept from learning English and afraid to speak up. They know nothing of the local laws.

Finally, the owner of the truck comes walking out of the convenience store. I recognize the round, well-fed face of a landowner, a colored mixture of the races common among the bourgeois of my native country. He's wearing clean, dry sport clothes that set him apart from his sodden, mud-spattered workers.

He smiles like he enjoys the prospect of setting the dogs on troublemakers like me.

"What's the problem, miss?" he says in English.

"How could you exploit your own people like this?" I accuse him in Ecuadorian Spanish.

"These aren't my people, they're Indians. Besides, I'm doing them a favor, bringing them to America. Their kids can go to school here."

One of the huddled men says to me, in Quichua, "We will forgive him some day."

I say, let God forgive him. That's His job.

I give a buck to the white-bearded old man who I happen to know is a World War II vet, wrapped in a thin blanket, crouching in the cold, granite doorway of the Queens County Savings Bank, and continue walking past the black teenager playing Freddie King licks for the evening shoppers on 103rd Street. I can only spread the wealth so far, you know.

I get home and find my daughter having dinner in the Kyriakises' kitchen. I must say, it's really nice to get such grandparent treatment from our landlords, but then I have to put up with them quizzing me about my extra long day and looking over my shoulder as I go through the mail, while the kid plays random horror movie chords on their piano. There's a note from Senator Clinton responding to my recent letter in opposition to abortion, politely stating that she respects my opinion, but remains committed to a woman's right to choose. That's just great. Only problem is, I never sent any such letter, which means some anti-abortion group is using a mailing list with my name on it. I'll have to look into that at some point.

And everything in the sexy women's underwear catalog should just carry a label that says, "WARNING: THIS CLOTHING WILL LOOK AWFUL ON ANY WOMAN WITH A NORMAL BODY." I head upstairs, flipping through the catalog. I notice there's only one model in here who doesn't pluck her eyebrows—not that anyone's looking at their eyebrows.

I glance out the window and the neighbor's teenage son waves at me through the window in exactly the same location on his family's house. I wave back. Jesus.

I never wanted to live in one of those lower-middle-class rabbit warrens where you can see what the neighbors on your right side are having for breakfast and who the neighbor on your left is screwing while her husband's at work.

No, I'll just take the hilltop estate overlooking my personal fiefdom. Just as soon as my fairy godmother finishes her gig with that Cinderella babe.

I make it upstairs and collapse on the couch, flick on the

TV, and wait until I can get up the energy to move. Some fully pumped men are running around trying to throw a basketball through a couple of opposing hoops while a season ticket holder with an orange towel over his head yells at them from the sidelines. The shot goes up: Air ball! Well, it was a great jump shot, but there's a *powerful* crosswind at Madison Square Garden that sometimes blows the ball off course like that.

I switch to another channel, which is broadcasting a TV-14 cartoon about a sullen, cynical high school girl and the group of social outcasts she hangs with.

I call out, "Tonia, that show you wanted to watch is on."

"I want to finish this video game," she yells back from her room.

Kids today. "Don't you know that watching television is more important than video games?"

I hear a growl of disapproval at my joke. First her "terrible twos" lasted three years, now she's having a ten-year adolescence.

I suppose I should think about dinner. Twenty minutes to make rice, and what do I have to go with it? Not much. I've got to go shopping *again*. There's one egg and a piece of cheese that's getting moldy around the edges. Very little left after I cut that off. But it will hold me until tomorrow.

The downstairs door buzzes. Mrs. Kyriakis answers it, speaking English, emitting the sounds of recognition, then a heavy tread creaks up the stairs and Stan shows up at my door looking pale and distressed and I ask, "What's the matter?"

He doesn't answer, just walks past me and sits on the couch, waiting for me to sit next to him. It's a ritual. I oblige him.

"What's wrong?"

His hands are shaking.

"Someone threw a rock through my window," he says.

Is that all? He's shaking with rage, not with cold. I know the signs. Is it something I—

"Today is November ninth," he says, his chest tight as if short of breath.

"And?" I wait. "I'm sorry, what's November ninth?"

"The anniversary of *Kristallnacht*. The Night of Broken Glass."

"Oh."

And he says, "I didn't think we still had to deal with this in America in the twenty-first century."

"Stan, I have to deal with it every time I step out the door."

He looks at me.

"I just don't tell you about it all the time," I confess. "Especially when it—"

"When it *what*?"

"Especially when it comes from Jews." I really didn't want to say this. "Some of it comes from Jews."

He takes a moment to process it, then he coolly admits, "Jews can be racist, too."

I nod.

"There was a guy I knew in med school who totally burnt-out on drugs," he says.

"What a shame."

"No, it isn't. It's good."

"Why?"

"Because there's no telling how many people he would have hurt, or harmed or destroyed if he had become a doctor. He was a real self-centered prick who always had his eyes on the money. One time he said to me, 'You know, sickle-cell anemia is a great disease.' And I'm trying to give him the benefit of the doubt, hoping maybe he means it's scientifically interesting, so I say, 'Why?' and he says, 'Because it kills black people.' Some doctor he'd have been. A racist, money-grubbing Jew. So you see, it's better this way."

We both know I don't need to answer. Instead, my lips find the fragrant feast of his neck, and my fingers stroll merrily down that salty back-country road to the mysterious black forest of his flesh, and soon my tender breast is jabbed by sharp, metallic points. I push him away slightly until my fingertips discover an unfamiliar thick and heavy Star of David dangling around his chest.

"Good God, you smite the Philistines with this?"

"You want me to take it off?"

"Just be careful with it."

He starts leaning in again when suddenly I'm giggling and rattling him on top of me.

"Now what?" he asks.

"I was just thinking, what if Jews had a sect of 'born again' devotees? What would they say? 'You must be circumcised *again*!'"

"Ouch."

"What's left to cut?"

I laugh some more, and eventually Stan pulls back and asks, "You want to get some dinner?"

"Everything I want is right here," I say, hugging him closer.

"Filomena!" calls Mrs. Kyriakis. "Someone at the door!"

Shit. I didn't even hear it buzz. Stan sits up and watches me go, eyes glancing over the pile of mail with the sexy women's underwear catalog on top.

"I'm going to dust that for prints when I get back," I announce.

I go downstairs thinking, who the hell is coming by at this hour?

It's Georgio, from the squat, dreadlocks packed into an African tricolor wool-knit hat.

"You hear the news?" he asks.

"No, I just got back into town."

"The cops have changed the classification of Manny's death from an 'assault' to an 'accident.'"

"What the hell does that mean? Someone accidentally hit him over the head with a pool cue?"

"We don't know. And we want you to find out."

CHAPTER TEN

**There is nothing more stimulating than a case
where everything goes against you.**
—Sherlock Holmes

IT WAS THE SUMMER before last.

I remember the skidding of the shiny wheels, the
smoking black rubber, the shrieking brakes, the thunderous
crash as the huge tanker ate up three cars flipping onto its
side, loading lines snapping off to prevent a fuel tank rupture,
the whole jagged ganglion sliding and scraping and sparking towards the heavy stone divider and slamming into it,
popping a hatch and spilling thousands of gallons of gasoline
onto the Grand Central Parkway at rush hour.

And I remember the first uniformed officer at the scene
wading ankle-deep through the gasoline to swing closed
the open hatch and prevent the other ten thousand gallons
from spilling onto the hot pavement, without thinking about
what he was doing, because if he had, it might have regis-
tered that the hot metal and the heavy summer traffic could
have ignited the fumes at any moment and, contrary to what
Hollywood would have you believe, it's not that easy to run
away from an exploding fireball.

The police officer's name was Ed Kaltenbach.

Why do I remember? Because last night I had to convince
Georgio to take up a collection and have the community hire

me through the agency, telling him, "You need two-fifty as a retainer by the end of the business day tomorrow, and five hundred minimum for a couple of days of investigation, *then* I can devote my full energies to the Manny Morales case."

"Okay. Can do," he said.

But I already started unofficially working on it and found out what time a neighbor found Manny lying in a heap of broken bones and blood and called 911, which car was dispatched, and the name and badge number of the first officer on the scene.

The police officer's name was Ed Kaltenbach.

This is a man I've got to see.

But he doesn't come on shift until four o'clock. So in the meantime—

"Fil, we got a case." Lonnie the lawyer sounds excited. "The tests came back and Tesoro's got mercury levels up the kazoo."

I'm sure the lab phrased it differently.

I switch the phone to my other ear so I can continue typing up—excuse me—keying in my travel expenses for the EPA account.

He says, "This case has got mental incompetency written all over it, and we're looking at some serious reduction of charges. I don't know how you came up with a wacko idea like testing for mercury poisoning, but it worked, baby, it worked!"

"So we can get an expert to testify that the levels of mercury in his system were enough to cause neurological disruptions?"

"It's in the bag, doll-face."

"Any more cute names and I'm getting a new identity, Lonnie."

He laughs in my ear like I'm such a kidder.

"Seriously, so how's this family going to raise the money for his defense?"

"Like you said, Lonnie. They'll come up with it."

"You sure? 'Cause their phone ain't working, I tried—"

"You're officially hiring me, right?"

"Uh, yeah, sure, Fil—"

"So arrange it with Davis. I'll go over and talk to Mrs. Tesoro right now."

"Ouch!" shouts Karen, jumping away from her screen. She's been jacked into an interstate background search for nearly an hour.

"What?" says Len, looking over at her.

She's gotten a splinter from a metal screw in the CPU case, but Len looks at the screen and says, "I think you just tripped over Alabama."

"Huh?"

"Well, what do you expect? They just left it *lying* there right next to Mississippi!"

"Someone needs a long weekend," opines Katwona.

I never wanted to do murder duty. I wanted to be on the NYPD's rape crisis detail. I wanted to help the living, not the dead. And I don't like visiting death scenes—they're *nothing* like in the movies. They're a million times worse. Twelve-year-old boys frozen in death, face down on some rancid mattress, with their once-innocent naked butts in the air. Shotgun wounds that blow heads across thirty cubic feet, yet which still remain attached to the body. A victim who's been in a tub long enough for the blood-filled water to thicken to aspic and for the maggots to begin chewing the skin off his skull. And the ones who fought for life, blue-black bruises detailing the exact route they traveled to death's land, fingernails scraping the skin or shedding the blood of their attackers, pitiful four-year-old drowning victims being held under water, fighting the whole way against the strange perditious force of an adult bent on evil. And ninety percent of the time it was someone they knew.

And they haunt you for weeks. When you eat, when you make love, when you look into your child's eyes. Who needs it?

But first, the far pleasanter task of informing a young wife that her lover man should be getting out of jail sooner. I take the F train and transfer to the Q23 bus up 108th Street, where I sit and read an abandoned *Newsday* with a cover story about a mom who suffocated her own daughter to "drive the demons out of her." The poor kid looks like she was the only normal one in the family.

But when I get to the old factory site, the barricades are already up and some of the squatters are leaning out the windows threatening to hurl broken cinder blocks and other debris down on the first person who crosses the line and approaches the front door. Slogan-filled banners and a shredded rainbow of knotted rags are gallantly streaming from the parapets in a declaration of defiance. Cops are holding back a small group of protesters, including some of the folks from Manny's building, while a lawyer representing the owners addresses a few microphones and flashing cameras, all from radio and print. No TV yet.

"They're not tenants," says the lawyer. "It's not a habitable building."

"They put in a new roof!" yells someone in the crowd.

"And electricity—!"

"And running water—!"

"Plus we have evidence that some of the illegal squatters are drug dealers," says the lawyers, as half-a-dozen pens dutifully scribble this information down.

Looks like I picked the perfect day to drop by. I push my way to the front of the police line and check out who got stuck with this lousy detail. I don't recognize any of the pink-faced recruits, although I study their faces and nametags for future reference. There's also a couple of hardened veterans, one donut-consuming Mr. Softee and, standing authoritatively in front of a light-blue sawhorse with her legs apart but her arms crossed indifferently, Officer Vanessa Cordero of the 110th Precinct, who was one of the cops standing around the day Sonny lost it. Sure, she remembers me, and after some sincere statements of intention, negotiation with the two veterans, credentials checks and verification, and some coaxing from the rent strikers, they let me through the police line to approach the building.

I walk in close enough for them to recognize me from the fifth floor, stopping just out of standard projectile range, leaving myself a few seconds of maneuvering time should someone get uncommonly crazy.

A couple of people are screaming at me to stay back, but Lucas recognizes me from a fourth-floor window and yells out my name. He tells me to come closer, and suddenly I'm on a vast, impromptu stage, trying to have a conversation that can be heard by several hundred people within a one-block radius.

"Filomena! *¿Qué tal?*"

"*Hola*, Lucas!"

"What you want?"

"I need to see Camille!"

"What?"

"Camille!"

"Camille Tesoro?"

"Yes! It's about Sonny!"

Lucas's head gets sucked inside the window. I suppose some high-level tactics are being discussed inside, because after a couple of moments his face reappears, and he tosses a knotted, white handkerchief out the window towards me. I reach out to catch it, then a sudden shred of instinct makes me recoil like a sea anemone and the weighted bundle hits the pavement with a muffled *thunk*. I don't know what they're throwing. It could be anything.

It turns out to be a note, weighed down with a couple of chunks of concrete. Right. I was going to break a finger to catch this? It tells me to go around the north side of the building and knock on the big metal door. I follow their instructions and locate the door, seven steps down from sidewalk level and surrounded by a railing. Safe from the evictors' battering ram, this door is not barricaded, merely triple-locked from the inside. I knock, and an anarcho-squatter with a bandana wrapped around her face lets me into an abandoned boiler room, through another metal door into a space that's been converted to the laundry room. Boy, this brings back memories.

A pair of sidewalk-sale washer-driers have been gutted

and refitted with various scavenged parts, but the things work, as testified to by the bearded rasta who's sitting under a shelf-load of powerful cleansers, chewing on a root and reading a magazine while waiting for the spin cycle to end, as if this were a regular neighborhood Laundromat and not a fortified outpost under siege. I wonder, if I went up to the rooftop, would I end up sharing a final smoke with a couple of cheerfully tragic fellows in Foreign Legion hats?

We walk through a low, dark room full of crouching dinosaurs that must be the original boilers. I guess the factory had three underground boiler rooms, and the squatters have managed to get one set of them working again. It would be a shame to have it all turned into a squash court, for members only.

Lucas meets me on the rusty metal steps, escorts me up to the Tesoros' fifth-floor apartment, then heads back to the front lines.

Camille's drawing a bucket of steaming, hot water from the kitchen sink. I give her the good news, and she clasps her hands together and praises God, so I'm very carefully choosing my words, trying to tell her the down side, that there's a danger of mercury poisoning in the entire building, when she takes out a little metallic capsule, cracks it open and pours a couple of grams of silvery liquid into the water bucket right before my eyes. And it swirls around and billows menacingly like a dark cloud rising from a firestorm, turning, rolling, spinning, gyrating, widening to fill the pail as she readies her mop for a dunk in the infernal brew.

"Camille! Is that *azogue*?"

"*Claro que sí.*"

"You've been mopping your floor with mercury-water?"

"Of course, every day I—"

"You've been exposing all of us to *mercury vapor*? If my shoes test positive—"

"It brings good luck," she says indignantly.

"How could you be so—so—Jesus!" A fiery red rage surges through my arteries and blows all my right-thinking circuits.

I want to dump her head in the bucket and hold it there 'til the bubbles stop rising. No, no, but I've got to smash *something*. I look around the room and my fractured glance falls on the baby's crib. Get a grip, girl.

Camille's droning on in that high, flat housewife-from-the-country whine of hers while I try explaining what she's done.

"I use it to treat colic, stomachache, constipation—"

"It can make your baby get leg cramps, peeling skin, itching—"

"—men inject it for strength—"

"—swelling, rashes—"

"—sprinkled in cars for good luck, and you can keep your man by bathing with it—"

"—apathy, anorexia, fever—"

"—or writing the man's name on a piece of paper, putting the paper in a glass, and sprinkling some *azogue* on it—"

"—kidney damage, painful blistering, and peeling of the skin—"

"—it prevents evil from sticking to you—"

"—on the hands and feet—"

"Or you can put it in cologne."

Maybe it's been affecting my behavior. Have I done anything exceptionally irrational, lately? Whoo, don't want to think about *that* at this moment.

"The woman at the *botica* adds a bit to each prescription because it brings good things."

I finally get it under control enough, and manage to explain to her, without once calling her a fucking idiot from the back-country, that if she tells anyone about this and the police hear about it, it'll blow our whole defense and her Sonny will be sent away for fifteen years.

She nods, wide-eyed. Incomprehending.

*

Gina. Gina. Come in, Gina. Mayday. Mayday. We've sprung a leak. Starboard engine on fire. Losing altitude rapidly.

Knife-wielding psycho on a rampage in the forward compartments. Aliens attacking. Mayday. Mayday. This is not a test. Repeat: This is not a test. Come in, Gina. Come in.

I call, I page, I send up smoke signals. I'm heading down the GCP to Jamaica in a black cab-company sedan when she finally calls me back.

"Jesus, Filomena, what's the problem? You paged me three times in the last eight minutes—"

"Gina, you've got to move on the lighting factory squat."

"The what?"

We pass under the expressway.

"Corona. A Hundred and Eighth Street. Mercury. Remember?"

"Fil, I'm in a meeting, and I'm trying to clean up the freaking Hudson River—"

It's not too kosher, but I doubt if anyone of my enemies is close enough to eavesdrop at this precise instant. I cover my mouth with my hand so the driver can't hear.

"My client's wife has been mopping the floor near the baby's crib every day for the last year with water containing several grams of mercury."

"Oh."

Nothing shocks Gina.

"So his mercury levels are high enough to cause mental instability, but if the source is his own wife, the judge is going to be a lot less sympathetic," she says.

"Exactly."

"So what do you want me to do?"

"How soon can you get over there and start taking air samples?"

"I can't do it at all, but we can have an emergency crew out there within a day."

"Oh, shit."

"Somehow, that's not the reaction I expected—"

"No, it's just that there's no way for them to get in. The building's being blockaded."

"By—?"

"By everybody. The cops are out front keeping people back and the tenants are inside waiting for the tear gas to start flying. It's a total state of siege."

"But other than that, everything's fine?"

"I might be able to negotiate with them to let you in."

"Just once I'd like an easy case from you."

"I'll leave you one in my will."

There's a pause in our conversation as the driver swings past the Maple Grove Cemetery, which voted overwhelmingly for Senator DiCatania in the last election. Dozens and dozens of tombstones are piled up, waiting for the gravediggers' strike to end.

Finally Gina asks, "Fil, can you tell me why on earth she was mopping the floor with mercury-tainted water?"

"She believes that mercury contains magical and curative powers."

"You mean, it's used in religious practices?"

"Not by most *latinos*, but yes—"

"Then we have to be careful not to take any regulatory action that could be viewed as an infringement of religious freedoms as protected under the First Amendment."

"We've got to worry about violating *the First Amendment*?"

I'm beginning to feel like I'm in some crazy ill-fated indie movie being filmed on location deep in the jungles of Thailand. What next? Malaria? Typhoons? A visit from Dennis Hopper?

All right, don't panic. All we need is a little containment.

I tell Gina, "Look, we're dealing with people who aren't even sure if mercury's legal or not. They're not going to sue the government for interfering with their religion."

"Sure, 'til some lawyer tells them about the First Amendment."

Look who's trashing lawyers now. What happened to that guy in legal?

"Just focus on the residual mercury in the building," I say. "That's the greater danger, isn't it?"

"I suppose we could spin it that way, for now. But I can't keep it under wraps forever."

"What took you so long?" asks Lonnie Ambush, as I walk up the windy courthouse steps to meet him.

"I had to squeeze through a police line."

Lonnie looks worried.

"Relax, it doesn't affect our case. Although there's a bit of a complication there."

Famous last words.

I tell him what's going on, and assure him that as long as we can keep the spotlight away from Camille Tesoro's insane and potentially lethal housekeeping habits, everything's going to be fine.

I'm not sure I believe it, either.

As I'm turning to go, a phalanx of defense lawyers in long, dark trench coats starts marching up the steps in tight formation around Charlie "Cheeky" Wendorff, whose right arm is in a cast. He points me out to a young woman next to him with long dark hair, who breaks off from the group and climbs determinedly up the white, stone steps towards me.

"That's his daughter, Lara," Lonnie informs me. Oh, great.

I stand my ground, my heart quickening against my will, awaiting the outcome of this confrontation. As she gets closer I can see the dark circles and streaks of mascara bleeding into the crevices under her eyes like the blackened rungs of a rope ladder.

Lara walks up to within an arm's length of me, looks me right in the eye, and says, "You're Filomena Buscarsela?"

I have to clear my throat to say, "Yes?"

"I just wanted to say that I'm really grateful you didn't kill my father, that you only shot him in the arm."

I say something like, "Oh, sure. You're welcome."

And I'm ready for my close-up now, Mr. DeMille.

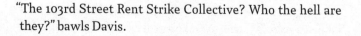

"The 103rd Street Rent Strike Collective? Who the hell are they?" bawls Davis.

"It's a neighborhood committee in Corona. They want me to solve a murder," I say, anticipating his inevitable question why, "because they don't trust the cops with it."

"Anything to it?"

"The cops haven't turned up a lead in three days."

"Well, they only came up with four hundred and twenty-two, which buys them exactly one day of investigation. Even you can't solve a cop-stumper of a murder in a single day."

"Right. That's why I need four or five days."

"For four hundred dollars? Are you kidding?"

"Yes, Chip, I'm kidding. Take it out of the EPA money."

"What EPA money?"

Katwona calls in through the door, "Fil, you got a call on line three."

"Take a message. According to this," I say, holding up a copy of the invoice, "Davis and Brown is billing the EPA *twenty-four hundred dollars* for two days' work."

"A big place would charge twice that."

"Yeah, and I'd get twenty percent. So how much is my cut?"

"Fil, he doesn't want to leave a message, he wants to talk to you," says Katwona.

"So put him on hold for a minute!"

"We're paying you for fifteen hours at your new rate," says Davis.

"A hundred and fifty dollars? You're charging them twenty-four hundred and you're paying me one-fifty?"

"That is more than the number of hours you put in on this particular case."

"The hours I *logged*. I put in twice that much—"

"Fil, he doesn't want to hold—"

"All right, I'll take the damn call already," I say, grabbing Chip's phone and punching the third button. "Yes?"

"It is about time." Dvurushnik's voice. He starts badgering me about finding more ways to protect his business and get more control over his workers, until I say, "Could you hold for just a second?" and go make a deal with Karen to take this guy off my hands *now*, redeemable for one major favor, at anytime, anyplace, under any circumstances.

"Mr. Dvurushnik? I'm switching you over to Karen Ricci."

"I am working with you, am I not?"

"Yes, but your case calls for a much closer examination of your specific business needs, and I'm sure you'll agree that it's better to send another person, someone with a different face this time, just so no one on the premises gets unduly alerted."

"Yes, that is good thinking, possibly. You will put me through to Miss—"

"Miss Ricci." *Click. Buzz. Click.*

Maybe I should just drop out of sight and rejoin the rebels. Jungle fighting is easier than this.

Except Antonia's an American.

When I get back to Davis, he's had time to think about it, and he offers me *sixteen* hours' pay for the EPA job. I'm about to tell him what he can do with the lousy ten dollars extra, and with several pieces of high-tech office equipment as well, when he reads my mind, it seems, and finally concedes.

"You got three days," he says.

"Including Monday?"

"Good luck."

I'll take that as a yes.

I'm rummaging through the supply closet, getting out some pads and a new battery for my phone, when a shape presses against my curved spine. I straighten up and turn around, and Len is standing there pretending to be absorbed in one of my files.

"Yes, Ms. Buscarsela, about this claim on your resumé that you can make it rain 'whenever you want it to . . .'"

"Are you trying to be funny?"

He just stands there staring at me until I ask, "What?"

He smiles. "Oh, I'm just wondering what you look like when you're having sex."

"Just like I do now. Satisfied?"

"I am nowhere near satisfied."

"Len, I've got a boyfriend."

"And I've got this desire to lick raspberry syrup off your body."

That does it. I grab Len by the collar, mention something about a "coffee break" and drag him out into the hallway for as much of a private conversation as you can get around here.

"Len, can we talk?"

"Sure."

"Okay, listen. You're a really nice guy. You're young, and cute, and you've got the brains to be a great detective."

"And?"

"And I'm sure you're a terrific cook, also."

"And?"

And part of me would love to . . .

"And part of me is very flattered by your attention."

"But?"

"Well, yeah: *But*. But it's not going to happen. I promised myself. And—it's just not going to happen, so—"

"Wait a minute. What's not going to happen?"

"*You know*. Something physical between us. Let's just keep the membranes dry, shall we? So please stop pressuring me."

"Why? Because of Doc Boy? He's probably boinking half the night shift while you're out there in the company car with your teeth chattering."

"Len—he's a terrific guy. We work well together. He fits in with who I am and what I need right now."

"In other words, you're comfortable with him, so don't rock the boat. Is that it?"

"No, there's also my daughter."

"Oh, yeah, right. Mommy can't fuck around in front of the little one. What kind of example would that be?"

"Len, this is *real*. She's twelve years old, and *very* aware of the idea of sex and its consequences. So, yes. It is partly a question of example."

"So who has to know?"

"Len, *I'd* know."

Pause. I think he's finally getting it.

"Look, Len—"

"Yeah, I can see you're very conflicted," he says, disgustedly.

"Look, Len, part of me would like to—"

"To do what?"

A surge of primitive desire, an irrepressible urge.

"*This*."

I seize him by the shoulders and bring him towards me, my head turning to the side to drink in the natural scent of his neck. I don't shy away from such contact that can begin to feel the real throbbing beneath. My grip tightens. Our hips touch.

I hear a door open down the hall.

Oh, great.

It closes again. But it's enough to bring out the other part of me, and we separate.

"Len, the beast in me says do this, but the single mom says no freaking way. Dig?"

"Dig? Who the hell says 'dig' anymore?"

"My point exactly. Len, this is real. Okay?"

"Okay . . ."

I touch his cheek lightly, then reach for the doorknob.

"I guess you're right about responsibility and all," he admits, "but I sure gotta say I *like* the law of the jungle." He follows me in, saying, "I mean, 'Til death do you part' used to be a much *shorter* proposition."

"Yeah, life's too short not to eat French pastry whenever you get the chance, but you don't see me stuffing my face all the time."

"No more pastry talk from you guys," says Katwona.

Then I suppose she doesn't want to know what a jelly donut reminds me of.

I suit up and head out, but before I run over to the 110th Precinct I go down to Jamaica Avenue, find a shoe store and buy some new cross-trainers, double-wrap the old ones in plastic bags and toss them into a Dumpster. I don't want to bring any more traces of mercury home after work.

Then I catch the R train and sit there sorting out my priorities. First I'll get what I can from the cops, then I need to interview all the witnesses, plus Manny's co-workers, his neighbors on 103rd Street and anyone else who strikes me as necessary once I have the previous taken care of.

There's a photo of some crabby-looking candidates on the front page of a crumpled *Times*, alongside an article detailing how the American Medical Association endorsed a House Republican plan to slash Medicare only after the doctors were promised that *their* payments under the plan would not be reduced. But it's wrong to suggest that their endorsement was contingent on billions of dollars, claims a senior vice president of the AMA. Right. The actual figure is closer to $400 million.

I get off at the Elmhurst Avenue stop, and walk along 43rd Avenue to the precinct house.

"I'm looking for Officer Ed Kaltenbach."

The desk sergeant points his thumb over his left shoulder while writing something down and talking on the phone uninterrupted. Yonder lies a bucket of sand full of cigarette butts under a NO SMOKING sign, a utility closet, and a hallway. I figure I'll take a shot at the hallway, and follow it to the briefing room, where the 4:00 P.M. meeting is just breaking up. I pick out the likely faces and check their badges until I find the right one. Ed Kaltenbach is a twenty-eight-year vet with thinning, straight reddish-brown hair, five feet ten inches tall, only slightly rounded with maybe fifteen extra pounds.

"Officer Kaltenbach?"

"Yeah? Who are you?"

I start to tell him, but he turns and starts walking towards Australia.

"Um, Officer—"

"Fuck off," he says.

CHAPTER ELEVEN

**As long as we haven't been able to abolish a single
cause of human desperation, we do not have
the right to try to suppress the means by which
man tries to clean himself of desperation.**
—Antonin Artaud

"**ANYONE WHO'D RISK** walking through fire like you did ought to be the type of guy who'd stand me to a favor."

He turns and looks at me again, running his eye over the length of my raincoat, as if the seamwork will reveal some previously overlooked detail of my character.

"How'd you know about that?" he asks.

"Give me some credit, please." He starts walking away again. "Listen, a lot of cops in this precinct will vouch for me. Last week I helped collar three perps for Officers O'Brien and Chen. Go ahead and ask them."

"That's their business."

"Officer Kaltenbach, you don't have to prove how tough you are, I already know: You did two tours of duty as a Marine in Vietnam, then twenty-eight years on the force, and I was there watching when you waded into a puddle of gasoline and snapped the hatch shut on that overturned tanker like you were closing a refrigerator door that someone happened to leave open."

"I'll give you this, you sure talk a better line than the usual parasites."

"What parasites?" I'm following him towards the open door and the cool, misty air of night.

"The ones she always sends. Now fuck off, I'm busy." He's almost out the door.

"Who? Your wife?"

"Ex-wife. As if you didn't know."

"No, I didn't know. I don't work for divorce lawyers, I work for a private investigation agency and this isn't about you, it's about the murder of Manny Morales."

We stand there on the wet concrete steps as cops push past us and claim their vehicles, shiny new all-white cars with blue-and-red details that come to life with bursts of red-and-orange light and a testy squawking of radios.

I show him my card and ask, "What law firm did she hire?"

"Lewis and Jacobs," he says, studying the print on my card. He's probably got their name and number memorized. "Those leeches give me two minutes of phone access per day to my kids. My ex-wife actually has a timer attached to the phone set for one minute and fifty-nine seconds, then it cuts off."

"Well, I'm not here to serve you a subpoena or anything. I'm here because the community hired me to investigate the murder of Manny Morales, and you were the first officer at the scene."

"Hey, Eddie, let's move!" shouts his partner, standing by the open door of a squad car.

"I gotta go," he says. "Come back after shift."

"You want me to come back at midnight?"

"Nah. Better make it 1:00 A.M."

I guess my exasperation shows, because he says, "You wanna talk or don't you?"

"Okay, I'll be here."

"Not here. Clancy's bar on Claremont. Know it?"

"I could find it in a London fog."

And he's gone in a swirl of dead leaves and paper cups and a bluish hydrocarbon haze.

Now I've got eight hours to interview people who are just getting home from work, and they'll be tired and resentful of my intrusion at this hour, so I won't push it. Better let them have half-an-hour in an easy chair and a second bottle of beer before I come knocking on their doors. And some of the people I need to talk to aren't even up yet. Also, Officer Kaltenbach saw me in my professional getup and thought I was some kind of segmented worm, so I should probably go home and change first. *El hábito hace al monje*, as we say in Ecuador. Clothes make the man, or in this case, "The habit makes the monk." Curiously enough, we have exactly the opposite saying as well: *El hábito no hace al monje*, "Clothes *don't* make the monk," which either demonstrates the brilliance of our folk wisdom at interpreting the contradictory nature of the human experience, or else it shows that we really don't know what the hell we're talking about.

Or both.

I have plenty of time to ponder this epiphany as I walk up to Roosevelt Avenue and take the Orient Express two stops, trying to save my pavement-pounding energy for later. Two blocks north, just in the door and barely started up the stairs, I get recruited by my elderly landlords to read their latest homeowners' insurance and property tax statements and to translate these documents into basic English and annotate the entire contents for them. Then Mr. Kyriakis asks me to help bring the ladder up from the basement and support it while he changes the kitchen light, and help carry it back downstairs again while they bicker the whole time about the two bills. Finally free of them, I trudge up the stairs wishing for a better situation.

Better in what way? They're not mean to us, of course, or screwing us financially. We moved in because the second floor apartment is so affordable, and it's a place Antonia can come home to after school without me being there to watch over her. It's just not easy living with a couple of irritable old folks. But I guess that's the price.

As always.

You'd think my coming home early would be cause for celebration, but Antonia is in one of her dark,

I'm-going-to-take-poison-now moods, brought on by some-thing apparently undisclosable to me. For all I know it's my own frequent absences, so I sit on her narrow bed holding hands with her and try to tell her how important it is to com-municate with me about what's bothering her, because pretty soon she's going to have teenage problems and I want her to be able to talk to me about them so I can help her resolve them, instead of some pimply-faced video junkie who's had a hard-on since the sixth grade who promises to do the same.

"I don't want some guy telling you—" I slip into my nasal, disaffected Gen-Z voice to illustrate him: "'Don't worry, you can't get pregnant on a Sunday, babe. I read that in a comic book, y'know?'"

"You think I'm going to fall for that?"

"No, it's in your contract: You can never leave me to fall for some jerk."

"My 'contract'?"

"Yeah, we signed a pre-natal agreement, don't you remember? I'll have my lawyer contact you."

She smiles and stares out her window at the unnatural glow of the city lighting up the underside of some low-lying clouds like an orange ion storm. Then I tell her I have to go back out and work late tonight.

"I've got three or four intense days coming up, but then I'll—"

"Then you'll be off on some *other* case," she says.

"No, I'll ask my boss for a few days off after this case. Okay?"

"And what about Sunday?"

"I don't know. I might have to work part of the day, but I promise we'll do something together."

"Can you check my math assignment?" she says, reach-ing for her books.

"Sure," I begin, reluctantly.

"Filomena!" Mrs. Kyriakis calls up from below. "I need some help."

Everybody needs my help. I feel like a huge storage

battery that a dozen people are tapping into with separate lead wires, robbing my electrical current and draining me, leaving me with nothing for my own little battery right here at home.

I go downstairs and follow Mrs. Kyriakis's outstretched finger to the back steps, where a small, grayish-brown rat has breathed its last. Her husband has gone out, so the task of rodent removal falls to me. At home in the Andes, I'd just toss the remains into the woods, but needless to say, the woods are not an option deep in the heart of Queens. Neither is the garbage can, since there's no collection until Monday morning and you don't want to breathe this thing after four days. So I opt for "burial at sea," by which I mean flushing the corpse down the toilet. But not so fast:

"I want to see it," says Antonia, ever fascinated with vermin of all kinds.

So I show it to her, dangling the stiff-legged thing over the watery maelstrom by its shiny hairless tail while Mrs. Kyriakis voices her disgust. I flush the ex-rat and wash my hands and try to explain to Mrs. Kyriakis that I'm not shutting my daughter off to anything, giving the example of how one time when Antonia was three or four years old, she pointed to a scab on her knee and said the word "chocolate," and my first instinct was to say "No," but I stopped myself and changed it to, "Well, it's the *color* of chocolate," because maybe that's what she meant.

"Pchh! What do you know?" is Mrs. Kyriakis's unvarnished summation of my parenting skills.

I guess what I'm saying is that child-rearing *can* be liberating and deviant behavior, as long as you raise them to think for themselves. So back upstairs we go, where I scrub my hands thoroughly and then pan-fry everything in sight and sit down to a real meal with my daughter. Then I change into a gray turtleneck pullover and the old leather jacket and bind my hair back under a broad-brimmed winter cap for that let-your-hair-down transformation when I meet later with Officer Ed Kaltenbach. It's simple, uniform-like, yet feminine. Just what I need for this guy to take me seriously.

On my way out I get a surprise hug and a heartfelt, "I love you," that pretty much makes everything else fade into the background where it belongs.

I carry that hug with me for several blocks, until I get to the scene of the crime, one block north of Roosevelt Avenue. It's a forlorn stretch of grimy concrete on a shadowy side street about fifteen feet from the dim lights of 104th Street.

It's dark. I check my watch: 7:15. About the same time as the murder three nights ago. I look around, wondering who might have seen anything. There are plenty of potential witnesses on a residential block like this, but most folks are sitting comfortably inside the warm, yellow glow of their dining rooms or watching TV, windows sealed against the chill wind and bone-piercing mist. In the summertime, there would have been a hundred people on the street at this hour. Now it's just a couple of scattered figures, scurrying to get inside and shut out the frost. A pair of new arrivals from the Caribbean walk past me, hunched over and complaining about the cold.

You think it's cold now, just wait two months.

Anyone would have had to act awfully quickly to kill someone on this spot, barely one avenue block from Manny's building, and beating seems like a particularly risky way to go about it. It takes a long time, makes a lot of noise, and the possibility of resistance and even escape is quite great. They must have been some kind of experts, unless they didn't intend to kill him, in which case they screwed it up royally. That sure narrows it down for me.

I'll have to come back and examine the area during the day, but right now I want to take a look around and see who's got a clear view of me standing here. The clothing store whose solemn portal was smeared with Manny's warm, vibrant blood is dark, gated and locked. Two side windows across the street look directly out at me. The right one is dark, the left one frames a gloriously illuminated wall dappled with the ever-shifting cool-green-and-yellow lights of an altar to the great god of television. There must be a hundred families within fifty yards of this spot, but until I read the police reports, I'll start with these two.

The TV worshippers first.

A quiet boy about ten years old answers the door. He's got the reddish-brown skin of a *caribeño* and the frightened eyes of a sensitive kid with a domineering father. And sure enough, as I open my mouth to ask,

"Excuse me, is your mother home?"

A voice booms from the other room: "Punch the bitch's face in!"

The boy jumps. My hand jerks closer to my pistol grip, but it might pass for a jump, too.

"Kick her fucking ass!"

This command goes unheeded, and the boy leads me into the hallway towards the other room.

"Who's there?" he asks the boy, who runs in ahead of me and says,

"There's a lady here who's asking for *mamá*."

The living room comes into view. Bare walls, bare floor, no furniture besides a 27-inch color TV and a white couch that his wife must have picked out but couldn't take with her. He's wearing a T-shirt and boxer shorts, with four empty beer cans scattered around his feet. If she were anywhere around here, I'd help her carry the couch out.

"Who the hell is—?" The man looks away from the TV screen and the dominatrix-bashing climax of some flaccid adventure movie, and stares at me, red-faced, uncombed, unshaven. All that's needed is a flickering fire casting eerie shadows on some hand-rendered paintings of a herd of Ice Age caribou along the walls to complete the image.

"Who are you? What the fuck do you want with my wife? 'Cause I threw the bitch out last week, and you can go tell all her stupid-ass friends that I don't need her back. You got that?"

Boy, if ever a guy needed the shiny silver barrel of a gun shoved down his throat, this is him. I try to tell him that I'm working for a private investigation agency, but he keeps yelling, walking towards me—I angle my dominant side away from him—then he grabs my left wrist and drags me towards the kitchen where he's got some dirty clothes soaking in the sink.

"See? What do I need a wife for? I can wash my own freaking underwear," he says, reaching into the dirty water and holding up a fistful of dripping wet grungies for me to bear witness to his accomplishment.

Gun down the throat, says the little voice inside of me, which never seems to be the voice of reason these days.

Eventually I manage to persuade my paleolithic friend that I don't know his wife or any of her circle of supportive women and that all I want to know is if he or his son was home Monday evening between seven and seven-thirty, and if they saw anything.

Slam!

I'm back on the front porch, knocking on the right-hand door, where an immigrant family from India lives, just the parents and their college-age daughter. They invite me into their hallway and explain that they were still at work and that their daughter was taking an evening class, so no one was home at the time of the assault. I try the next two houses with no further luck.

I step outside as an arriving jet roars by overhead, and look down the street, which butts into 104th Street at this end, to a flat row of buildings overlooking the block. There's a windowless biker joint across the way on 104th whose forbidding black steel doorway is just out of sight, but a dim light is emanating from a lone, dusty window that probably gets pried open once a year to ventilate the back room on those nights when the temperature goes above 100 degrees. Maybe.

I walk up and try the door, but it doesn't open. Then there's a low buzz and the cold brass doorknob releases from the catch. They don't let just anybody in here, I guess. I walk straight up to the bar like I've been here a million times, my feet find the rail, and I order a beer before my eyes get used to the light, since I don't want to do that stand-in-the-doorway-and-survey-the-scene bit that tells everyone in the place who you're working for.

I have a few swallows and slide a crumpled five across the dented sheet of hammered zinc that laminates the ply-wood-and-pine beneath. It sits there for the rest of the evening. I arch my back and massage my neck, then hunker down around the bottle and listen to the voices around me.

"Man, ten minutes with me, I'll teach you more about conga drumming than you learn in a year from those stupid white boys," says a heavy-set *cholito* with a thick mustache.

"Doesn't do shit for me," comes the answer from a latter-day headbanger. "No disrespect, but there's too many fuckin' beats in it for me. Basic rock drumming, man," and he demonstrates a heavy-handed 4/4 on the pockmarked zinc: "The left one is mom, the right one is dad, the bass drum is the coach you never liked and the snare is the girlfriend that left you." *Thumpa-thumpa-thumpa-thump. Ting.*

And there's nothing like getting a whore's-eye-view of true sleaze: "So the guy's got the money to hire three of us, but he wants us to put on these pig masks and crawl around naked on the floor squealing like freaking pigs with our asses in the air while he stands there like Farmer John throwing bacon bits on the floor in front of us."

"Did he have anything worthwhile?" asks her friend.

The first woman makes a pinched face and holds her thumb and forefinger about an inch apart. "But he's got plenty of dough. He wants to do it again with five of us next time."

"Where's he get the money?"

"He's a bank president."

"Call me?"

"Sure."

Now that's a true friend.

The smoke in here is starting to irritate my lungs. I nurse the beer and watch a group of leather-bound biker dudes playing pool until my attention is seized by a big guy coming out of the back room. He's got a fleshy, pitted face, long, stringy brown hair with a couple of shots of gray in it, and carries a little extra weight under his T-shirt and leather jacket. His jeans are tucked inside his high leather boots.

"Hey, Ice," says the woman who was telling the story.

He nods and mumbles something, and continues over to join the assembly of cycling enthusiasts, having shut the door to the back room definitively behind him, but some light is still peering out through the cracks. Okay, let's see, I could drink up the bar's supply of licorice schnapps and force the bartender to go back there for more and follow him in, or maybe, just maybe, there's an easier way.

I'm rejecting the alternatives one by one when suddenly one of the biker dudes grabs my man Ice and throws him against the wall, but the biker dude's girlfriend quickly intervenes and begs Mr. Ice, "Please don't kick his ass. He just got out of jail and he hasn't adjusted yet."

There's a long pause before Ice answers, "Okay."

And the tension eases.

A good use of what the police psychologists call "verbal de-escalation techniques," and what everyone else calls "talking your way out of trouble." But it gives me my in.

As the pool balls begin clattering once again, I drift over to the edge of the game, watch a few rounds, then quite visibly drain my bottle, note its emptiness, turn towards the bar and tell Ice, "You want one?" as I go. I order two beers without looking back.

When he comes up behind me, I hand him a beer and say, "Nice move, Ice. Shows understanding. When I got out of the freezer I was so horny I'd have humped a fire hydrant at that point."

He stands there looking at me, then swigs half the bottle in about a second, and goes back to looking at me. He's playing with silence, so I keep going: "I just mean your point-of-view gets all screwed up. And if you've never been in a South American *cárcel*, don't freaking talk to me about how tough you've had it, you know? There were places even the guards were afraid to go."

The smoke finally overwhelms me and I start coughing.

A real deep, dredge-up-the-hot-phlegm three-dimensional hack that gouges out whole chunks of my lungs with fiery claws and confirms my claim of long years spent in dank solitude, though in fact the greatest damage was done to them during a criminal act committed by the hired thugs of an industrial polluter who's *still* on the loose.

Somebody hands me a glass of water, and eventually I recover.

Ice stares at me, then tips his hand up and empties the bottle. I notice the name tattooed on his wrist.

"So, your nickname: Ice Pick. How'd a big guy like you get such a cute name?"

"What do you want?" he asks.

I can be direct, too.

"I want to know who killed Manny Morales."

"What the hell for?"

"'Cause I'm getting five hundred bucks for it. It wasn't you guys, was it?" I say, gesturing towards his circle of friends with the neck of my beer bottle. He snaps the bottle out of my hand and waits, holding it in a tightening fist.

"That's okay, I didn't want it anyway," I tell him, indicating the beer that's foaming over his knuckles and dripping onto the floor.

He waits a moment.

"You're either really smart or really stupid," he says.

"So are the people I'm looking for, and I'm starting to think they ain't a bunch of rocket scientists."

He makes no attempt to wipe the beer off his hand.

"Why's that?"

"'Cause they did it in full view of your rear window," I say, tilting my head at the door to the back room.

A ragged smile cuts across his face, revealing a line of teeth like a grit-clogged motorcycle chain.

"So that's it," he mutters. "Go ahead and ask me."

"Okay, was anybody in that room last Monday night between seven and seven-thirty?"

"Sure, you wanna go talk to him?"

This is too easy. What's the catch?

"Yeah, I want to talk to whoever works back there."

"Oh, he works there all right," says *Señor* Ice Pick, leading me to the heavy wooden door. He opens it a crack and calls in, "Got a minute, Vic?"

I hear some low mumbling response, but I can't make it out.

"He says he can spare a moment," says Ice.

"Thanks."

I duck under his arm and plunge headlong into a poorly lit maze of beer cases, feeling my way to the creature's lair in the center of it all, a psychosensory dungeon with that dead-body-in-the-garbage smell that most self-respecting animals instinctively recoil from in disgust. There's a partially burnt mattress on the floor with food and other garbage strewn around it, such as empty bottles and plastic bags, a crumpled packet of rolling papers, two glass pipes and a metal one, a charred spoon and a burnt-out candle, an ashtray stuffed with roaches and cigarette butts. Vic is slumped in a chair at a battered metal desk with a similar garbage saturation index, wearing filth-encrusted pants and a ratty T-shirt that some seditious musicologists suggest may have been white sometime around the year the Sex Pistols first swindled us with "Anarchy in the UK," his outstretched arm listlessly wiping a tiny section of the cloudy window before his eyes with a stiff brown rag.

"Why does the dirty clean?" he asks.

"I beg your pardon?"

He turns his glazed eyes towards me and asks, "Why does the dirty clean? We use rags to clean things, right?"

"Oh, right."

"And rags are dirty," he says, holding out the indisputable evidence.

His runny nose begins to twitch. Then his mouth draws open in a silent snarl, quivers, and explodes helplessly with a ferocious sneeze, followed by another. Then another. When it's over, he blows his nose and with the filthy rag. Actually, having an impaired sense of smell is a distinct advantage in this place. Then he has a coughing fit. He coughs until his eyes start watering.

He looks up at me, blinking, then jerks his head quickly to one side and says, "Wo!"

"You may not know this," I tell him, "but ducking at after-images is considered suspicious behavior by most people."

He blinks at me, then screws the top off some cough syrup and takes a swig straight from the bottle, spilling some down his chin. He wipes it off with his fingers, and looks at the label on the bottle. "Look at this freaking stuff, will ya? 'Non-narcotic' it says, and they act like that's a good thing!"

"Listen, uh, Vic—"

"How come you know my name?"

"Your friend Ice Pick told me."

Vic laughs, more of a wet snort, really, with plenty of snot in it. "He's nobody's friend. Ha! Ha! *Hochh—ptoo!*" Right on the floor.

"He seems to trust you."

Vic's eyes bulge out at me. They're pretty bloodshot, and in this smoky yellow light, his skin looks translucent, as if it's been hand-stretched over his bones by one of Dr. Frankenstein's second-year graduate students. And not one of the brightest ones, either.

"He knows I won't cross him," says Vic, with what appears to be lucidity. "We got a good deal set up. Catch a squeeze bottle full of acid at a buck-fifty a hit. Cut it up and sell 'em for ten. It's a sure thing."

"There are no sure things when you're messing with acid."

He looks at me like I've just recited the Preamble to the Constitution.

"Too true, girl, too true."

"You going to drop the hits on blotter paper, or good old-fashioned sugar cubes?"

"Sugar is bad for you," he says, completely without irony. "Say, what's your name, anyway?"

I tell him.

"Fill-oh-what?"

"Just call me Fil."

"You wanna smoke a joint, Fil?"

What is this, one of those two-dollar-budget drug-education films they used to show in school thirty years ago? I feel like the walls are made of canvas and if I bump into them they'll ripple and the camera will pick it up.

But he's already gotten out a torn piece of brown paper bag and is unfolding it on his knee. He uses his most advanced engineering skills—it's called an opposable thumb—to close around a clump of shake, convey it to the desk, and dump it. He picks out a couple of twigs and rolls a fatty with rolling papers the size of a sheet of newsprint, specially made for the chemically challenged.

And yet, there is something about the atmosphere in here—the week-old-pizza smell of spilled bong water, the familiar ritual motions of tubular envelopment, of licking the gummed edge, the hissing match, the crackle of burning paper and the aroma of semi-decent weed—that pierces the layers of silt burying the pleasure centers within my deepest memories like an angler's barb and hauls with enough force to reel in a sperm whale. Only the sight of this scorched shipwreck of a man and the ego-driven memory of why I'm here keep the hooks from ripping out a bloody chunk of my gray matter.

To some people it's just weed. To me it's a grappling iron, dragging me straight down.

And this isn't exactly an idyllic setting. Although maybe that's part of it, the uncivilized desire to chuck all responsibility and take up residence in an artificial paradise, the irrational fiend that tempts us to peer over the edge of the abyss and listen to the wind and the waves roaring beneath.

But I withdraw from the summit, and tell the human shell sitting before me that a man was murdered right across the street three nights ago, and does he know anything about it?

He takes a deep drag on the bone, and reaches way, way back in his mind, and eventually he answers, forming the words through a puff of pot smoke, "Yeah, I seen a guy hanging out like he was waiting for something. Seemed weird 'cause it was, like, kinda cold, you know?"

"Just one person?"

"Coulda been more. It was dark, like it is now."

Anything this guy says is going to need some serious corroboration, but here goes:

"What did he look like?"

"All I saw was the cigarette, man. A cigarette where his face should be."

When I finally come up for air outside the bubbly walls of the beer-bottle labyrinth, Ice Pick's heavy arms fall around me like a drift net and he asks, "Find anything out from Vic, lady dick?"

"Yeah."

"And? Get what you need?"

No. Not nearly.

But the night isn't over yet.

CHAPTER TWELVE

Cynicism is merely a developed sense of reality.
—Katherine Anne Porter

"**SORRY I'M LATE**," says Ed Kaltenbach, scraping a wooden chair back and sitting down opposite me. "They were filming a Fellini movie on Baxter Avenue."

I take a sip of club soda and lime and wait for his explanation.

"We had a little trouble at the Roosevelt hotel," he says. Nothing further.

I'm not going to beg for details, so I just sit there and stare at him.

"A father-son suicide," he says.

"What is it about hotels, anyway? Seems like sometimes people just check in to check out," I say. "Why the circus?"

"Because something doesn't feel right about it."

More silence. Time to remove my cap and shake my hair down. I'm brushing it away from my face and watching his eyes follow the flowing hair as it catches the ephemeral glow of the magenta-colored neon "BUD" sign behind the bar.

I can use silence, too.

"The old man was one tough *padella* from the mountains of Sicily," he says. "Not the kind of guy who'd hang himself from a shower-curtain rod."

"He was a frying pan?"

"Huh?"

"You just said he was one tough frying pan."

"Ah, crap. What's that word they always use?"

"I don't know. *Paesano? Padrone?*"

"*Padrone*. What's it mean?"

"Boss. Master. Protector. Like the Spanish *patrón*."

"Hey, Miranda, it's about time," he says to the approaching waitress. "Get me a beer, honey. You?"

"No, thanks."

"Why not? This is a bar, you know. Sign outside says so."

"Because I had one earlier this evening."

"You had *one* beer earlier this evening?"

"Congratulations, you passed your hearing test."

"Very funny. You know, prohibition's been lifted. What are you, on the freaking wagon or something?"

"I'm working."

"Yeah, right. You probably took the pledge."

He sees something in my eyes that I hoped wasn't there.

"You *did*," he says, smiling to himself for having read me so easily. "Well, it looks like you made it up all twelve steps just fine to me, honey."

"Thanks."

"You know, the way things are going, pretty soon we'll have the designated drinker. Then what am I supposed to do with my honorary degree from the Betty Ford Center?"

I smile at his joke.

"I mean, I'm the kind of guy whose idea of health food is multi-grain bourbon."

"I'm fine, thanks."

"Sure you are."

I don't know why, but somehow walking into a bar doesn't do that whole swan-dive-into-the-flaming-pit thing to me. Alcohol just doesn't have the same pull other drugs do. I can keep that particular demon chained up, for some reason.

Kaltenbach's beer arrives, in a tall wet glass. He takes a

gulp, pats his mouth with a napkin out of courtesy to me, and asks, "So what'd you want to see me about?"

"You remember."

"No, I don't. It's been a long day."

"The Morales case," I prod him.

"Oh, sure. What about it?"

Everything.

"How's it going?" I ask.

"Not so good." He makes me wait as he takes another long pull at his beer. "They arrested four kids from one of the gangs Morales pissed off while he was trying to chase the drug dealers off the block. But we don't have enough evidence to hold them, so we're back to square one."

"Too bad. Four gangbangers seems like a good bet."

"Why do you say that?"

"It's cold now, but it was warmer three nights ago. It's like they wanted to make sure people saw them kicking the crap out of him, as near to his turf as possible. They wanted to intimidate everyone, send a message, know what I mean?"

"They sure sent a message, all right."

"Well, that's the thing. They were supposed to smack him up and leave him on the doorstep. Instead they ambush him in a dark spot a block from his house and mess him up so badly, he dies. They probably weren't supposed to do that, either. You don't normally kill someone in front of witnesses. It looks really bad in the quarterly report."

"So we're looking for a bunch of amateur fuck-ups."

"They failed to follow orders and they fucked up *twice*."

"Who hires such cheap labor?"

"Everybody. More specifically, the same people who think beating the crap out of someone is an effective business strategy. So tell me, what was the scene like when you got there?"

"Why should I tell you?"

"Because you're back at square one."

He clears his throat gruffly and gulps some more beer to wash it down, then he calls the waitress over.

"What'll it be?" asks Miranda.

"You know what I want."

"Scotch with a soda behind it."

He clicks his tongue and shoots his index finger at her.

"Everything's in the report," he tells me.

"Can I see it?"

"It's a case in progress."

"You telling me I have to file a Freedom of Information Act request? I'll be lucky to get an answer in a decade or so. The trail will be mighty cold by then."

He buys some more time by tipping up his glass and taking the last swallow of beer for the second time. Then a third time.

"That glass is not going to get any emptier," I say.

He puts down the glass and meets my gaze. "You know, I hear there's a tribe of natives down in South America that has no word for 'patience.' You related to them?"

"No, but I hear there's a tribe of natives of Long Island who have no word for 'shut the fuck up or I'm going to kick your fucking face in.'"

He blinks, then stares at a spot in the space between us. Then he says with a twinkle, "You know, honey, the Freedom of Information Act doesn't mean the information is free."

That one bounces off my armor so hard you can hear a palpable *ting*! I guess he figured it was worth a shot, and it doesn't faze him one bit.

"I'm sorry, honey, but you know I couldn't possibly show you those files even if I wanted to. You know the regulations."

"Yes, I know the regs. I also knew the victim and I probably know at least one of the suspects, too. Think of me as an expert witness and let me look at what you've got."

"If you know something, you better tell me."

"How do I know what's useful if I don't know what you know? What ground you've been over already? I just spent half the night listening to contradictory testimony from a bunch of tired and crazy people, and it would sure be a lot easier if I could just see the reports—"

"I can't get you the reports. What do you get out of this, anyway?"

"Credibility with the community." Something you should try for sometime, Officer Kaltenbach. "And investment for my business," I say.

"What business is that?"

"My own private investigation agency. Some day."

His eyes narrow skeptically, boring into me like he's taking a core sample and reading the growth-rings. I can almost see the words, "Aren't you a little old for that?" forming inside his cranium.

"Yeah, I've had a few false starts." I've tried everything, too: office work, factory work, guerrilla warfare . . .

He shakes his head, unable to hide a smirk. "You women, you want everything handed to you on a platter."

"What did I just say? And stop playing 'bad cop' with me. I know all about that shit."

"Yeah?" It's a challenge, the way he says it.

"Officer Kaltenbach, cooperation is the norm these days between public and private branches of law enforcement."

"So start cooperating with me."

"Fine. Where do you want me to start?"

"You see? Now that's more like it. Why don't you start by telling me how come you know so much about bad cops."

I guess I got myself into this, and I'm not turning back now.

"Okay."

He waits.

"Most of this was a pretty long time ago."

"What, you got some sealed juvenile records?"

"They don't bother with that where I come from. They just lock you in a hole for a year and tell your family you disappeared."

"Is that so? What'd you get busted for?"

"Feeding people."

For once, he doesn't throw it back at me.

"First I had the bad luck of getting nailed. Then I caught the eye of these two hard-assed guards who just couldn't get enough of bruising me inside and out whenever they felt like it. Then there was also this other guard who more or less left me alone, and that made her the 'nice' one at the time, right? But pretty soon I realized that the so-called nice one was hanging back, doing nothing while the others went after me. Sure, the worst part is that the others enjoyed their power to manipulate, dominate, and control me. But she used to stand around and watch. So I guess what I'm trying to say is, not shoving your nightstick fifteen inches up somebody's ass doesn't make you a good cop."

His reaction?

"Hang on, I gotta go to the can."

And he's off to relieve himself. Well, this is going swimmingly, I think to myself, covering my eyes with my hand and shaking my head. Maybe I should just concentrate on Officer MacKenzie, who seems to be thawing on me, or Officers O'Brien and Chen, who still owe me one, supposedly. But none of them are remotely connected to this case. Still, I've been through worse, and I might as well brave this out a little longer.

Kaltenbach comes back and says, "Can't believe they've still got a sign up in the men's room saying, 'No cigarettes in the urinals.'"

"Oh, that explains the sign in the women's room saying, 'No urinating in the ashtrays.'"

"I mean you haven't been allowed to smoke in that half of the bar for ten years now."

"What a shame."

"You used to be a cop, am I right?"

"A detective, actually, but I don't want to get into it right now."

"You made detective? How come you didn't stick with it? Couldn't handle the pressure, sweetie?"

"I got tired of being the world's one-stop colonoscopist."

"Aww, ain't that too freaking bad?" He makes a sweet-and-sour face at me like I've just proven why women are unworthy of competing with men, then he chases it with a swig of scotch.

"I had one of the toughest gigs in Manhattan, Officer

Kaltenbach," I tell him, "jammed up between the armies of North Harlem skells who'd ice you for a nickel and the equally hostile hordes of narcissistic Wall Street assholes who think it's their birthright to boss people like me around."

"Narsy-what?"

"In love with themselves."

"What's that supposed to mean?"

"It means that I've earned a little consideration."

"Yesterday's news."

I can see that he's unimpressed.

"All right. Let me tell you a story," I say, sipping my soda and suddenly wishing it were a double bourbon. And it all comes back, the scream ripping through the air, the high-wire feel of your heart being sucked through a hole in the bottom of your chest like it's been dropped from the cargo bay of a B-52 bomber, the people scattering in panic, the blood on the sidewalk, the horrible jostling through the crowd.

"We were chasing an armed robber along 181st Street at about ten o'clock in the morning in the middle of June. The guy likes to cut things—purse straps, earlobes, loose fingers— anything that gets in his way. He tries to lose us by ducking down into the subway. It's the tail end of rush hour, and he's holding a bloody boxcutter in his hands. So we're pushing our way down the stairs, following the trail of blood and sig-naling to the transit cops to stop the train. Sure enough, the red trail stops at the edge of the platform, so we get them to stop the train and keep the doors sealed. We gain access, and we're going through the cars one by one, expecting this guy to start slicing off ears and taking hostages any second now, when this prick in a business suit starts telling me, 'I've got to be at my appointment in half-an-hour.' So I say, 'I'm aware of that, sir, but we are trying to apprehend a danger-ous criminal.' And he says, 'Listen, you stupid f-word b-word, I've got a *very* important appointment at ten-thirty with Mr. Gary So-and-so, Vice President of the Big Freaking Bank of America' and blah blah blah until I finally say, 'Where's your appointment?' 'Fifty-ninth Street.' 'Here's ten dollars. Go take a goddamn taxi to your goddamn appointment and get the fuck out of my face.'"

"Did he take it?"

"He took it. SOB probably earned five hundred grand a year in pre-Clinton dollars to my thirty-one, but he took it. I had to pry the damn door open for him, too."

He smirks. "Never happened to me."

"Maybe not. But don't tell me you've never been caught in the middle with nobody backing you up."

"Sure. Lots of times."

"Yeah? Tell me about it."

He clams up and tries to brush me off, but I cling to his natty pelt like a burr.

"Come on, Officer Kaltenbach, don't give me the strong, silent treatment. I told you one."

"I don't recall making any deals."

"Fine. I don't need this, anyway—" I start gathering up my things to leave.

"Hey, hey, that's what I mean. You just crack right away. What kind of detective gives up on the first try?"

A detective who's got no income, a kid waiting at home, and who's getting nowhere with a recalcitrant piece of old horsemeat like *you*, Officer Kaltenbach.

"You can call me Ed," he says.

I'm about to say what a fine fucking privilege that is, but I think better of it. Let him think he's won the first round of this Punch-and-Judy battle of the sexes. I sit back down, which appears to give him tremendous satisfaction.

"My first couple of years on the force . . . we were still fighting the war in Vietnam, with the protests and everything, and, you know, I had been there. So it was kinda rough."

I nod to show appropriate female empathy.

"Anyways, a bunch of longhairs were hanging around the McDonald's on Queens Boulevard. I personally never understood what they had against that place—I mean, it wasn't Dow Chemical or anything, we weren't dropping hamburgers on the freaking Vietcong, you know. But the next thing we hear they're taking over the place, handing out leaflets and—" he pauses for effect "—they pull down Old Glory and raise the Vietcong flag in its place."

He eyes me, trying to determine if I'm able to gauge the gravity of the situation. I stare back in awe.

"So the next thing I know we're in the middle of a stand-off. A dozen potheads are threatening to torch the place if we try to take the freaking VC flag down, and about twenty-five or thirty construction workers who used to live around here are threatening to torch the place if we *don't* try to take the freaking flag down. This goes on for nearly two hours."

"How'd you finally resolve the situation?"

"All this time, there was a delivery truck trying to get through. So I exchange uniforms with the guy and put on the white coveralls with the golden arches on the pocket, and I smash the truck right into the flagpole and knock it down. End of story."

"How King Solomon–like of you. I guess that's what they call a smash delivery."

He laughs and helps himself to a substantial portion of his drink.

"So what's this about you and the Morales case?" he asks, trying to catch me off guard, I imagine.

"I don't know," I say, playing the part he clearly wants me to play. "But from the bits I've heard, things aren't jelling. I've got an instinct that it goes deeper, and I'm sure you understand what I'm saying, Offi—I mean, Ed. Like your response to that tough *padrone*'s so-called suicide, it just doesn't feel right. But I can't put it all together if I don't get a look at the physical evidence you guys have gathered, the crime scene photos, interviews with the neighbors—"

"I'll see what I can do."

"Really? You're not just saying that?"

He looks at me like I've insulted a man of honor.

"I said I'll see."

Suddenly my dreams of darkness are pierced by a fierce, chest-rattling hum, and the dawn's first light pours in on plaster falling from the ceiling, walls vibrating with the heavy *whup-whup-whup* of a fleet of helicopters and distant voices warning us to take cover and to prepare to repel the tanks. For a moment I'm back in the jungle, being hunted by the ignorant, ruthless armies of a corrupt and hateful government. I instinctively reach for my rifle and my hand closes around—nothing. I'm not in the jungles of Ecuador, I realize, blinking my eyes out the window and surveying the legendary concrete habitat of the borough of Queens. But there certainly is a convoy of police helicopters blackening the sky, heading south towards 108th Street, and the pre-dawn raid has already begun.

This is not going to make my job any easier, especially on—what time is it, anyway? Jesus!—four hours of sleep.

It's practically over by the time I get to the squat house. A rising column of thick gray smoke shrouds the police tank sitting in the shattered portal as the last holdouts are led out in plastic handcuffs. Police in full riot gear who dropped from the copters are patrolling the roof of the factory armed with high-powered rifles. A couple of the die-hard anarchists are dumping buckets of red paint out the third-floor window onto the sidewalk below, spattering the hob-nailed boots and really bringing out the natural relief of the building's facade, which was carved during a time when architects and stonemasons still took the time to plant embellishments on factory walls. But they are soon pulled inside by the multiple flailing arms of the dreaded police colossus. A few paint-filled balloons come flying halfheartedly from the group of early-bird protesters, splashing the sidewalk and cornerstone with red paint, before they are forced to flee to avoid arrest.

Through the forest of dark blue helmets I catch a glimpse of Lucas being trundled off by two heavily protected cops, his arms spilling over with hastily gathered jewelers' supplies, and I manage to get next to him for a second—

"Where's Camille?"

"I don't know."

"Where's Georgio?" I ask.

"Crashing at a friends. Try Manny's—"

—before we are rudely separated.

And I had it all planned out so nicely. Wake up, get Antonia off to school, then begin a methodical house-to-house investigation of everyone who was familiar with Manny's numerous struggles. Instead I find myself playing front-line advocate to a neighborhood under siege as hundreds of innocent Coronians are stopped and frisked by the police and taken to jail for offenses ranging from resisting arrest to spitting on the sidewalk. Don't yell, "I have rights!" at the arresting officer, I advise them. Remain calm and polite, no matter how rude the police get, and don't ever touch them. Don't invite the cops into your apartment, this constitutes a consent to search, and you should never consent without a warrant, because if they had enough evidence they'd have gotten a warrant in the first place. Cops *are* allowed to stop you and ask for ID. If you go, "Holy shit, the cops! Let's get the hell out of here!" that's considered suspicious activity. Needless to say, resentment runs up and down the street like a crackhead with his pants on fire as I try to stop the cops from combining the last two sentences of the Miranda warning into one "trick" question:

"Do you understand and waive these rights?"

"Don't say yes!"

"Who the fuck are you—?"

"Get her the fuck out of here—!"

"Officer, I—"

"Jesus, fuckin' bitch—!"

You ain't seen bitch yet, boys, I'm just too smart to take a swing at a guy who's got eight burly friends in body armor watching his back. I've got plenty of experience with Third World–style "justice," and I avoid arrest by some miracle and make my way through the battle zone to Manny's old job a few blocks north, finding sanctuary within its quiet walls.

This wasn't supposed to be my first stop, but the Lord obviously had other plans, and who am I to question His methods? It takes several minutes for anyone at the Isaiah School to notice me, but pretty soon I'm jotting down statements in my notebook. It seems highly unlikely that Manny's death was related to his work with disabled children. Some outraged parent? No hint of impropriety there. Fraudulent petty cash disbursements? Co-worker rivalry? Sexual harassment? Not a whiff of scandal. No apparent peccadilloes. Nothing. Everyone testifies that Manny was a straight-shooter in the workplace, and a fighter for the rights of the disabled.

I see that Jerry's working with someone new, a dark-haired woman named Rosemarie who looks like she's descended from the Borgias of Naples. Jerry hasn't adjusted to the loss yet. I'm not even sure he understands it, as he sits there innocently asking, "Ma-nee? Ma-nee?" in a way that would pierce a healthy heart with a thousand daggers. I talk to Rosemarie a bit, then it's time for her to give Jerry his breakfast. He attacks the cold cereal, shoveling it into his gaping mouth and making crunching sounds like a shark ripping into a dolphin. Lower-functioning autistics aren't big on table manners, I see.

I watch The Great American Eating Machine and suddenly remember the four guys who mistook Manny and Jerry for a gay couple, and wonder if the cops have investigated the possibility that Manny was attacked in a misdirected act of gay bashing. Yeah, but who are they going to question? Four guys in a black Camaro that I saw a week ago? That's not much to go on. But I'll mention it to Officer Ed the next time I see him.

I cross under the Roosevelt Avenue El and walk up to Manny's building, but this morning's police activity has made my job considerably harder. The tenants are all stirred up, as if possessed by demons, and nobody wants to chat dispassionately about what may have happened during a few crucial minutes four nights ago, they're too full of rage and conspiracy theories:

"The landlords killed him, man!"

"Who else could've—?"

"Nobody—"

"The fuckin' city killed him."

"Fuckin'—"

"Get me the name of your landlord," I say.

"Where?"

"What for, mon? They'll just deny it."

"Yeah, and Pazzerello's fuckin' storm troopers will protect him—"

"Do you have a copy of the rent receipt?" I ask.

"Don't show her anything—"

"Yeah, pretty fuckin' late for that now—!"

"Where the fuck were you when we needed you—?"

"When Manny fucking needed—?"

"Could you all stop saying 'fucking' every third word?" I request. There's a momentary lull. "Where's Georgio?"

"He's—"

"Don't fuckin' tell her anything!"

"Shut the hell up, ya fuckin' faggots!" comes a chorus of voices from across the street.

I spin around on full alert, but I quickly see that it's a different group of guys. No. Sadly, virulent gay bashing is *not* limited to murder suspects.

"Ah, ¡callate la boca!" an older, more sensible woman commands. "He's up on the fifth floor," she says, taking me inside.

"He barely got out in time—"

"No thanks to you!"

Another walk-up. Doesn't anybody I need to see live on the first two floors?

"Me llamo Roberta," she introduces herself. "¿Y tú?"

"Filomena."

"Ah, so you're the one we hired." We trudge up the stairs, past the familiar smells of Spanish coffee and fried eggs, through the realm of mysterious Middle Eastern spices, past Puerto Rico and the Dominican Republic and, finally, to Jamaica. All the while she's filling me with her dark thoughts about the housing situation, and how the big wheeler-dealers use hired muscle to terrorize the tenants. It's no different than it was in her homeland, she says, where the big landowners periodically hired men with machetes to hack up some peasant who didn't keep to his place.

"*No hay buenos y malos aquí. Sólo hay malos y más malos.*" There's no good and evil here. Just evil and more evil.

The sound of reggae, the smell of sacramental herbs. Somebody's keeping the pandemonium at bay. The door swings open and a young, dark black man smiles back at me. No checking the peephole first?

Georgio's inside, ranting about the forced "mass exodus" from the lighting factory.

"There's my girl," he says, coming over, slapping my back and giving me a hug. "Zaïd, this is Filomena. She's gonna save our collective asses."

Zaïd grips my hand warmly.

"She's gonna plant her staff in the road and part the evil armies of Babylon that are united against us," shouts Georgio, holding up his arms in a Mosaic pose.

"I don't do partings," I apologize. "I only do that straw-into-gold thing."

"We shun their gold," Georgio declares. "We the people invoke the power of Jah!"

The room seems luxuriously decorated to me, but then I've been looking at nothing but bare sheetrock for the past couple of weeks. There's a sleek, new sound system pumping out the rebel music, with plenty of room at the bottom for thick chunks of bass. The flag of one of the central African nations graces the wall. I'm not sure which one. It's definitely not Rwanda or the Congo. Cameroon?

"And we are going to use that power to take back our homes!" Georgio yells out the open window into the street. "Do you hear me, servants of the pale white God? We are going to take back our homes!"

I hear whistles and cheers of support, mixed with other responses from the angry neighbors down below.

"Maybe they won't get the variance," I suggest. I haven't mentioned the EPA yet.

"Are you kidding?" says Georgio. "This is Babylon, mon. You could build a highway through Our Lady of Sorrows on 104th Street if you paid enough people off."

Zaïd agrees.

"Let the free market rule, they say," Georgio continues. "Let the free market decide how much the rent's gonna be."

"Ever notice when they swear in the Prez," Zaïd says conspiratorially, "and he puts his hand on that Bible, they don't make him swear to tell the truth, the whole truth and nothing but. They make him swear *to uphold the Constitution*. Ain't nothing in there about him not lying to us. All that stuff about how competition is good because it means better products and low prices—yeah, when was the last time you saw a car that'll run thirty years and costs $750 new? When was the last time you saw that? But they're still trying to feed us that shit."

"They were feeding us that shit when we were growin' up on the island, mon."

"So your big revelation is that capitalism sucks?" I say.

"I would rather be toiling in the cane fields under a master who whips me every day in front of the TV cameras so that everyone could bear witness to my oppression," says Georgio, "than to keep on living in this pretend world of smiley-faced capitalism, always presenting the finely polished image that they're bestowing nothing but comfort and good cheer, faster Internet access, cheaper plane tickets, better hot dogs. But the image is fake."

"The reality in other places is just as fake, we're just more skillful at hiding it," I offer.

Georgio waits for me to say more. I explain: "The CIA knows how to steam open your mail, read it and put it back and re-seal it just like nothing ever happened. Where I come from, the secret police rip it open, paw through it, stuff it back in the envelope and deliver it to you as is just so you'll *know* they've been through your stuff."

"Or you come back to your room," says Zaïd, jumping in,

"and five guys with dark green uniforms are going through your stuff and they're like, 'We're the laundry staff. Where's your dirty laundry at?'"

"That's the way it is, sister," says Georgio.

"It's better than them strapping you to the electric table, but it still sucks," I say.

"And I'm saying it's *not* better, it's *worse*—"

"Anyway, I'd love to debate this further with you, but I actually came to investigate Manny's death."

"Yeah, what up with that?"

"Well, I'm working on a couple of theories."

"Like what?"

"One: It was one of the drug gangs he chased out of the area. Two: It was some of the landlord's hired goons. Three: It was somebody else."

"That only two theories, girlfriend," says Georgio. "Somebody else don't count."

"So help me out."

"How?"

"What happened that night?"

"What are you asking me for? I wasn't around," says Georgio.

"Were you?" I say, turning to Zaïd.

"Well, I've got my own theory," Zaïd says. "Our *amigo* Manny was messed up by some white nationalists out cruising the 'hood looking for some ass to kick, black or brown."

"Anything's possible," I say. "Although they'd have to have some real balls to come up here and try that, and somebody would have noticed a posse of skinheads tooling around Corona carrying baseball bats. Has that been a problem? Was Manny getting any threats?"

"No more than any of us, but he was a spokesman. The brother made enemies. You know, some uppity spic who don't know his place."

I bristle at his use of the term.

"Sorry, sister, but that's the word."

"Race could be a factor," I say, considering the implications.

"But with all the heat he generated, all the flames he kept feeding, it seems awfully convenient for the people he was barbecuing to be rid of him and have it look like a separate racially motivated attack."

"See, that's why I came to you," says Georgio. "We both know there's got to be some money behind this. Same motivations as in the bestsellers, mon: Money, power, greed. Only thing missing is the sex."

"And racism just ain't sexy," says Zaïd, bitterly.

I switch topics: "Can you tell me in your own words what happened Monday night between seven and seven-thirty?"

"You know, I really don't remember all that well," says Zaïd. "Just a regular Monday night is all."

"Manny came home from work the same time as always?"

"I guess so."

"You know why he went back out?"

Nobody knows.

"Could I see his apartment?"

"That could be a problem. Someone's already living there."

"We needed the strength in numbers," says Zaïd, as if he needs to apologize to me for their weakness. "We couldn't keep the resistance going with an empty apartment, especially Manny's."

So much for uncontaminated evidence. Great. A cold crime scene, no witnesses, not even a shot at tangential evidence from his apartment.

"Well, I might as well talk to whoever's there, just in case."

Roberta leads me down a flight of stairs, warning me not to listen to Zaïd. "That kid would steal from himself if he could," she whispers in Spanish.

More music and smells, only this time it's a street band called Hooverville playing their mayor-bashing ode to the squatters, "A Thousand Pounds of Nails," and the aroma of freshly made coffee. Manny's old apartment is occupied by a Jewish ex-hippie with wild thinning hair, although he's only in his mid-forties.

"You thought I looked older, right?" he says, letting me in.

"I don't mind going prematurely gray. It's a sign of . . . mental instability."

He offers me a mug of that strong, strong coffee, and it takes him three mugfuls just to keep his eyes open. We find common ground bitching about the politicians who all seem to get their material from the National Joke Depository in Canton, Ohio, then I ask him what condition the apartment was in when he moved in.

"You mean, was there a message on his answering machine from someone saying, 'Meet me at the corner of 104th Street and 39th Avenue at seven-twelve in the evening'? No, sorry about that."

He sure has his facts straight. He lets me look around, but I have to say that it's a lot easier to sift through the deceased's effects *before* someone has moved in and packed them up in boxes and carried them down to the basement, where they await distribution to the neighborhood's neediest. So any potentially meaningful association between the items has been thoroughly destroyed, and as for going through storage boxes full of Manny's stuff—well, I'll save that for later. Talk to the living first. The only things he kept around are Manny's health food supplies, and no, there's no message inside the jar of granola. I checked.

The next apartment belongs to large family of Pakistani immigrants. Everyone's rushing around to get ready for the day, so it's hard to find a quiet spot to interview people. I settle on the hallway, under the stairs. The father shakes his head and agrees that it is a terrible shame about Mr. Morales, but that he has seen much worse violence and oppression back in his country, and then, uninvited, offers me his observation that American women are unhappy because they have too much freedom, and the son concurs, but after they've gone the daughter quietly tells me that she finds American culture liberating, even as she puts on her veil. Soon everyone's gone except the grandmother, and I have to use one of the phone company's by-the-minute interpreters to get the story from her.

It comes out slow and rambling, but she thinks she might have seen two guys following Manny down the street that night.

Wish I had more reliable witnesses, but so far the little pieces suggest that two people went after Manny from this end, while two more waited for him at the other end of the street. That's no wandering gang of teenage racists. That's organization.

I'm ready to go online back at the office. I'm stepping off the curb when someone calls my name. I turn and look down at little Angelito Muñoz, asking me to come and see about his grandmother.

"What's wrong?" I ask.

"Just come see."

The inside of their apartment is quiet and still. The adults have gone to work and the older children have gone to school, leaving a few faint swirls of dust behind them. Angelito leads me into the kitchen, where I find the elder María Muñoz sitting alone in the dark, the table covered with dirty breakfast dishes, except for a pristine place set in front of an empty chair.

"It's been there all week," Angelito confides to me. "Every time we try to take it away she says to leave it there."

I draw closer. Mrs. Muñoz gets no warmth from her coffee, which has gone cold, no comfort from the almond cookie on her plate, the sight of which makes me unexpectedly and supremely sad. What a lonely pleasure. This woman needs so much more than a cookie can offer, and I can't give it to her.

"*¿Cómo le va, Señora Muñoz?*" I say in my softest, sweetest voice.

She looks up at me, seems to be piecing me together bit-by-bit like a blurry pointillistic image, until she's sure it's really me. Then the corners of her eyes turn down and her face darkens.

"*You*," she says. "You work for them but you don't work for me?"

"*Señora Muñoz*, I told you there's nothing more I could have done. This other case, it's for the good of the community—" I know. It sounds hollow as soon as it's out of my mouth.

"'For the good of the community'?" she says.

"Please forgive me."

"I should spit on you."

"It's your right."

I stand there and wait for it.

But the only thing that comes from her is a tear that slowly drips down her cracked cheek.

And she waits a long time before wiping it off.

CHAPTER THIRTEEN

Fiction carries a greater amount of truth in solution than the volume which purports to be all true.
—Thackeray

EVERYONE'S a little self-centered, but some people have raised it to an art. I'm trying to run a background check on some of the witnesses I spoke to, and Len, at the other terminal, keeps reaching across my chest for the reference manual and ever-so-lightly brushing up against me, until I cut into him and he responds, clearly miffed.

"Okay, Fil, only next time you get in touch with your inner bitch, just send me a postcard, huh?"

Jeezus, somebody give this guy a shot of estrogen. I thought we got everything straight between us. I've been trying to be nice about it, you know, not rubbing his face in it, but to no avail. I give up.

"Pick up line two, Fil," says Katwona.

It's Lonnie Ambush, reminding me to be at the courthouse at 9:00 A.M. on Monday, when Sonny Tesoro's plea is going to be entered.

"Don't forget," he says, needlessly.

"I won't, I won't."

As long as I've been interrupted, I take a moment to dial the EPA and press Gina for results.

"Fil, the constant stream of environmental concerns in

the New York–New Jersey area make it impossible for the government to take a special interest in an abandoned lighting factory in Corona."

"But people are living there—"

"Not anymore, they aren't. The city took over the building in order to revert ownership to the landlord, and now we're fighting them for jurisdiction over the site. It'll probably take 'til Monday."

Monday is sure filling up fast.

"Why so long?"

"You call that long?"

"Fine, fine, the bright lights and big city have gone to my head. Now tell me why."

"Because it can cost $20,000 to clean up a single contaminated apartment, so everyone is searching for every excuse not to look too closely—"

"I like that: Everyone's searching for an excuse not to look."

"—And because we're operating under a security alert."

"A security alert? What does that mean?"

"It means all the mail's got to be X-rayed, all non-government-employee visitors must be confirmed by phone and escorted by an agency employee at all times—"

"What on earth's going on?"

"Threats, Fil. What do you think? I've already said too much, but even as I speak, the NYPD is setting up concrete roadblocks on Duane Street and Broadway. Don't forget: We're the federal government. Some people think *we're* the enemy."

"Hmm. That was Zaïd's theory, too."

"Who?"

"Never mind. Something else. Something I better get back to."

"Me, too. Check with me later."

"Will do. Sheesh, Gina, that sucks. I mean about the threats."

"'Sucks' doesn't quite cover it. We even have a day care center in the building, just like the one in Oklahoma City."

I cancel my background search to take a quick look at the map of racial incidents in the borough. There's a lot of activity, I'm sorry to say, but nothing of obvious use to me right now. If this were one of those weekly TV dramas, this would be the moment for me to pinpoint one particular group of vigilantes who go around taking out politically active minorities and leaving a signature at each scene big enough for an intelligent cat to make the connection. Too bad the reality is that there are tons of racists out there who don't need any other motivation to torment people besides hearts hardened by hate for anyone who happened to come to this country ten minutes after they did, on the very next boat in some cases. Well, it was just an idea. What if it's not race hatred but our old nemesis, money? Give 'em enough cash and people will sell their own brothers into slavery. Just ask Joseph. Maybe I should run a financial check on some of the key players in Manny's life.

I start with his co-workers at the Isaiah School, curious to find out if any of the kind, helpful people I was speaking to at the institute this morning are secretly milking the pension fund. Sure, they all seemed like dedicated people working with developmentally disabled children, but you can't always tell by appearances. Every now and then you find yourself interviewing some smiling old woman who turns out to have her husband down in the fruit cellar soaking in several jars of formaldehyde, and you learn to trust your instincts. Anyway, just as I'm getting up a head of steam, in walks Sherry Aksakalova, the black-haired bombshell from "Gonzo" Mendieta's club. She storms right up to me.

"I want to sue my boss for sexual harassment."

"Then you need a lawyer, not a private detective. And you can't use us, anyway, Gonzo's an active client."

"What I really want is to kill him."

"Well, for that you need a hit man," I say. "Maybe we better have this conversation in private." Abby's office is empty for the next hour.

"He will not keep his hands off me."

"Yeah, I know the type," I say a little extra loudly, as I lead her into Abby's office and shut the door.

"He is kind of man who will not take 'No' for an answer."

"Honey, Gonzo's the kind of man who won't take 'Fuck off' for an answer."

"The only time I have ever seen him laugh is when I ask for more money."

Gee, I know *that* type, too.

"I do not even like men that much, you know?" she says.

"No, I didn't know, but I kind of figured."

"How you figure?"

"Maybe it has something to do with that tattoo on your arm that says, 'If you can read this you're standing too damn close.'"

She laughs. "I have that since I was technician in gay theater."

"You mean gay sex shows?"

"No, legitimate gay theater."

"Or, as we like to call it, straight gay theater. Now, *Swan Lake*: There's a sick story for you. Some guy wants to screw a swan, for Christ's sake."

"Yes, is *very* romantic."

She looks at me, her eyes shining, radiant, penetrating me with sonar power.

I confess to her, "No, Sherry, no. We're talking prison-house stuff. I've been gay and I've been straight, and believe me, straight is better. For me, anyway."

"You mean you are bisexual?"

"Not really. And bisexual is such an ugly term. It makes you sound like some kind of fuse box or something. Personally, I prefer 'omnisexual.'"

"Yes, yes, I agree. Why should I be called a 'lesbian' simply because I love women? Why should you be called 'bisexual' simply because you like variety?"

"Sherry, I'm not—"

The intercom buzzes, startling me. Sometimes the

button sticks and the whole office can hear everything that's being said in here. Thank God it's not engaged. I've hardly ever told anyone this stuff outside the great, gray walls where we all did time together.

Katwona's voice: "Phone call, Fil. Line three."

It's Dvurushnik. What is this? Pushkin Day?

"I want to thank you for sending me such a well-shaped young lady," he says, and he begins describing Karen in every topographic detail. Great: Another guy who needs a libido transplant.

"It's nothing," I say.

He wants to discuss full-time security arrangements.

"It'll cost you," I caution him.

"Cost is no object."

"That's Chip Davis's favorite phrase in the whole world. Let me patch you through to him."

"No, I prefer young lady."

She'll hate me for this.

"She can be the operative liaison, but Mr. Davis has to make the arrangements."

"Ah, yes. Of course."

Of course. Now, where was I? Oh, yes.

"I better get back to work, Sherry," I say, walking around Abby's desk. "I'm really in the middle of some shit right now. But give me a couple of days and I'll be happy to light a fire under Mr. Gonzo Mendieta for you."

I've got my hand on the knob when she thanks me with a big, wet smack on the lips. There's some tongue in there, too. I spend a moment being taken aback, but sweetly so.

I hold the door open for her, and the office seems awfully quiet all of a sudden, all eyes on me. After Sherry leaves, Len speaks up: "You didn't really hire yourself out as a hit man, did you?"

"Oh, is *that* all. Of course not." But the eyes stay on me.

Back on the computer, getting lost in my work, soon I'm sniffing out the enzyme-filled scent of money and drawing awfully near the source by the smell of things. I've just found a $12,000 cash deposit, dated three days ago, in Mr. Zaïd Ngala's checking account, with the promise of more to come in adjacent areas, when Karen calls out, "Hey, Fil, listen to this," and turns up the radio in time for me to catch the news announcer's voice:

"—have arrested reputed mob associate Vincent Giordano in the murder of Queens resident Manuel Morales."

Then we get a fast edit and one of the precinct's senior detectives saying, "Mr. Giordano has twice been convicted of similar enforcement-style beatings, and he is unable to account for his whereabouts at the time of the murder."

"Looks like they trumped you," says Len, enjoying my apparent defeat.

I pick up the phone and call Ed Kaltenbach.

"I said—" Len begins.

"I heard what you said!"

"What's going on out there?" Davis calls to us from his office.

"Nothing," Karen answers.

"Don't worry, Chip, we're working hard. I mean, we're not just out here jerking off," says Len.

"Speak for yourself," says Karen.

He's not in. I try his home number. Finally.

"What are you still investigating?" Kaltenbach protests. "Last time I checked they caught the guy."

"You mean because he can't 'account for his whereabouts'? Jeezus, how many of *you guys* does it take to screw in a light bulb? Is that the best you can do? Shouldn't you have something a little stronger than that?"

"Hey, you wanna come do my job?"

"I'd be delighted, 'cause then you'd have to let me look at the freaking reports. How long are you going to keep me on hold about that?"

"It looked like an old-fashioned union beating to me."

"Oh, fuck."

"Whadaya mean, 'fuck'?"

"Fuck. Push. Thrust. Copulate. From the Middle English

fucken, probably akin to the Dutch *fokken* and the Swedish *fock*. Because it's starting to smell like a work-for-hire, that's why, and you don't hire organization unless you're—"

"What? Who?"

A big, fat greedy landlord.

I leave him dangling.

"Katwona, what was that call we had on Monday? The one that wanted me to dig up some dirt on a pain-in-the-ass tenant?"

"Oh, umm—" She's got four phone lines flashing, and it's right on the tip of her tongue. It takes her a moment, then, "It was Abe Fleischwolf's office."

"Thanks."

I do a quick title check with the Queens County tax assessor's office and find out who owns Manny's building: Abe Fleischwolf Associates, Inc.

I get their number and dial.

"Mr. Fleischwolf's office, how may I help you?"

"Is Mr. Fleischwolf in?"

"Yes, he is."

"Have him stay there."

I'm putting on my coat when the phone rings for the millionth time.

"Hold it, Fil," says Katwona. "It's for you. Line one."

"Now what?" I pick up the phone. "Hello?"

"We know about your past," says the gruff, digitally modified voice.

"What about my past?" I ask. The felonies I committed on Long Island a few years ago? My young adulthood as a riotous renegade?

"Enough to keep you from getting your license." *Click*.

Unlikely. Granted, the New York Secretary of State can investigate violations of the licensing laws based upon the complaints *of any person*, but most of my "youthful indiscretions" are buried mighty deep in the records, and I was never convicted of anything in the U.S., not like *that's* a ringing endorsement of my character.

But still, someone's got my number, and I try to get theirs, too, but the phone system's automated voice tells me that the number of the party that just called me is not available because it is either unlisted or new, and to please check my records and don't forget to Have a Nice Day.

Yeah. Thanks.

All I can say is, Abe Fleischwolf's office is not what I expected it to be. It's a cramped, airless office with institutional beige walls dulled by the years and shrouded beneath a grimy film of five-for-a-dollar cigar smoke.

No highly polished steel-and-glass.

The all-powerful Abe Fleischwolf is a former garment worker, with nut brown skin and white hair, who wore the same shoes and ate the same half-a-can of tuna for lunch and dinner every day for the better part of thirty-five years until he saved up enough to buy his first tenement, and from there he slowly built a small empire that today encompasses nearly forty apartment buildings.

But he's also a tired old man who keeps telling me there's no room in this world for his kind anymore, the small-time neighborhood landlord who scrapes by on a profit margin of one or two percent, and the only pleasures left to him are the shrink-wrapped cigars he buys at the drugstore.

"Why such a shallow margin?" I ask.

"I got tough tenants. It's hard to make a profit around here. You see this building?" he says, pointing to a stack of invoices. "I got a family of crack addicts in apartment One-F. Every month, they rip out the copper pipes and sell them, and I gotta replace them. Every month."

He denies that he or anyone else in his office made the call. He even lets me use the phone to call the agency.

Len answers.

"Where's Katwona?" I ask.

"Hey, even receptionists gotta take a piss once in a while, Fil, you're such a harsh taskmaster—I mean taskmistress—"

"Len, this is important. Check with the phone company and find out who called us Monday morning around ten-fifteen."

He calls me back ten minutes later and says, "Their records indicate that the call came from a phone number that's been inactive for three months."

Cue: Eerie music.

I've been chasing the wrong landlord. Manny's actions were also instrumental in slowing down the factory-to-condo conversion. Who else would want him hurt, or dead, and be willing to pay for the privilege?

"Who owns the lighting factory?"

"The what?"

I give Len the address and do some more waiting. Eventually he comes back on the line and says, "Not an easy one, Fil. Gonna take at least twenty minutes."

"Fine, I've got some people I need to see."

***

"Man, they already changed the locks," says Georgio, leaning against the retaining wall on the roof of Manny's building, looking south towards the heavily patrolled roof of the empty factory. "You know, why bother with that? How am I supposed to get my keys in the door when they've got a twenty-four-hour watch on the front, the back, and the roof. *The roof!* I mean, what are we gonna do? Get a fleet of helicopters, parachute in, and take the building by storm?"

"And you'd think taking eighteen police officers off regular patrol duty would be pretty hard to justify politically when you're trying to keep the crime statistics down."

"Unless there's something valuable in there that none of us know about."

"More outrageous conspiracies, Georgio? No, I'm afraid this is standard Pazzerello overkill."

"How you mean?"

"I mean, we've got an open murder case in the neighborhood, with four killers on the loose since Monday, and they've got three rotations of six officers apiece watching an empty building."

Georgio says, "Where you been? They say they caught the guy."

"What guy? Vinnie Giordano? I know Vinnie. He may conduct the occasional midnight dig on Staten Island, but he hasn't publicly beaten anyone with a pool cue since the dawn of the disco era. No, we're talking about some tough-but-stupid amateurs, three or four guys with maybe half a brain between them. And I want to find out who hired them."

"If you say so."

"Where's Lucas? Have you seen him yet?"

"No, they're gonna make him spend the night in a holding cell."

I shake my head at the familiar injustice, so like my native Ecuador. Not supposed to be the way it is here, though.

"What about Camille?"

"She found a place on 41st Avenue, near the highway."

"Do you know which one, exactly?"

"No. One of the houses near the end, she's on the top floor."

"And Ted?"

"Don't know. He's probably crashing with one of his girlfriends."

"And where's Zaïd?"

Georgio looks at me curiously. "What do you want to see him for?"

We're climbing down from the roof when my phone rings. It's Len: "Yeah, Fil, listen, we got temporary receivership by the City of New York, previous owner Manganaris Associates, subdivision of Spinnaker Works, a holding company for St. Lawrence Tool and Die Manufacturers, division of Kidd Guaranty and Trust, another holding company, half-a-dozen other corporations-on-paper—but here's the owner, as far as I can tell: Sullivan and Krauss Realty, Inc."

That's a big place. I'm not going in there cold. I'll have to go into the office first thing tomorrow and see what I can dig up on *them*.

"Have Katwona make an appointment for me sometime tomorrow afternoon."

"Under a pretext?"

"You bet your ass, fanboy."

"Fine. What's the pretext?"

That stumps me for a moment. Then: "Security. Tell them we're offering a free consultation—no, scratch that. Tell them we've been observing their current security arrangements, and we *guarantee* them better service at a lower price. That'll get their fucking attention."

"Sure will. You're a genius, Fil."

"Say, Len."

"Yeah?"

"Thanks for running that down for me."

"No problem."

I knock on the door to Zaïd's apartment, and ask him point-blank where he got $12,000 from.

"Growing the ganja, sistah."

"Where?"

"All over. Some of the boys rent out a couple of apartments, but with the right tools and know-how, you can grow a few thousand worth of bud that ain't no schwag in a two-by-three-foot closet."

Just like Sonny was doing. Somewhere out there is a thread connecting these events. I can feel it.

"Prove it," I say.

"Prove what?"

"Prove to me that you got that money selling buds."

"Hey, what is this?"

"It's a murder investigation."

"Oh. Okay, here." He goes and opens a desk drawer. My hand is inside my coat, but he pulls out a pile of receipts and starts going through them. "You see, to make it in this business, I gotta take the cash and hop a bus down to Atlantic City. I trade it in for chips, play a few hands and win or lose a few hundred, whatever, then I turn in the chips, *pay the Man's taxes on the winnings*, get the receipt—" he holds a genuine

IRS-approved casino receipt in front of my eyes for $12,464, dated last Monday "—and everything is legal as sea salt, sugah."

This from a guy who failed tenth-grade math.

One more stop, then I'm calling it quits. Back under the el, left on 41st Avenue, two long blocks east. A series of row houses, well-kept. Yards raked. Newly painted trim. Garbage pails lined up neatly along the walls. But there are two near the end that look somewhat the worse for wear. Rotting window sashes, paint peeling, scraps of paper clinging to the rusty steel mesh fences. There's a teenager on a bike having a screaming match with an older man leaning out a second-floor window, about keeping the noise down at night when people are trying to sleep.

"*¡Niño malcriado!* We have to get up early and go to work, but we can't sleep with your parties—!"

"*¡No soy un niño! Tengo diez y siete años.*"

I'm not a kid! I'm seventeen years old.

"Bah! What do you know about being a man?" he continues in Spanish. "When I was your age I worked in the fields all day, and if you made any trouble, you got *la corbata*!" He punctuates this statement by drawing his thumb across his throat and making a *cuic!* sound.

"Kids today!" he yells, looking at me for sympathy.

I smile. The kid regards me through narrow, slitted eyes. "*Perdónenme, señores*, but do either of you know where I may find Camille Tesoro?"

The older man starts shouting at someone in the room behind him.

"Upstairs," says the kid. "Room fourteen."

"Room *fourteen*?"

I walk in and go up the narrow stairs to the second floor, where I have to scrunch down because the ceiling is only about five feet high. It seems that the second floor has been divided in half *horizontally* to create a third floor with five additional rooms, where the ceiling is barely four-and-a-half feet high. I know prisons roomier than this.

I stoop over and find Camille breast-feeding the baby in the last room on the left—and I'm using the word "room" generously. I crawl through the opening and I sit on the floor across from her. Our backs are against opposite walls and our knees are practically touching. We speak in Spanish, as always.

"Jesus, when does the hunger strike begin?" I say.

Camille does not laugh.

"Look, I know this has been a bad day for you but I need to ask you a few questions." She doesn't tell me to stop. "Has Zaïd Ngala ever been to your apartment? I mean your old apartment in the factory."

She looks at me a long time before saying, "No."

"Any of his friends?"

She shrugs. "Probably."

I try to get her to be more specific, but she just sits there staring at a stain on the floor.

"What about Georgio?"

"What about him?"

"How come he didn't spend the night at the factory?"

"How should I know?" She's getting irritated.

"You know where Ted Hocks is?"

"No."

"When was the last time you saw him?"

"Oh, I don't know."

"Days? Weeks?"

"A couple of days ago, I guess."

"Know where he is now?"

"No."

"Okay. Was your apartment ever broken into?"

"Yes."

"When?"

"It was at night."

"I mean how long ago."

"Oh. A couple of months ago. The end of summer."

Hmm. No point dusting for prints from two months ago, and I don't have the money or time to do the whole place with police lab–level scrutiny.

She's just sitting there like a doped-up mental patient.

"Camille, it's going to be okay."

"You told the city about me," she says flatly. It's an accusation, not a question.

"No, Camille, I—"

"You told them I was using *el azogue*, and they came and threw us out."

"Camille, listen to me: *I swear* I did not tell the city about you. The city doesn't know about the mercury contamination in the building yet, otherwise they'd know the place is worthless, because the EPA is going to condemn it."

"Who?"

"The U.S. Environmental Protection—" Oh, shit.

"So you *did* tell them! And now look at us, sitting in this hamster cage because of you!"

Damn. I keep trying to avoid it, but once again someone is screaming at me, red-faced with rage. For all I know she might have mercury poisoning too, and it's gone to her brain. And the kid—

"At least now I'm living with people I trust! *Sí, señora,* we're safe here," she declares.

Thirty-three people crammed into a two-story house.

"Now get out," she says.

"Okay, I'll come back in a couple of days, when you—when things are better. Sonny's case is coming up on Mon—"

"I said get out!!"

Time to go home. It's been a long day. I know I've asked this before, but why aren't there more Friday nights in a week? On my way home I pass a small group of grim-looking gravediggers pacing around in the cold, the plain printed signs hanging from their necks declaring this to be the fifth day of the strike. A few more blocks and I pass by a stack of marble headstones and empty coffins piling up outside the funeral home. What a city: Even the dead don't have a place to spend the night.

CHAPTER FOURTEEN

When murders are committed by mathematicians,
you can solve them by mathematics. Most
of them aren't and this one wasn't.
—Dashiell Hammett, *The Thin Man*

As poet *and* mathematician, he would reason well; as
mere mathematician, he could not have reasoned at all,
and thus would have been at the mercy of the Prefect.
—Edgar Allan Poe, "The Purloined Letter"

EVERY CASE IS DIFFERENT, but every case is the exact same. There are a million ways of getting into the maze, but you always end up going down the same pathways, searching for the same type of information—assets, titles, who owns what and who did what to whom, digging up a past that they would rather have you forget about.

The real estate firm of Sullivan and Krauss is no exception. But a little archival archaeology—hours of painstaking excavation, classification, and reconstruction—turns up a pattern of abusive tactics constantly weaving in and out of legality: Threats of eviction even when the rent has been paid on time (and we've got copies of the cancelled checks to prove it), cutting off heat and hot water, damaging the outer doors, removing people's possessions and dumping them on the street, leaky faucets and old dishwashers being cited as "violating the terms of the lease" and, in one case, a warrantless search of a tenant's apartment conducted by actual police officers. I wonder who those cops work for, and if they have my name and number on file.

I have to make some calls, but I manage to set it up.

Officers O'Brien and Chen agree to meet me in a back booth that the waiters will ignore at a Cuban-Chinese diner on a gray and unassuming street.

The formalities are few.

"Thanks for coming," I say, and get right to it. "I've got credible, corroborated testimony that a couple of precinct cops hired themselves out to a real estate firm called Sullivan and Krauss for the purpose of intimidating the legal tenants of 84–02 Elmhurst Avenue. You know anything about that?"

"Hey, we're the new kids," says O'Brien.

"We're the FNGs," says Chen.

"And we ain't opening up to anybody on that stuff. Maybe next time. Talk to Kaltenbach."

Chen says, "Yeah, lean on Kaltenbach for that stuff."

"Oh? Does he know something?" I ask.

"Talk to Kaltenbach," says O'Brien.

Okay. But trying to reach Kaltenbach is a short road to nowhere until he comes on shift, so I head back to the office, where I discover that by some cosmic confluence everyone else is either still on their way here or out on an assignment and I'm alone in the place with Len.

So I guess we might as well talk.

"I thought we went over this, Len," I tell him.

"We did, we did, I just—I don't know. Hyperactive hormones just wouldn't let it go. I guess I'm over it, sort of."

Remarkably honest.

"Look, sometimes there can be weird moments between two people who can still go on to be great friends. Believe me, I know. Okay?"

"Okay," he says. "So what have you got?"

I tell him I've got a pattern of harassment by Sullivan and Krauss at several locations, and credible allegations of hired goons being used to harass the factory crew as well.

"I thought landlords stopped using hired goons for that."

"They may not deploy them anymore to get into a swanky apartment in Manhattan, but for a squat in Queens, why change a successful formula? Especially when you're targeting immigrants who don't know their full rights under the law."

"Nonsense," says Len. "Immigrants know the law better than anybody, studying all the time for that citizenship exam and stuff, it's fresh in their minds. I mean, how many Americans know what the freaking Eighth Amendment is all about?"

"No cruel and unusual punishment," I answer.

"See what I mean?" Len poses this question to the rest of the office, which echoes in its emptiness on this chilly Saturday morning.

I've spent too much time on this already, now I've got to gird myself to go out and face the wily herd of bull marketeers, and I don't even carry a stun-gun, unlike the poor schmucks who had to deal with a genuine escaped rodeo bull this morning. The rodeo was illegal, naturally, and the mistreated bull broke free and ran through the streets of Rego Park scaring the crap out of people until the police finally cornered it and kept shooting at it until it finally gave up and died. Now everyone's blaming the cops for not handling the situation properly. "Why'd they have to shoot it?" they're all asking. Uh, excuse me, sure it's a shame, but how would *you* deal with an angry 1,700-pound bull? Play it some Mozart, no doubt. I mean, give the beat cops a break once in a while, save your venom for the corrupt pigs out there who shoot unarmed teenagers and help greedy landlords terrorize people whose only crime is having the bad taste to earn less than $500,000 a year.

After many days of clouds and rain, a vaguely familiar yellow object appears in the sky. That's the sun, I'd recognize it anywhere. But the sky is swept clear by an icy meat cleaver of wind so fierce and biting I find myself envying the Muslim women walking up Kissena Boulevard, all bundled up—and man, that veil is starting to look pretty good right about now.

Screw waiting for the bus, let Davis & Brown pay for my heated taxi ride to the onyx-and-chrome-plated offices of Sullivan and Krauss deep in upper-crusty Forest Hills, on a street so well-groomed it looks like it must get vacuumed and buffed every Tuesday and Friday.

I haven't had time to piss twice in the same spot all week and now I have to endure sitting still and watching the rest of the morning slip away, all for the privilege of being seen by a low-level bureaucrat who acts like I have my whole life in front of me, so what's so bad about wasting a few hours of it with him? If life were four or five hundred years long, maybe I wouldn't mind sitting around like this, but what makes you think *you* know how many hours I've got left, mister?

I also happen to know that the primary purpose of the bureaucratic system is to dissipate blame, to cover butts and make it nearly impossible to pinpoint the inevitable screw-ups in the chain of command, because I've worked for some mighty big bureaucracies. When something goes wrong, you just say, "The B-1 forms got hung up in purchasing," or "The paperwork's still with the state agency in Albany" or something equally unverifiable.

So when they finally show me into Assistant Auditor Andrew Murtaugh's office and he says, "Be with you in a minute," without looking up from his computer screen, I know I've made a new friend. I spend another ten minutes silently watching him juggling the numbers and digging into a plastic bag on his desk for oral gratification. His jaws don't just chew food, they *destroy* food. He's gnawing on bite-sized beer pretzels as if he were chomping on his enemies' fingers, ripping the sinews from the bones and grinding them up with his teeth.

Now *this* is what an evil landlord looks like.

Finally: "Yes, Miss Busharella, so tell me how you're going to help my company."

My company? Pretty big dreams for a guy in a windowless cubicle halfway towards the alley.

"Your company is leaking money from a variety of sources," I say, in my most businesslike voice, pulling out a two-inch file folder with the top three pages on Sullivan and Krauss and the rest gleaned from the recycling bin next to the copy machine.

Grasping the first one authoritatively, I continue, "For start-ers, last month hundreds of nonpayment notices went out to occupants who had in fact paid their rent on time—"

"Our bookkeeping office uses a lot of paralegals," he says, defensively. "Unfortunately, they make a lot of mistakes, but they're not expensive ones, and they certainly cost less than hiring full-time professionals or else we wouldn't do it this way."

"Right," I agree. Fortunately, one of the most useful skills I learned from working in an office was how to hold polite conversations with people *I can't stand*. I primly pluck out another document between my thumb and forefinger. "You had a case in July and August of this year involving a rent strike in Jackson Heights where you spent a great deal of time and money trying to force several evictions by catching the tenants committing illegal acts—by installing security cameras in the hallways, which the tenants promptly disa-bled, by gaining access to apartments under false pretenses—when you could have simply reported them to the police for hiring an unlicensed electrician with a criminal record to steal gas and electricity from the power company after you cut off the utilities."

"And what are you recommending that we should have done under those circumstances?" he says, mixing two meas-ures of snooty and just a dash of defensive this time.

I notice he doesn't deny the illegal entry charges.

"Hire a private investigator and plant them in the build-ing as a tenant—undercover, of course."

He appears to be considering this. Then: "No. We'd have to support an empty apartment in addition to your agency's fees. Too expensive."

"Not compared to what you'll make when you take back the building and raise the rent *for each apartment* from seven thousand a year to sixty thousand a year."

"Hmm. Can I see that?" He reaches for the sheet of paper in my hand.

"I don't have those precise figures with me," I say, dancing the old bureaucratic tango. "This is only a comparison of your typical expenses and what we think we can save you."

Our rush-to-print fact sheet is good enough to survive the two-second glance he gives it.

"So you're saying we could hire a private detective to spy on tenants who might be breaking the law."

"It's perfectly legal."

"And what about getting credit reports on them as well?"

"That's . . . not so legal."

"But it could be done, even if the—the research costs were higher?"

He said it, I didn't. Woohoo! I've been in his office for fifteen minutes and he's already asked me to do something illegal. Oh, I'm going to have fun reeling these guys in.

"Oh, yes," I say, raising my eyebrows ever so slightly and giving him that up-from-under look. "We can do many things."

Like take down Sullivan and Krauss, save the factory squat and maybe sink a couple of dirty cops, too.

I was beginning to wonder where the homeless World War II vet was going to go when it got *really* cold later on, but now I don't have to agonize over it, because the mayor's police are busy arresting the white-haired man for living in a card-board box as part of the city's crackdown on quality-of-life offenses. His crime: Not disappearing like he's supposed to. I didn't have a buck for him anyway, this time. I barely have enough for myself.

I keep walking.

That teenager is out here again, playing the electric blues for dimes and quarters, clutching the guitar like it's the only thing he has in the world. I don't know how he keeps it up in this frostbite-inducing weather. I've got to keep my fingers balled up into fists inside my gloves and thrust deep in my pockets just to retain some heat in my frail extremities—something I learned the hard way in the south central highlands of Ecuador.

The shadows are getting long, but there's still enough daylight for me to revisit the crime scene and get a feel for the layout. Some early birds are out stringing up lights and getting a jump on the holiday season, though I've always noticed that the gaudier the Christmas display outside, the more dysfunctional the family inside.

The clothing store is open, garlands of flickering lights draped around the garish hand-painted border on the picture window, drawing the eye to the specials, but I'm not paying attention to those. I'm observing a recess in the wall wide enough for a couple of guys to hide in, and where you can just see the rear window of the biker bar, so that if someone were standing here smoking cigarettes, an onlooker—even an extremely stoned onlooker—could theoretically see the orange glow from the tip.

There are dozens of cigarette butts strewn across the ground and swept into the corners. It must be a popular place to get out of the wind and light up. The cops probably bagged a bunch of them, if they were doing their jobs. But it's hard to know what's going to be important in a sunny courtroom eight months from now. I'd need a complete team of lab technicians and some divine guidance to find the right one. A gust of wind comes up to kick dirt in my face and remind me just how frustrating it is to be out here looking for a four-day-old angle while nearly everyone around me, it seems, is collecting regular paychecks for staying inside and keeping warm.

And suddenly I feel awfully lonely out here. Lonely, cold, depressed, wondering what Manny felt like, lying there like a specimen wiggling around on the petri dish, the vivisectionists patiently waiting for him to stop kicking so they could get back to work, in a world drained of color. Fortunately, such bleak thoughts are normally limited to my waking hours, but I know myself well enough to know when it's time to get my frozen circuitry back inside a nice, warm house. A big, purple electric church of love where I can thaw out and plug in, the marquee shouting out in hooker-pink neon:

Uncle Sam's Red-Hot Rooming House.

That's right.

This country is also my house. I live in this great big two-hearted house with the four-car garage called America, but I live in a small room in the back where sometimes the spring rain leaks in through the roof and the winter wind howls through the cracks in the walls, and the basement floods in the summertime. But when I try to tell someone that the basement's flooded and the roof is leaking, and ask for a helping hand to fix these minor flaws together, I am usually told that the house rules are to love it or leave it. But I *do* love it. I love my big American house, that's why I want to fix it. The place needs some serious repairs, although I guess a lot of people find it easier to ignore us—even though we all live on the floor below—or simply move to a big, new room that's further away from us, close the door and pretend the cracks in the foundation are *our* problem or, stranger yet, pretend there's nothing wrong. But I want to fix it.

Fix the house. Plug up the holes. Repaint.

Red paint.

Spatters. Blood...

And suddenly it's clear to me that this has nothing to do with the rent strike at his building, that this was about Manny's unique ability to unify public opinion against the landlord's plan to evict the squatters and convert the factory into lofts and condos, and God knows what other projects, which are ultimately worth much more money than that hundred-year-old tenement he called home.

I've been thinking two inches in front of my nose the whole time here, trying to act logically. But as any good organic chemist will tell you, the elusive cyclical shape of the benzene molecule came to the nineteenth-century German experimenter Friedrich Kekulé in the form of a dream—a snake with its tail in its mouth—decisively demonstrating that creative or "irrational" thinking is essential to scientific or "logical" thought. Sometimes, it's when you're supposedly *not* thinking about a problem that the solution comes to you. And it's time to listen to what my intuition is trying to tell me.

An eccentric male detective once noted, somewhat inappropriately by today's standards, that women subconsciously observe a thousand little details, without really being aware of it, eventually adding them up and calling the result intuition. Well, it's time to take the proverbial bull by the horns and act on it.

Hey: If I could predict the future, all I'd need is six numbers between 1 and 54, and the Lotto jackpot is mine.

"So I gather that pickled eels are a delicacy where you come from."

Elisha Kalinin is cooking with great intensity. Manny's former comrade-in-arms at the Metropolitan Council on Housing looks up from the steaming pot she's stirring and shakes her head. "You Americans won't eat anything different, will you?"

Great. Someone finally calls me an American, and she means it as a put-down.

"Well, that depends. Do Russian politicians have to work the rubber Chicken Kiev circuit?"

"I am not a politician. I work with the Met Council, advocating for the poor—"

"I know, that's why I'm here. I want to know your opinion about what happened to Manny Morales."

"Ah yes, that too. You are always giving your opinions on everything. Too many opinions in this country, that's why nothing ever gets done. What kind of justice do you expect in a place where the police have to get a warrant to search your garbage?"

"That's only in New Jersey and D.C., but I guess it's all part of being a democracy."

"Voting in America isn't democracy, it's damage control."

Now who's got opinions?

But Elisha adamantly believes that Manny's death was not about race or drugs, though race never fails to bring out that extra bit of viciousness in people. It was political.

"Manny was killed for stirring up too much trouble for the landlords."

"That's my feeling also," I say.

"So when do we attack?" she asks, picking up a carving knife.

I waggle my finger, cautioning her. "*First* sticks, *then* stones."

It's ringing.

"Yeah? Who? Kaltenbach? Ed Kaltenbach?" says the voice on the other end.

No, Ebinezer Kaltenbach the Third.

"Yes, I'm trying to reach Officer Ed Kaltenbach," I say.

"Can't reach him. He's in a radio car."

"Well, find him for me."

"Say, who is this?"

I cross my fingers. "This is Virginia Jacobs, his ex-wife's emasculative lawyer. I've got a child support agreement that has to be signed before 12:01 A.M. tonight or it's going to cost Officer Kaltenbach another fifteen hundred bucks and I will personally make sure that he knows it's your fault for not finding him quickly enough."

I spend a minute on hold.

"He's responding to an incident in the park between 103rd Street and 41st Avenue."

"I'll be there in five minutes. Tell him to wait for me."

I find him near the swing set, trying to talk a shivering addict into spending the night in a shelter. Well, well, hard-hearted Officer Ed ministering to the homeless. He probably just doesn't want the guy to die on his watch.

"What do you want?" he says to me.

"You know what I want."

And he actually says, "Fugeddaboutit."

"I don't think so, Officer Kaltenbach. You see—ahem—I know about a few of your fellow boys in blue renting themselves out as enforcers for an overeager landlord, something that's going to piss off an awful lot of people when they hear about it."

"They weren't enforcers, they were just—" He stops.

"Doesn't matter what they were, does it, Officer K? Long as you and I both know they were doing *something* that could get their badges turned in. It's the kind of thing I like to see through to the finish, unless I get a little cooperation."

He straightens up, emits a monosyllabic obscenity and tells me to meet him after shift at the Mets Restaurant, Roosevelt and 112th, and a long way from the precinct house.

The junior guitar hero is still working his turf, trying to make some sandwich money by wailing through one of Jimi Hendrix's signature blues progressions, the one from "Red House," I think. Officer Ed is about to stop him—unauthorized street musician, noise violation, panhandling—but I hold up my hand and say, "Wait 'til the end of the solo."

And so we do. Play it, brother.

"Hey, I was just talking to the lieutenant from your old precinct," says Ed, cramming himself into the chair with a groan.

"You mean no one's fragged the lieutenant yet? Gee, I didn't know human will was that strong."

"Can't you say anything good about your old boss?"

"Yeah: He always kept his pencils well-sharpened."

"You are totally unforgiving," he says. "Here, I got some goodies for you."

He hands me a thick manila envelope.

The police reports are worse than I expected. There are a lot of mistakes, missing witnesses, times and locations screwed up. I talked to some people who aren't even in here.

Hey: You want textual accuracy, go read your gas bill.

There's a batch of fuzzy Polaroids and two sets of glossy Crime Scene photos. The photos show what I imagined. Plain black-and-white for placement, triangulation, distances, ratios. Full color for the total feel. Golden brownish stains drying on his jacket and streaking his pale, bruised forehead, hair stiff and floating in the shiny blackening pools of blood spreading out across the sidewalk.

The forensics report is better. Manny fought back valiantly. They've got skin cells under his nails, hair samples between his fingers, and bloodstains on the clothes—and not all of them are his.

"Good," I say out loud.

"Good? What's good about it?"

"Oh, sorry. It's good that we've got some of their blood on him."

"You mean you're glad he messed them up a little before they whacked him. You are a vengeful woman, you know that?"

"I mean we've got enough samples to analyze and run through CODIS." The Combined DNA Index System, courtesy of the FBI. "We might even get a cold hit."

"There's a chance of it. They've got samples from three different suspects."

"There were four," I say. He looks at me. "Well, probably."

The final set of photos is the contents of the evidence bags, since Officer Ed obviously can't sneak the bags themselves out to me. It's mostly garbage from the street, collected without any knowledge of what might prove to be important evidence later. Cigarette butts, a wad of chewing gum, a crushed coffee cup, anything that might leave us a fingerprint to go with the DNA samples.

There's a group of six matching cigarette butts, identified as very recently deposited in the area, possibly the ones that one of the killers smoked. Hey, these guys are good.

I tell Ed, "I've got a witness who saw somebody smoking on the corner, minutes before the attack."

"We've already matched the saliva on those cigarettes to one set of bloodstains on Manny's clothes. It wasn't any of the kids we picked up."

I nod. I keep looking.

"What's this?"

"It's a can of soda."

"I can see that," I say. "What is it?"

"His clothes revealed some stains which were later determined to be this brand of soda, and his prints are on the can. So that's it. His last soda."

"Manny didn't drink soda."

"Everybody drinks soda."

"Not him. He called it 'garbage.'"

"So?"

"So? So maybe one of them was drinking it and he grabbed the can during the fight. I think it's significant and if you don't check it for secondary prints and saliva-borne DNA I'll have to report you."

"To who? Or is it to whom? Look, you know how many partials you get from a can of soda—?"

"All right, just have them run the contents through the mill, and check any saliva against the bloodstains on his clothes. Maybe we can ID the fourth attacker."

"Maybe." He shrugs.

"It could be our best lead. The lead that busts the case wide open." Sure, I'm being a little dramatic, but I'm playing to a tough audience. "And it'll have come from you."

That's the penny that tips the scales.

"All right, I'll give it a shot."

"Great."

"Yeah, this is a great case, all right. Too bad our star witness got smeared across the sidewalk."

CHAPTER FIFTEEN

**If boys destroy life about them in a kind of frenzy, it
is in revenge for their inability to bring forth life.**
—Simone de Beauvoir

"**YOU GUYS** are still up?"

"Well, I—" Stan starts to say.

"Mom, it's Saturday night," says Antonia. "Besides, I was
reading."

"It's one-thirty in the morning!"

"And you must be tired," says Stan. "We'll get a fresh
start tomorrow. Maybe go for a walk in the park, do some
food shopping—"

"Yeah, I'm tired of rice and beans all the time," says Antonia.

"All right," I submit. "Maybe I could make grilled tuna."

"Okay, but doesn't the can get really hot?" asks Stan.

I've got a whole family of comedians to come home to.

"So what were you reading?" I say, sitting down on
Antonia's bed. She shows me the three adult-sized books
that she has finished this week while waiting for me to come
home. I tell her I'm sorry that we don't always spend enough
time together. She describes her favorite story of the three,
and we talk about it, then I tell her that Plato and some other
mighty famous jerks believed that art and literature are
"useless" because they have no actual real world value, no
material economic utility.

"That's stupid," she says, turning over the latest in adolescent fiction and showing me the bar code and price. "Somebody charged us seven ninety-five for this."

"Well, I guess they meant that sitting around reading is not supposed to be a productive use of your time, especially since Plato believed that all artistic representation fails to fully reproduce the world, that it's all a poor copy, like shadows flickering on the wall of a cave, which aren't real. But I suspect that all those predominantly male thinkers were really frightened by the strong emotional responses it provokes in people. Men fear anything they can't control," I say, stroking her hair. "Like you."

That gets a much-needed smile.

Soon I drift off into blackness and dream that I'm extracting a few dozen hard, stiff, calcified cartilaginous eyelids from my nostrils and yards and yards of stringy black entrails from my mouth, but they will not come out—their roots are attached. Glue in my lungs. I pull, gagging, ready to vomit, and they tug on my insides. They won't come out. They're still rooted deep within me. I wake up.

Christ. I've been getting these dreams ever since I nearly died from a lethal dose of poison gas.

I hear sirens in the distance. Typical. There's a bright orange glow on the horizon to the southeast. It takes a moment to realize how dark the rest of the sky is. I look at the clock: 2:31. That's not dawn, that's a fire. Well, you're not getting me out of this bed. That's what we have firefighters for. Only . . . I get up and look out the window again, clearing the sleep from my brain. It's only a couple of blocks south, and one block east, right on the highway. Oh, no.

I'm zipping up my coat as Stan asks, "Filomena? Where are you going?"

Out then, with a rush of cold wind, swiftly covering several hundred feet before the frigidness starts penetrating my personal cocoon of warmth. A fearsome premonition, which worsens as I get closer to the overcrowded house where Camille lives, other possibilities and explanations evaporating as I approach the spot and there it stands, blazing red, engulfed in flames.

The top two floors are gone, sucked into a raging fire-storm. Ambulance crews are pulling in, as neighbors stand around gawking at the stunned survivors shuffling around wrapped in dark gray blankets. I can't see Camille among them. The police keep me back. Reporters are already there:

"Reporting *live—*"

"Thirty people homeless and three dead—"

"Rooms divided with sheets and cardboard, feeding the flames—"

"Kept their cash under the mattress—"

"Bodies coming out now—"

"—helping her down the smoke-filled stairs, but at the last minute she screamed, 'My baby!' and ran back inside. The mother and child both died in the fire."

I lie there motionless. Drained. Staring at the bare walls.

"Shouldn't you be getting up?" Antonia whispers, off in the distance.

Why bother? Lately, God seems to be staying up nights coming up with ways to keep blocking my path with obstacles. How can I stand up to that?

"Filomena?"

What kind of person, what special kind of all-American boy, can attack and kill someone *he's never met*? Here we are sending messages blipping through space to globular clusters somewhere out there beyond Alpha Centauri and meanwhile we can't even communicate with our own children.

"She needs her rest," Stan whispers.

I'm curled up in a fetal position under three blankets,

"Could you pass me a tissue?" I ask.

"When will you feminists stop your demands?" he says, trying to cheer me up. Not this time, I'm afraid. "Fil, come on. What's wrong?"

I'm worthless. I fuck up everything I touch. The world is better off without me.

"Fil?"

"I don't know," I reply, my eyes shimmering with salt water, my voice gliding out across the thinnest ice and crackling, as if I were playing the lead in some sappy melodrama from the 1930s. "I feel so . . . down. Angry. Depressed. Pick one. AC-DC. Emotionally volatile. I'm flip-flopping like when I was pregnant."

Oh, shit. "I'm not pregnant, am I? No, I can't be. I know what that feels like. This is . . . different."

Stan rolls me over and gently prods my abdomen with his firm, restorative fingers. "I recognize your problem." His official diagnosis: "You've got *shpilkes* in the *kishkes*."

"Is that the standard medical terminology?"

"It means your stomach's tied up in knots."

And why shouldn't it be?

It's in the paper. The landlord claims he "didn't know" there were thirty-four people living in the house. There were only supposed to be fifteen, he says, paying $800 a month rent for each apartment, even though they had to run extension cords up from the first floor because there weren't enough outlets on the second and third floors, and the bathroom ceilings were lined with plastic to prevent leaks—and a host of other ills that no legal resident would tolerate. "If it was so deplorable, why didn't they leave?" he asks, not expecting an answer since the people he's discussing were not invited to the press conference. Then he sends the city officials scampering for cover when he produces copies of a notice issued by a city inspector three years ago, citing the building for numerous violations, including illegal apartments, which indicates that the city was fully aware of the conditions in his building and failed to act.

So I guess when he claimed he didn't know, he meant, Sure, I had illegal apartments, but it's the city's fault for letting me get away with it.

"Why don't more people care about this?" I ask.

"For the same reason people eat more jelly donuts than bran muffins," says Stan. I look to him for an explanation. "It's a lot easier to swallow something sweet and fluffy and hollow than something that's good for you but which tastes like sawdust. So football games and talk shows and sit-coms are always going to pull in more viewers than a documentary on the short, unhappy lives of Peruvian coal miners."

Yes, of course. Lives of intense poverty. It explains the apparent lack of emotions from the survivors, so perplexing to the Anglo observers. Whatever the U.S. throws at them, they've seen worse. Charge them $800 a month for a four-by-six cubicle? Hey, these are people who made a forty-nine-day trip from Jucuapa, El Salvador to Houston, Texas by hiking over the mountains at night, canoeing across thundering snake-infested rivers and riding through the desert for thirty-six hours locked inside a hot, dusty panel truck. Burn up their life's savings?—the $4,800 in cash they kept under the mattress because they couldn't open a bank account without a social security number? "I'll just have to work harder," they say. As always. But take away their children's lives? What can you do to replace that? Is the dream of having a family just too much to ask?

Stan turns on the TV, and I get the tail end of some Sunday morning pundit saying, "—More accidents on the ski slopes and white water rafting because as a culture, we're sick of all the safety and luxury we have. We're sated with wealth and opulence—"

"Turn that shit off," I instruct him.

He channel switches rapidly to the Spanish news, where a cop from the 110th Precinct, speaking English under a voiced-over translation, says, "The fire erupted on the stairs, quickly spreading to engulf the stairwell and second-floor landing. The suspect has burns on his hands, arms, and face which are consistent with someone who started such an explosive fire."

Now they show the seventeen-year-old kid with the bicycle I spoke to yesterday being led away in handcuffs as the voiceover explains, "Police and neighbors believe that the suspect deliberately set the fire, hoping to save a man who he had argued with only hours before, and somehow regain his friendship."

So that's it. No crazed skinheads from Bay Ridge. One of our own.

Stan's putting on his coat. "Where are you going?" I ask.

"I'm going to seek out new life and new civilizations."

"Well, could you bring me back some eggs?"

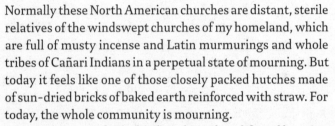

Normally these North American churches are distant, sterile relatives of the windswept churches of my homeland, which are full of musty incense and Latin murmurings and whole tribes of Cañari Indians in a perpetual state of mourning. But today it feels like one of those closely packed hutches made of sun-dried bricks of baked earth reinforced with straw. For today, the whole community is mourning.

Lucas is out of jail, clutching bitterly to life and hugging his old friends, all praying for the souls of Manny, Camille, and so many others. The nuns are leading in a group of blind and disabled parishioners, including some foul-smelling winos from the local shelter. The nuns are all over sixty, I notice. No young women are joining the order these days. What's to join? Asking them to give up materialism is enough. Why does the Church ask them to give up a healthy desire for passion, too? I mean, if you're going to turn your back on all the opulent consumer comforts permanently on display in this society and devote your life to working with the poor and downtrodden, the least they can do is let you have some hot sex once in a while.

But a life of religious devotion is apparently the only permissible way to keep an eye on human misery, now that those wily watchdogs of public decency have taken to cautioning parents that excessive preoccupation with social causes, race relations, environmental issues, and the like is a possible warning sign of drug use among teenagers. Then perhaps they want us to conclude, after all, that religion is indeed the opiate of the masses?

The preliminaries are ended, and the priest sweeps his arms into the sanctified, smoky air over the ass-numbingly hard wooden benches, and delivers a sermon on the homeless.

"You shall not oppress the stranger," he says, conveying God's commandment from the Book of Exodus. "For you know the heart of a stranger, seeing as you were strangers yourselves in the land of Egypt."

I put my arm around Antonia, hugging her to me. This is the most time we've spent together all week.

And now, a word from the Son: "There shall come a time when the King shall say unto you, Come, ye blessed ones, inherit the heavenly kingdom whose foundation I laid for you before the earth began: For I was hungry, and you gave me meat; I was thirsty, and you gave me drink; I was a stranger, and you took me in. Naked, and you clothed me. I was sick, and you visited me; I was in prison, and you came to me."

And I think of Sonny, all alone, in there . . . I haven't visited him, either. My excuse? I'm trying to help him. No, I've *got* to help him. I can't screw this one up. Help me, O God. While he's still alive—could You please tilt the pinball game of life in my favor just one more time?

"Then shall the righteous answer him, saying, Lord, when did we see you hungry, and feed you? Or thirsty, and give you drink? When did we see you a stranger, and take you in? Or naked, and clothed you? And the King shall answer and say unto them, Verily I say unto you, Inasmuch as you have done it unto one of the least of these my brethren, you have done it unto me."

Yes, that's it. Religion is the opiate of the masses.

All the other opiates are illegal.

*

"*¿Cómo vas? ¿Estas bien?*" I ask. How are you? Okay?

"*Sí, estoy mejor,*" says Sonny, his voice echoing around the hollow chamber. Yes, I'm feeling better.

"Are you sure?"

"It's not so bad, if you stay out of trouble. Besides, I pulled a gun on nine cops, so I'm down with the crew there."

It was more like five cops, but I leave it alone.

Poor Sonny. His wife and child just got incinerated and he's looking at a fifteen-year stretch as one more nameless prick among the vast sea of black and *latino* faces populating the state prison on drug charges—ninety-four percent at last count. But to hear him tell it, things have never been rosier.

"I'm as free as I've ever been," he says.

"Okay, Sonny." *Bueno*.

"*Bueno*."

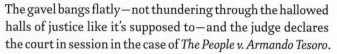

The gavel bangs flatly—not thundering through the hallowed halls of justice like it's supposed to—and the judge declares the court in session in the case of *The People v. Armando Tesoro*.

I've got a ringside seat for this contest right behind my man Armando "Sonny" Tesoro, the bottom half of the bill. My hands are nervous and clammy. I rub them together for warmth.

Lonnie Ambush starts off well, presenting the argument that "the defendant, Mr. Tesoro, was exposed to abnormally high concentrations of elemental mercury, as the blood and urine tests will demonstrate, as a result of his living in a refurbished factory loft where mercury vapor lamps were manufactured for fifty years, and we will introduce expert testimony that will confirm that Mr. Tesoro's blood-mercury levels were high enough to produce the behavioral abnormalities noted by the officers of the New York Police Department. We therefore will be requesting a reduction of the charges of attempted murder, felony gun possession, and resisting arrest based upon our establishment of the fact that the defendant was incapable of behaving rationally at the time of the incident."

Not a bad speech for a guy who thumbtacks his business card to utility poles.

But the assistant district attorney gets up and says that the defendant's alleged inabilities are immaterial, because the mercury was self-administered.

"With the defendant's knowledge, his wife applied between one to four capsules containing approximately nine grams of liquid mercury each near their baby's crib, every day for eleven months, producing an estimated mercury vapor concentration of point-three milligrams per square meter in the area of the crib—an amount that is *six times* the permissible exposure limit for adults. And of course it's even worse for children."

What? How did they know about that?

"How were they able to obtain capsules of pure mercury?" asks the judge.

"Ninety-three percent of the drugstores in the Hispanic communities, where they're known as *botánicas*, sell these capsules for about a dollar-fifty each."

I'm whispering into Lonnie's ear. He gets up: "Your honor, we ask for an adjournment pending the U.S. Environmental Protection Agency's report on the mercury contamination throughout the entire factory complex, which was delayed because of the city's recent action to evict the residents—"

"They're not residents, your honor, they were trespassing on private property," says the ADA.

"Motion for adjournment denied," says the judge.

More whispering.

Lonnie: "Your honor, the Consumer Product Safety Commission was informed of this practice of employing mercury among certain members of the Hispanic community—"

"I heard they swallow it to enhance virility," says the ADA. There's some laughter in the courtroom, and the judge bangs his gavel and calls for order, just like on TV.

"Your honor," Lonnie continues, "this community is exceptionally diverse, and the ethno-religious use of mercury has not been fully documented. But one thing is known: These capsules are sold without warning labels. There was no way for the defendant or his wife to know about the potential hazards of mercury poisoning. The U.S. EPA was asked to consider proposing legislation requiring the use of warning labels on capsules of mercury, but they failed to act. Instead, they deferred to the Consumer Product Safety Commission under Section Six of the Toxic Substances Control Act, and now the CPSC is moving *very slowly* because they're afraid of being accused of interfering with religious practices."

"Counsel, are you suggesting that this is a First Amendment issue?"

"Uh, yes, your honor, we are." That's news to me.

There's a brief moment when it seems like we may actually get a reprieve, or at least an adjournment to the judge's chambers for a dispassionate consideration of the matter. But—

"No. I find in favor of the prosecution." *Slam*.

I tell Sonny that the EPA should be testing the air in the factory sometime later today, and that we can appeal based on their findings. And as they lead him away, he turns and thanks me for helping him.

"*Gracias por todo*," he says. Thanks for everything.

Lonnie's turn to glad-hand me. "Thanks for helping me out back there. You're pretty darn good, you know that? You should partner with me and stick to white-collar crime. The pay's better and it's a lot less dangerous than your basic criminal investigations—"

"Who knew about Camille's use of mercury?" I demand to know.

"The whole *latino* community, apparently," Lonnie concedes.

"Yes, but how did *they* know about it?" I say, pointing to the prosecutors.

But there's only one answer. He lives right upstairs from them. The man who hears everything through the cracks in the floor. Mr. Lucky Charms.

Ted Hocks.

CHAPTER SIXTEEN

At eighteen our convictions are hills from which we look; at forty-five they are caves in which we hide.
—F. Scott Fitzgerald

"**YOU GET** the DNA results yet?" I say into the phone.

"Yeah," Kaltenbach growls, clearing the phlegm from his throat. "It's a fourth suspect all right. So now we got *three* nobodies we gotta find out there, and Giordano sure isn't going to give up their names. His lawyers keep getting in the way. They're real good at that."

"Why are they still pushing Giordano? There's *no way* it's him."

"Yeah, I think everyone's going to figure that out real soon."

"Listen, Ed—"

"Oh, so now I'm Ed?"

"You've been called a helluva lot worse, I bet."

"What about it?"

"While I've got you here, did you ever hear of a guy named Ted Hocks?"

"Who's that? He got a record?"

"I don't know, you tell me."

New York State will not conduct a statewide criminal record search without a signed authorization from the subject. You can imagine how often *that* happens.

"All right, I'll look him up. What's the problem?"

"He's missing. But I think I can find him."

"You're not going to do something dangerous, are you?"

"Heaven forbid."

You'll notice I didn't say, "No."

"I'll let you know as soon as I locate him," I promise.

"Well, God help him, whoever he is, if you're looking for him."

"Gee, thanks, Ed."

"Don't get too cocky about it."

"I believe that's anatomically impossible."

"It's better than what I was going to say."

I hang up and start flipping through my notes for the names of Hocks's clients. Here they are: Cynthia Beck, Gerta Wolf, Monika Heppner, Lisa Otto, Elizabeth Penzler, Genny Vogelfänger. Hmm, I think a pattern is beginning to emerge.

Yeah, it's all a plot by Wagnerian opera singers to take over the world. One major drawback is that our national anthem will be four hours long, a real problem at night games.

Len comes up behind me.

"So, what's the plot so far?" he asks, in his jolly way.

"I'm going to need some backup, that's what."

"Well, as long as it's just stupid, and not dangerous."

"It's not stupid, Len."

He looks at me. I open my mouth, but he cuts me off—

"I just wanted to say that I've been kinda acting like a jerk lately," he says.

"Yeah, I know."

"Oh. Well, anyway, I wanted to let you know that I'm sorry. So . . . I'm sorry."

"Hey, at least you're admitting that you've been acting like a jerk. I like that in a man—but not enough to start stocking up on spermicidal gel or anything."

"Okay."

"Good, now let's nail this bastard."

In your typical action/adventure movie, the bad guy is always a "mad genius"—you know, some renegade former

Green Beret who can make a devastatingly powerful bomb out of a cup of lard and a tube of toothpaste. Hollywood does that to justify the fact that it takes the hero two hours of screen time to catch the sucker. But most criminals are dull-witted people. Stunted. Uncreative. Brutal. They just have a tight bunch of friends, and there are a lot of places to hide in a city this big. Of course, that doesn't make for pulse-quickening drama, but that's how it goes.

We track down the addresses of all of Hocks's women friends, and it is suggested that we make our way through the list, but I say that'll tip him off. We've got to go for the most likely one, the one who was worried about him eating too fast, Ms. Genny "Slow-Down-Honey" Vogelfänger. 43–06 National Street.

I start by going through the garbage.

"Why are we doing this?" Len asks, fingering an empty action figure box.

"Because I'm not sure what he's done yet, or how to handle it, but if we get a bunch of cops sniffing around, it'll only push him deeper underground."

"Oh."

I come up with several empty boxes of sugary-sweet children's cereal, including four boxes of Lucky Charms. Close enough for my purposes.

"So how does this work?" Len asks, walking up the steps with me.

"I go in and talk to him, you stay out here and freeze your ass off."

"This is a punishment, right?"

"It's the right tactic for the job, Len."

"That, too."

I push the button next to the name VOGELFÄNGER.

"Who's there?" His voice, garbled by static. He's actually in.

"It's me, Filomena. You know, Genny's friend."

"She's not here."

"That's okay, I'm just dropping off something for her kids."

He waits a moment, then buzzes me in.

I walk up one flight and knock on the door. Hocks opens it about a foot and stands there blocking the way. He looks completely different from the fuzzy-haired Mr. Natural I first met only a few days ago. He's clean-shaven with a buzzcut and he's wearing a muscle shirt and he looks strong enough to break a pig's neck.

He holds out his hand for the thing I'm supposed to be dropping off. I take out some coupons torn from the empty cereal boxes.

"I know the kids love this brand," I say. "Can I come in?"

"Yeah, sure."

He lets me in and shuts the door. "You want some coffee or something?"

"Sure."

He goes around the low counter to the kitchen area and lifts the lid on a double-chambered espresso pot. He dumps out the dregs, rinses the pot out with warm water, then tries to unscrew the two halves, but they won't budge. They're stuck. He wipes his palms on his pants, grips the two halves of the pot, and shows off the crushing strength of his hands, grunting with exertion, his face and arms turning red except where the tendons rise up white like steel cables connecting the muscle to bone. His low growling crescendos to a Hemingwayesque lion's roar until the top finally twists loose. They must have felt that one all the way over in Africa.

"I didn't know coffee was so much trouble," I say, apologetically.

"Genny always puts this thing on wrong," he complains, dumping out this morning's grounds. "So what'd you want to see her about?"

If I were working with the police, I'd have to read him his rights now. Good thing I'm not working with the police. I put the coupons on the counter.

"Oh, yeah," he says.

I look over at his old TV. He's watching the St. John's game in black-and-white with the sound turned off.

"You like basketball?" I ask.

"Fuck no, I'm waiting for the hockey game."

"Oh." He's washing out the filter. "So you don't like basketball?"

"I hate basketball." He dries it, then reaches into the pantry for a can of pre-ground coffee.

"What do you hate about basketball?"

"The fucking hecklers, man. The beer-talkers. They really get my blood flowing, ya know?" He scoops some coffee into the filter and screws it back into place. Then he fills the pot with water and puts it on the front burner, high.

"What else do you hate?"

"About basketball? What's not to hate? It's all right there in black and white, know what I mean?"

"I thought the only game that was all in black and white is chess."

"Yeah, right. Where've you been? Tennis has gone the same way, too."

"Tennis?'

"Yeah, I remember seeing the U.S. Open at the Tennis Center when I was a kid. Everything was regulation white. But now it's all messed up, you know what I mean?"

"Did your mom take you?"

"Yeah, actually, she did. What do you care about my mom?"

"She taught you how to cook, right? That recipe for lentil soup?"

"A little. I mostly taught myself. She wasn't around much."

"Did she take you to church?"

"Dragged my ass there every fucking Sunday until I was big enough to fight back. It was always so *boring*."

"I know how that feels."

"Yeah?"

"Sure. Same thing happened to me."

"So when'd you stop going?"

"Oh, I haven't gone in . . ." I'm racking my brain, trying to remember how long it's been.

"Yeah, I haven't been since I was fifteen. And there's no way I'm going back. All they do is tell me how fucking *bad* I am, you know? That I'm evil, I'm a sinner, I'm going to Hell if I don't straighten out."

He glares at me. I try smiling. Hey, it's worked in the past.

He goes on: "I mean, I've been fucked over by the system more times than you've had hot meals and they just keep coming back for *more*."

He swats a roach off the wall with surprising ferocity and wipes the remains on the counter. I wait.

"America used to rule the world," he says.

"We're still in the top ten," I say, edging away from the splattered roach.

"If you're not the lead dog, the view never changes."

"Yeah, well I had kind of hoped that humanity had risen above the level of a pack of dogs."

"See now, that's where you're wrong, Miss Fil-o-men-a. And don't look at me like I'm from Mars or something. Everybody says that Mars is the red planet, but it's not red anymore. There's no red in it."

I'm backing away, watching the bodies leap silently across the tiny TV screen. There is something strange about the TV that I hadn't noticed before.

"There's no color left anywhere, man. No color. They've robbed all the shades and hues, man. It's all black-and-white. Are you listening to me?"

I'm looking at the control knobs, which say, quite clearly: CONTRAST COLOR TINT HUE BRIGHTNESS. I turn the knobs, and a rich magenta floods the screen. A little adjusting with the green and blue, and it's a passable color image.

I look at him. "If you've got a color TV, why are you watching everything in black-and-white?"

And he just smiles. A wide, gap-toothed, crazy smile

that tells me he is no longer the kind-but-flaky hippie I thought he was.

Of course. He was exposed to mercury, too.

"Uh, Ted—"

Then he vaults over the counter and lunges through the air at me. I fumble for my gun but he crashes into me and smacks it away, and brings me down in a controlled fall to the floor.

"You fucking two-faced scab!" he growls, red-faced, on the verge of a meltdown. "I'm your worst nightmare."

"No, you're not. I see much worse stuff than you in my nightmares."

He spits on me.

"Thanks for the DNA sample," I say.

He's strong. But he doesn't want a murder just yet. Probably wants to truss me up and have a little fun, first, but I keep wriggling out of his grasp. So he grabs my arms and crosses them over my chest, the better to hold me down with. But this position allows me to thrust the widest part of my forearm into his mouth, and pinch his nose and pull down as hard as I can with my other hand, successfully cutting off his oxygen. He hammers away at me, getting redder in the face, but I can just curl up enough into him by ducking my head between my arms—the ones he's been trying to pin me with— and avoid the worst of it. Soon his body starts rattling, trying to break free of me. Good. His face is turning purple now and he tries to yank himself away. I give him a hard shove off, and crawl as fast as I can over to my gun, but he's up and out the door, sucking air before I can squeeze off a shot.

I chase him down the stairs, but he kicks open the outer door, knocks Lenny off the stoop, and tears off down the avenue. I can't shoot at him, it's a public street. So I take off after him, keeping him in sight for about a block and a half before I misjudge the speed and direction of a woman wheeling a stroller out of a Korean grocery store and collide with a few bushels of kale, nearly flipping over and landing on my feet like a freaking cat, but then I slip on the wet green leaves and smack my head on the sidewalk. Fortunately, I've got a winter hat on, but as I try to sit up, my head start swimming with momentary disequilibrium.

In a moment, Len's shape towers over me, upside down, offering me his hand.

"Shouldn't we be calling the cops now?" he says.

"Man, don't you know that your first line of defense is to walk away?" says Ed Kaltenbach.

"It wasn't an option," I say, adjusting the ice pack on my head. We're in the back of his squad car and everybody's listening to me, for a change.

"Going up against this guy by yourself is about as smart as picking a fight at a Kung-Fu tournament."

"Yeah, he seemed sort of sociopathic in a fairly major way," I admit, waiting for the throbbing to go down.

"That's not the half of it," says Kaltenbach. "I got the results of the criminal check on this Hocks guy. He's got six warrants out for a series of bank robberies."

"*Armed* robberies?"

"No, he's never been violent."

"Until today."

"Well, that's the thing. Bank robbery's a pretty ballsy scam, all things considered, so him and three other gutless losers hit on the idea of just backing a pickup truck up to an ATM machine, hooking up some chains and hauling the whole freaking thing away. No guns, no hysterical victims and a much bigger payoff—you know, your average bank robber only gets away with three or four thousand at a time. But even some chickenshit ATM can have fifteen, twenty thousand in it. I've heard of forty."

Len whistles appreciatively.

"So he's wanted on six counts of grand larceny?" I ask.

"He's still a freaking mutt," says Len. "He'll get picked up for rolling an old lady, the cops'll see the outstanding warrants and book him on that, too."

"Wait 'til the other shoe drops, kid," says Kaltenbach. "Two of his partners have disappeared in the last month."

That makes our ears widen.

Kaltenbach nods. "Yeah. I think this guy's gone over the edge."

Actually, I felt more like I was watching one of those hapless cartoon characters who's gone off the edge, standing on nothing and flapping his arms, but who hasn't started falling yet.

"We're checking that list of all his other girlfriends," he says. "Guy had quite a harem going for him, too. This one—this Genny Vogelfänger—she's a real beaut. We tell her we think her boyfriend may have beat a few guys to death and she says no, it couldn't be him, he once started crying when he accidentally ran over a cat."

"It could be true," I say.

"Man, with eyes like hers, she should be doing better than waiting on tables for three bucks an hour."

"Yeah, she could be waiting on tables for *four* bucks an hour."

I lie back and think about Ted Hocks and his twisted way of thinking, some of which was clearly a part of him before all this, but that extra push, that difference between being *at* the edge and going *over* the edge—it must have come from residual mercury vapor. How else do you transform a goofy hippie anarchist into the mad hatter who attacked me? Or was that hippie stuff all an act? Is everyone in that building going slightly bonkers? Camille didn't seem fully rational to me, either, towards the end. Was Hocks a standard low-life career criminal as Kaltenbach says, but nonviolent until he moved into the factory? I don't know, but it makes sense if all this time he was on mercury, not Mars, and what I thought was youthful exuberance could have been the beginnings of chemically induced madness and I just didn't take the time to notice it.

Of course it doesn't take much to push someone over the edge who already subscribes to that crazy kind of gun-of-the-month-club mentality, full of paranoid scenarios like:

What if you wake up with your assailant on top of you and you can't get to your rifle? Answer: You need to keep a semi-automatic pistol under your pillow. When the truth is, if you wake up with an assailant on top of you, *you're fucked*. You're lucky if he lets you keep breathing.

Oh sure, I've got this fantasy of always being ready, of being able to hear a sound downstairs and come out loudly cocking back on a short-barreled shotgun, but ninety-nine percent of the time it's the cat or your teenage daughter trying to sneak back in after a late night out and you end up blowing a hole in her stomach.

Action heroes never shoot the wrong guy. And people believe that shit.

Kaltenbach comes back and says they've looked everywhere that makes sense and they haven't found any sign of Hocks.

"Then look somewhere that doesn't make sense," I say. "He had no money, no weapons, and he was wearing a T-shirt in twenty-degree weather. He had to get inside fast, somewhere no one would notice him, where he could stay warm and think things through, assuming he's still capable of that."

Kaltenbach gets on the horn and says the units should check the Plaza movie theater on 103rd Street and the Universal Church of God on Roosevelt Avenue.

"He could also be hiding in the back room of any of a hundred stores," Kaltenbach says to no one in particular.

I say no.

"Why not?"

"Because every store on the avenue is owned by an enemy of the white race, the way he sees it. He'd sooner dive down the sewer than hide behind some shady *portorriqueño*."

"You're saying we should look in the sewer?"

"No, I'm thinking more along the lines of a secluded room somewhere in the abandoned factory."

"He can't get in. There's two cops on every entrance."

"Yeah, but the EPA is going to be in and out all day testing the facility for mercury poisoning."

"Hmm. Could be," he says. "You stay here."

"The hell I will."

Who says shadows aren't real? From where I'm crouching they are *plenty* real. Elongated shadows shredded by lumbering machinery and lanterns moving among the ghostly ruins, casting nightmarish shapes across the vaulted ceiling of the hollowed-out factory floor. The EPA tears up the planks and finds shiny liquid mercury flowing freely between the pillars and the soil. And we pick our way among them like souls on our way to Purgatory, passing through one of the colder rooms in Hell for a taste of what we've just barely missed becoming ourselves.

Len's flipping over chairs and tables just to let off tension, but what do you expect? Since this isn't a bit like sitting at a terminal electronically tracking cybercriminals.

I have to admit I'm jumping at shadows myself, and, as I said, there are a lot of shadows down here. I'm creeping up on a recess in the wall when some bizarre synchronization of the movement of twenty different flashlights animates the timbers and sends them shimmying towards me, alive and breathing thickly.

Get a grip, girl. He's just a man.

Yeah, a man who could jump out and slit my throat at any moment.

He may not even be in here. If I were him, I'd be trying to find somewhere warm, and there's no such place in this chilly shell of a building.

Time to put myself in the mindset of a pumped-up, desperate psycho.

I'd seek the high ground. Or—its opposite.

We each choose a path and explore the lower level of catacomb-like rooms, whose dark walls shine with mineral deposits nearly a century old.

"We already checked that way," says a commanding male voice. "It's clean."

Still I keep following a sloping trail across the laundry room and through a low doorway until I reach the edge of a thin stream that probably flows down to join the great, black river of forgetfulness. *Drip. Drip. Drip*.

But the water has been shut off for three days.

I follow the sound of the drips to a puddle of water on the floor. I tip my flashlight up and see several bags of ammonium nitrate, which must have been frozen before and are now thawing. Holy—

There's a flicker of movement to my right and I spin around. It's him, uncoiling from inside a gutted old washer-dryer, playing with a stun-gun as if he's fascinated by the arcs lighting up his face with an unearthly blue-green glow.

"What are you doing here? What's all this stuff?" I say, indicating the soggy sacks.

"A little arson goes a long way," he answers.

"Ted, don't do this. You have your whole life before you. Of course, the way you're going that's only about ten minutes."

"Same goes for you, *muchacha*."

I try to reason with him and explain that I can get the charges against him reduced due to temporary insanity caused by mercury poisoning, and he laughs at me.

"Are you kidding me?"

He starts coming towards me, zapping the fetid air with his steadily weakening lightning bolts. But this time I've got a second to get the gun out. I wish I could tell you we have one of those bad-guy-to-good-guy why-I-did-it-all scenes, but instead he just lunges at me and I swing the gun at his head. It's only a two-inch barrel and it doesn't stop him much. He grabs the gun with one hand and jabs me with the stun-gun. Lucky for me it's an older model that needs a couple of seconds to recharge, so I pull away from it and shatter the useless flashlight against his cranium. He winces like he's been hit with a rubber band and jabs me again, harder. And suddenly ten thousand wasps are dancing the tarantella on my nervous system and my trigger finger spasms and the gun goes off right next to his ear, again and again.

I manage to slam my left elbow down and knock the stun-gun loose for a second, then I stomp on his metatarsals and fire off another shot.

He forgets about the stun-gun and grabs my gun hand with both of his massive paws. It's normally pretty hard to wrest a short-barreled revolver away from someone, but he's got huge hands and a lot of anger.

My words come out a strangled hiss: "Christ, how much of that stuff did you breathe?" And I squeeze off another shot into the darkness around us just to let the rest of the world know where we are.

Then he wrenches the gun away from me and holds it up with a roar of triumph, and I turn and run, slamming the flimsy door behind me.

"Think this door can stop me?" he shouts, firing my last round through the diseased wood at me. Then I hear him clicking it and throwing it away in disgust while I rush to the shelf over the washing machine, hoping the stuff's still there, hoping there's still time before he triggers the explosion. Yes. I grab two half-gallon jugs, one of ammonia, one of bleach, and crouch down by the door and start emptying the ammonia through the crack under the door. It flows freely into the next room.

"What the hell—?" he says, sloshing around inside. Then: "Ha! You're going to have to do better than that, girl!"

I get out my handkerchief, cover my nose and start dumping out the chlorine bleach. Immediately the smoky tendrils of deadly nitrogen trichloride vapors start rising up. I lean as far away as I can, only getting a tiny bit, but Hocks's little ante-room is turning into a gas chamber.

"Damn you!" he curses. "What the fuck—arrgh! When I get my hands on you, you fucking—!"

I hear his keys jangling. Shouts and thunderous footsteps come running towards me, but they're not here yet.

"Damn it! What the—? Fucking—!"

Hocks is trying to unlock the door with a master key.

"They changed the locks, Ted," I tell him.

"*Arrrrrghch!*" He rattles the door, pounding against it, then takes a few steps back, launches himself, and finally bursts through and falls to the ground, clutching the dirt and gagging as the police crews arrive, guns drawn.

I alert everybody. "We better get out of here, guys, that room's full of poison gas."

Kaltenbach surveys the scene and remarks, "Jeez, I want you on my side in the next war."

CHAPTER SEVENTEEN

**If they love they know not why, they
hate upon no better a ground.**
—Shakespeare, *Coriolanus*

"**YOU FIND OUT** where all that ammonium nitrate came from?" I ask.

"He had the stuff stored there, somehow," says Kaltenbach, pouring himself a cup of bad precinct house coffee and sipping it with me outside the interrogation room.

He's been with Hocks all afternoon, and he goes back in for more. Maybe I'm not so surprised when Hocks's DNA matches the fourth suspect's, but we're all really surprised when he confesses to the killing of Manny Morales.

"You probably just meant to beat him up, right?" Kaltenbach questions him.

Hocks chuckles to himself. "We broke him, man. He was lying there, all torn up and bloody, and we just kept on hitting him until *he begged us* to kill him and get it over with."

"Who hired you?"

"Nobody."

"Don't give me that crap. Make it easy on yourself. Who hired you?"

He chuckles again and says, "Ain't nobody need to hire me to ice a freakin' spic."

Outside the door, I cringe. That's not him talking, that's

the poison talking. And I resolve to get it out of him during the trial. His brain should be working better by then.

Hocks is the only match they've got, but he won't give up the other three names no matter what kind of deal they offer him. And none of the samples fit Vinnie Giordano, who gets released.

I get a call about it that afternoon at the office.

"Are you Miss Filomena Buscarsela?"

"Yes."

"Well, listen up good. I got a message from Mr. Giordano's employer."

I stiffen reflexively.

"He heard you got Vinnie off the hook, and he's grateful for it and he don't like owing anybody any favors."

"So he'd like to know if there's a favor I need right now?" With all that comes with it, no doubt.

"Yeah."

Sure: Push through my PI's license in three days.

"Okay," I answer. "As a favor, I'd like him to owe me that favor. I don't know when I'm going to need to collect. Maybe never."

"Okay, I'll tell him."

"Thanks."

"I knew you were smart."

Davis and Abby both come out of their offices and congratulate me on helping the police solve a murder. Damn good PR for the firm. Then it's right back to business as usual. But at least I showed them I could serve the *latino* community *and* bring in some big-ticket clients.

Later on I'm taking a break, reading about a company in Texas that's been found guilty of selling cheap pesticides instead of medically approved chemicals for disinfecting toothbrushes used by Native American kids in a Head Start program somewhere out west, when Katwona interrupts me, announcing, "Fil, there's someone here to see you."

It's Ed. "You want to take a ride with me?"

"Sure. It'll be good to get out in the open air again."

Nothing like having a uniformed cop come by the office to enhance your reputation as a law enforcement specialist.

"Where are we going?" I ask.

He takes me across the street to the courthouse to watch Hocks go before the judge. It's only a pre-trial hearing, but because of the sensational nature of the case, a courtroom artist is there, sketching Hocks's likeness in pencil and pastels. At one point Hocks leans over, studies his own portrait and says, "Oh, that's coming out good." So he's an art critic, too. I wonder what he did to the last guy who sketched him.

Hocks is being transferred upstate to await trial in a maximum security prison, and Kaltenbach is one of the lucky cops who was ordered to escort the police van to the city line. He invites me to ride with him.

We're halfway across the Whitestone Bridge, complaining about the slow traffic, when somebody kicks through the rear window of the van about twenty feet in front of us.

"Jesus—!"

"Get on the radio!"

But it's too late. Hocks reaches out and yanks open the door, jumps out as the van screams to a halt, and, shackled hand and foot, he hops to the railing and leaps over it into the East River 150 feet below.

The autopsy reveals he had stashed a handcuff key and half a razor blade up either side of his nose. And there was a note in his pocket on which he had scrawled, with an artist's pencil, the words, "I WIN."

"I don't understand," says Ed. "Such a healthy guy. He didn't even smoke."

"One of his cronies sure did."

"Yeah, but which one?"

We never found out.

So that's it. With God's help, I have survived one more trip through the labyrinth. And I've finally gotten a little time to spend at home without being too tired for tiddly-winks.

Antonia curls up next to me and asks me to tell her a funny story about when she was little. It takes me a while to think of something, but then I remember the time she was four or five and she wanted to see her friend Lila, and I said, "Lila's in India," so she said, "I want to go to India, too," and I said, "It takes a lot of money," and she said, "I have money," and pointed to her jar of pennies, which probably had about two dollars in it.

I guess it's not as funny as it was at the time.

Then she asks me, "What does breast milk taste like?"

And I answer, "It's sweet, honey. It's very sweet."

"Is that why we all like sweets so much?"

"I guess so."

I'm cheerfully making a real meal for my growing girl when Sherry drops by with a copy of her group's CD, and shows me the review of a play she's doing the lights for. It reads, "Sparks fly during the scene between Raskolnikov and Sonia."

"Sparks fly?" I ask her.

"Yeah, we never could fix that loose dimmer plug."

The steel ball swings through the crisp, clean air and cracks the eggshell surface of the factory six stories above the roped-off sidewalk. Cinder blocks crumble and cave, and hundred-year-old dust rises from the gaping hole. Then the ball swings slowly away and prepares to smite the towering edifice again.

"Couldn't you just dynamite it?" asks Georgio.

"You don't dynamite a building full of liquid mercury," Gina tells him. "You've got to take it apart brick-by-brick."

Georgio and Lucas were lucky, Gina discovered, escaping the worst because they lived on the highest floor over what used to be the offices, where there was far less contamination than in other parts of the building.

"Sorta makes me feel like if we can't have the house, no one can," says Georgio. "Too bad."

"Yeah. It's too bad."

He contemplates the ruin, and says, "Not much of a happy ending, is it?"

"We did okay," says Gina. "We just didn't win the big one. It takes time."

"Spoken like a true compromiser," I say.

"Hey: I'm a government employee," she explains.

So what else is new in the world of environmental crusaders? Gina tells me she's developing a soil screening guidance system that she hopes will become standard throughout the industry, supplying the "acceptable" levels of contamination for 110 chemicals based on a one-in-a-million chance of excess cancer risk for the individual exposed, and procedures to follow for various different surface and subsurface soil conditions because, as she says, "There are sites we haven't even found yet."

Well, isn't that a cheery thought.

She and I congratulate each other on the success of our respective cases, but so far no promotions are in the offing for either of us.

So the EPA proves that the factory building has been contaminated by mercury vapor for years, slowly poisoning the occupants and increasing the risk of violent mood swings and even brain damage. But the city is arguing that they were never legal tenants, so the Tesoro case is still pending.

Sorry to leave you hanging, but that's how life is sometimes.

ACKNOWLEDGMENTS

Thanks as always to Alison Hess of the U.S. EPA for digging the dirt; to Abe Bunks, Roy Coakley, Susan T. Kluewer, John Westermann, and Steve Wishnia for technical advice on legal and police procedure; to Kelley Ragland, the original editor of this novel, for letting me get away with it; and to everyone at PM Press for giving this series a new home.

"All that Glitters" first appeared in *Alfred Hitchcock's Mystery Magazine* (June 2004, thanks to their *fa-a-abulous* editor, Linda Landrigan). I had a lot of fun writing this one because first, I had the basic idea kicking around in my head for more than a decade thanks to my "mole" at the U.S. EPA (it's based on a documented case), and also because it represents a transitional moment for me, from my Ecuadorian female detective (and cross-gendered alter ego) to Jewish-themed tales, which culminated in the novel that I was born to write, *The Fifth Servant*. Enjoy!

ALL THAT GLITTERS

NO ONE LIES ON THEIR DEATHBED and says, "I should have watched more television."

My great Aunt Celia never saw a television until she came down from the Ecuadorian highlands in the mid-1970s. She sat in our unheated home, wrapped in her stiff woolen shawl, the room dark except for the glowing glass screen before us, as the newsreaders told us how a flooded section of highway had given way and sent a busload of *cristianos* plunging into a ravine. She watch silently, then cautiously leaned over to me and whispered,

"Can they see us?"

I tried to explain that they couldn't.

"But they're looking right at us."

Then one day she left the mud-walled village and followed my wayward cousins to the U.S., where she beheld many more wonders, until, after eighty-four summers of service, that wondrous heart stopped beating.

That was three days ago, and the black-bordered card staring up at me from between the shaggy piles of white papers on my desk informs me that the funeral mass is at 2:00 P.M. today at Our Lady of Sorrows in Corona, followed by burial services at St. Mary's Cemetery in a neighborhood some overconfident pioneers were audacious enough to name Utopia.

I'm remembering the special flavors of Aunt Celia's kitchen, especially her *sopa de pollo*, which had a unique taste that is still unmatched despite all my attempts to reproduce it. I'm lost in a hazy reverie of olfactory sensations when the third button on my phone starts blinking and my boss hails me from the corner office.

"Fil, pick up!"

"Sure, whadaya got for me, Chip?"

"I'm trying to reach that customs guy in Puerto Rico and nobody in the freaking place speaks any English," Chip shouts back at me.

"Sure they do. They're probably just playing with you. *¿Alo?*"

"*¿Sí? ¿Con quién hablo?*" says the guy. I can hear metallic banging in the background, and I can just picture the guy wearing oil-stained coveralls, holding a socket wrench in his hand.

I tell him that I'm calling from Davis & Brown Investigations in New York, and that we're looking for a customs agent named Wilson Ortega.

"You got the wrong number," he tells me in Spanish. "This is a garage."

I thank him, hang up, and go tell Chip.

"Must be a chop shop," he says, not realizing how many car repair shops there are in San Juan.

"Just sounded like a garage to me, Chip. But you never know," I add, wondering if there's a subtle prejudice behind his response.

But Chip is already punching the hold button: "Mr. Theodorakis? My Spanish-speaking investigator is with me and she says you were given the wrong number," he says, crossing the number off his heavily scribbled legal pad with a thick pencil and waving me out of the office.

I stare at the papers on my desk for a few blank moments,

trying to recover the special smells of my great aunt's kitchen. But they are gone, dissipated by the air currents of time and responsibilities. I start going through the easy pile, mechanically putting papers in the right folders, filing reports where they belong and recycling old memos, and wondering if anyone else can hear the giant *whooooshing* sound as all the joy of being alive gets sucked out of me, leaving an icy whirlpool of survivor's guilt rushing through my chest.

I'm thinking that in Ecuador, cats have seven lives, and here they have nine—so where I come from, even the *cats* have it harder—when I look up and see a man standing a few feet in front of my desk. He's in his mid-fifties, with waxy skin sagging like sallow candle drippings and heavy bags of sleeplessness hanging from his eyes. He's wearing a long, dark winter coat and a thick fedora with a trace of shiny black yarmulke showing underneath.

"Miss Buscarsela?"

"Yes." I don't correct him with a "Ms."

"I'm Louis Koppelman. The architect. Mr. Davis said that you would help me."

"Nice to meet you, Mr. Koppelman." I extend my hand towards him, where it hangs for a second, then I divert it to the seat. "Sit down and take your coat off."

He looks the chair over before lowering himself into it with a tired sigh, and takes his hat off, revealing a wavy mat of black hair and a *yarmulke* clipped in place.

"It's my mother," he says.

"Wait, I need to get the details—" I say, reaching for a pad and pen.

"She's dead."

Two syllables that stop the clock in its tracks.

"I'm sorry to hear that."

"Are you? Really?"

"Yes. There's no way to fill a hole like that."

He can hear the ring of genuine emotion in my voice, I guess, because he stops contemplating the void just beyond my left shoulder and makes eye contact.

"Yes. That's it," he agrees. "A hole that will never be filled."

I nod. Nothing else gets said for a few seconds.

"Go on," I say. "Tell me about your problem."

"All right. Her name—my mother's name—was Laura Koppelman."

I write this down.

"She died of cancer. It started in her throat and spread to her chest. In less than three months, she was gone. Just like that."

"I bet she had a helluva good recipe for chicken soup, too."

He raises an eyebrow at my non-businesslike comment. Then he nods. "Yes, she put something special in it. I always thought it was the fresh dill, but I can't get it to come out the same way, not like hers—"

He stops as if one more word will crack open the thin layer of ice damming up his tears. I feel a surge of wetness rise to the rims of my eyes, as well.

I'm the one who finds my voice first. "So—um—what can I do for you as a private investigator?"

"Where do I start? My mother gave everything to us. And we're a big family. There's me, my three brothers and two sisters. She never worked a day outside the home when we were kids. Very traditional. But after we went to college and the girls got married off, she decided to go out and get a job. Something that, you know, she enjoyed doing. With a lot of stylish people coming and going. So she took a job in the fur trade, then after six months she switched to the jewelry business. She worked a long time for the same establishment."

"How many years?" I ask.

"Eighteen years. They gave her a pair of diamond ear-rings and a gold necklace as a retirement present."

"Wish I had a boss like that."

"No, you don't. He was also a chain-smoker who refused to ventilate the place properly."

Ah. I think I see where this is going.

"So you want us to find evidence suggesting that unhealthy work conditions contributed to her demise—"

He eyes me coldly as I slip into unfeeling bureaucratese.

I correct myself: "That second-hand smoke may have caused her death."

"Yes. It won't bring her back. But . . ."

"I understand. Where did she work?"

"Czernowitz Jewelers. In the diamond district. You know, West 47th Street?"

"Yes, I've heard of it, but my boyfriend tells me it's just a rumor."

Chip wants me to hop the subway into Manhattan right away, but I don't feel like beating the bricks along West 47th Street in this chilly weather.

"Too freaking bad," is his answer.

"Why me? Why don't you send Mitchell or Hrabowski?"

"Because you're the one with the Jewish boyfriend, remember?"

"So that makes me an expert on the diamond trade?"

"Get dispensation from the Pope and do it," comes the order.

Five minutes later I'm calling Dr. Stanley "my Jewish boyfriend" Wrenchowski at LIJ Hospital and asking him what I have to do to pass for an upper-middle-class Orthodox housewife.

"Well, first of all, I wouldn't go all the way to Orthodox, Fil. You better stick with Conservative."

"Why?"

"Because I don't think you could pull off Orthodox."

"I'm not going there for a ritual bath, Stan, I'm just going to have a look at the place. What's the matter? Don't you trust my role-playing skills?"

"Okay, okay. You're a master of disguise. But if you're going to try to pass as Orthodox, remember—you can't touch any male over thirteen. Or sing. Or show your hair."

"Why not?"

"Because it's erotic."

"Oh yeah, my hair's so charged with erotic power the hairband hasn't been made that can contain its frizziness."

"Stop. You're making me crazy."

"Stan, this is not a good time. Just help me out here. What's a good name for a Jewish gal?"

"With your coloring, you should try for something Sephardic. How about Hadassah?"

"Hadassah?"

"Sure. Senator Lieberman's wife is named Hadassah."

"What's her sister's name? American Jewish Congress?"

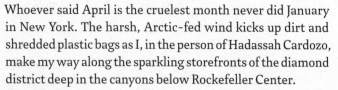

Whoever said April is the cruelest month never did January in New York. The harsh, Arctic-fed wind kicks up dirt and shredded plastic bags as I, in the person of Hadassah Cardozo, make my way along the sparkling storefronts of the diamond district deep in the canyons below Rockefeller Center.

All that glitter cuts through the cold air, refracting the midwinter sun into a thousand laser-like darts of rainbow-colored light. Since modern anthropologists have convincingly demonstrated that all humans, from Iceland to Tasmania, originally came from Africa, you've got to ask yourself—*why on earth did we leave*? A nice African savannah sounds pretty good right about now, especially after watching the high-fashioned ladies stepping out of double-parked limos and strutting around in clothes so shiny and asymmetrical and useless they look like they were designed by Edith Head's brother, Dick. This season's fashion statement seems to be: We'll go to our lonely deaths—but looking *really* sharp.

I pass the lone antiquarian bookstore on a block dedicated to diamonds, with the twenty-four-hour picture frame shop on the second floor. Screw the company, I'm doing some window shopping. That's what they get for sending me out here on a day like this.

Looking at the high-priced hardcovers in the store window reminds me of a case a few months ago where I had to punk out a sleazy book dealer who was passing off forged goods as mint condition rarities. Let me just say, as a public service, that you should be very suspicious of anyone who tells you that they have a signed first edition of Kafka's *The Trial*.

I move on, strolling past a window display that's got to cost a million dollars a foot. Yard after yard of diamond-studded Stars of David, menorahs, heart-shaped pendants, medallions, eye-in-the-palm fertility and Chai symbols, even a humidity monitor in the corner to make sure all that ice stays nice and fresh.

As I watch all these well-to-do Jewish men servicing the top one percent of society's economic ladder, an uncomfortable thought edges its way into my psyche. I know that this is an unrepresentative sample, but the way they all look to me, with their long curly black beards and their white shirts, black pants, black vests, and black yarmulkes, dressed in the uniform of perpetual mourning for their exile from the Promised Land, I can't help thinking that they all look like escapees from the Museum of Ethnic Stereotypes. Economically powerful, weirdly dressed Jews, big noses and all, as if drawn from some Nazi-era propaganda posters.

Of course, the stereotype of the *latino* as a slick-haired, leather-jacketed, switchblade-toting *vato* from East L.A. is alive and well in reality and on TV, but nobody ever dedicated a nation's total resources to annihilating us.

I guess I shouldn't complain. When put in that perspective, things are good. There are no hordes of Cossacks swarming across eastern Suffolk County, burning houses and raping women as they head towards the city, but—*ach*—troubles we have enough, I think to myself as I start to get into character.

I've got a pinhole-lens video camera concealed in a pager at waist level. I'd rather work with eye-level video, which gives me a lot more control over what gets recorded. Belt-buckle-mounted units tend to give you a shaky, silkworm's-eye-view of things, but the eyeglass and tie clip units were signed out on priority cases and I have to be back in Queens by 2:00 P.M.

I activate the recording unit, tell the wind what day and time it is, pass three more glistening storefronts, and push open the cold metal door to Czernowitz Jewelers.

I don't need a portable air sampler to tell me the place is full of carcinogens. The elderly man behind the counter has a three-inch cigar parked in his mouth and a patch of ash spotting his black vest. The ashtray on the glass counter overflows with dead butts like a lifeboat full of shipwrecked survivors, and a thick curtain of blue-gray smoke hangs a foot below the low ceiling, its shadowy wisps hungrily clawing for my tender air sacs.

Otherwise, the layout is as sterile as a suburban doctor's office—and actually, a blood pressure monitor wouldn't be a bad idea in here. The old guy's silk-embroidered shirt barely engulfs the wiggling fat of his arms as he strains, bending slightly to lift a tray of sparkling diamond rings from the thigh-level shelf in the primary display case. He gently places the tray in front of two well-dressed women, and turns to cough up something far less glamorous into a plastic-lined wastebasket on the floor.

I aim the camera at the scene for a few minutes while the two women discuss the aesthetic merits of beryl versus amethyst accents. A group of out-of-towners come in and gape at the wall-to-wall tinsel. They want to look at the low-end silver chains and pendants with tiny diamond inlays. Three of them leave before the man behind the counter turns to me, his face jovial and open. "How may I help you?"

"Thanks, I'm just looking. Besides, you're busy."

"Busy? I'm busy in diamonds like Picasso was busy with paint. Maybe some nice earrings?" he says, turning back to the two women, but they're not ready to make the leap.

Some homies in dark North Face jackets wander in to check out the goods, smiling at the brightly cut facets. They get the same courteous treatment I got.

It's time to go. I've got enough tape of this guy smoking and coughing up loogies to help make my client's case. I'm about to leave, when I realize that it's not enough to show this guy chomping on the end of a dead stogie. This is about a woman's life. I want to see how soon he lights another.

He's got his own version of a Wall of Fame going in the narrow space between two upright display cases. There are some interesting discoveries among them, like Lisa Kudrow and Goldie Hawn, for instance. But Moshe Dayan is Jewish? Who knew?

"See ya later, Pops," says one of the homies, as they bounce out the door, and the tourists see their chance to bail and grab it.

"Come back soon," the old man calls after them. "Looking is free."

He turns to me again. Time to try out my rudimentary Yiddish.

"*Vos makht ir, reb Czernovitz?*"

"*Men hot parnose,*" he says. "Business could be better, and you speak with a German accent, *chaverte.*"

"Oh, really? Well, that's because my parents spoke Ladino. I'm only just learning Yiddish from my boyfriend." Brilliant save. Applause from the back bench.

"Well, he's obviously Americanized," he declares, accurately.

"But you are Mr. Czernowitz?" I repeat for the benefit of the tape.

"*Dos bin ikh,*" he says, spreading his hands a little. "And this boyfriend of yours? Is he ready for a diamond ring yet?"

I smile and avert my eyes.

"Ahh," he says, happily chalking up another point on an invisible tradesman's chart. "I can always tell."

I look across the wide, bustling street and catch a glimpse of the twenty-four-hour frame shop in a store window.

"When was the last time you needed a picture framed at 3:00 A.M.?" I say to myself as much as to him.

"This is the city that never sleeps," he says with an upbeat intonation that's strictly for the tourist trade. "Except for us, right?"

I look at him.

"You mean closing early for *shabbes*?"

"Of course, *shabbes*. And *Erev Tu B'Shevat*."

Erev Tu B'Shevat. Yes, this is a test. Christ, I know all of the big ones—Pesach, Sukkoth, Rosh Hashanah, and the rest—but *Erev Tu B'Shevat*? What the heck is that?

"Right," I say, blankly.

He's all smiles. Then he lights another cheroot and—*bingo*—I get my money shot.

"What's *Erev Tu B'Shevat*?"

"The eve of *Tu B'Shevat*," Stan says.

"Right. What's *Tu B'Shevat*?"

"I have no freaking idea."

We're driving through the part of Queens that's nothing but power plants and cemeteries.

"Some source for all things Jewish you turned out to be," I say.

"Give me a break, Fil. You know my parents raised me on classic routines from the comedy team of Marx and Engels. That diamond district We Are The Chosen People thing is about as far from my edge of the Jewish universe as you can get. We're not all one type."

"I know that."

"You know where people get that idea from?"

I'm about to say, Sure, anti-Semitic propaganda—

"It's all Captain Kirk's fault."

"Come on, Stan. Every trekkie knows that Kirk and Spock are Jewish."

"Look, I know you're a fan, but you've got to admit that your beloved *Star Trek* has been projecting subtle racial stereotypes for years. Think about it. All those alien species that have one defining trait—you know, the Vulcans are all logical and unemotional, the Ferengi are all profit-driven wheeler-dealers—"

"I see what you mean. They all have one identifying racial characteristic."

"Like there's no gay Klingons who aren't into that whole warrior thing. Anyway, it's just that guys like that jeweler are much more visible than I am—"

"Watch the traffic cones."

"I see them. I mean, as far as I'm concerned, Jesus was a radical socialist rabbi from upper Judea who challenged the system and died for his beliefs. It wouldn't be the first time it's happened. But you guys had to go spreading His word across the whole damn continent."

"It pays to advertise."

"It sure does. I mean, how come you always have all these weirdos claiming to be Jesus—Charles Manson, David Koresh—but nobody ever claims to be Moses? That's because he was too human, he made real mistakes. He killed a man in anger and ran away because he couldn't face the consequences. Then he tried to back out of his obligations to the Lord. He even pissed off his family by marrying a dark-skinned Kushite woman."

"So you're saying that the image of Jesus as perfect actually makes it easier for false prophets to convince gullible people that they're Him."

"It's not so weird, Fil. You know how criminals think: The punishment's the same for stealing a couple thousand dollars as it is for stealing a couple million, so you might as well go for the big money. And that's how you become Americanized."

"By stealing a few million dollars?"

"By buying into our system." He swerves into the left lane to pass a shiny red sports car that is inexplicably refusing to exceed the speed limit.

"And bowing before the altar of Mammon like this schmuck is doing," he says, jerking a thumb at the scarlet-enameled prize.

"You mean worshiping money."

"Yeah. Consumerism is our established religion, and if you don't buy into it, they chuck you out of the temple."

We exit the highway and play dodge-the-pedestrian on the winding streets of Jamaica so I can drop the video gear off at the office and get myself a gold star for it. When I come back to the car, Stan's double-parked, putting on a tie in the rearview mirror. He wraps the wide end around the narrow one, making four complete circuits.

"My homage to the glorious House of Windsor," he admits.

"Yeah, how many families have a knot named after them?"

The spotlights high above illuminate the silver wine cup in the priest's hand, making it glow like liquid fire as he holds the wafer above the chalice and says a prayer for the departed soul of my great Aunt Celia Espinoza.

I see all the faces, hug all the cousins. Then we get back on the highway and head east in silence. The first piece of land you encounter upon leaving Utopia is a cemetery, then a golf course, then another cemetery.

The ground is so cold and hard they had to use a backhoe to open up our mother earth. Treadmarks score her grass-and-dirt-covered arms.

"We are gathered here . . ."

The ritual rhythms of the words drone on and on, seeming to stop for a moment because there is an *amazing* sunset—unmatchable yellow-white brilliance at the center of a wash of orange splashing the trees and gilding each bare branch like in some wine commercial or movie where the second unit spent a week setting up a shot like this, but no one in the picture even notices or comments on it. Well, we sure notice it. And in a few moments, it's gone. This moment has passed, but it lives on in us.

". . . beloved mother, cherished aunt . . ."

Within seconds the sun fades to a bright yellow disk, as if God had taken a big hole punch and poked a hole through the sky to let in a bit of heavenly light and then, in another few moments, it slips below the horizon, flat as a gold-rimmed dinner plate. And the dying light strikes the ribbed clouds drifting in with a pastel rose, like a celestial washboard.

The roads are jammed, but nobody is actually getting anywhere yet. My family has come from as far as Florida and Ecuador, and I haven't seen some of them in a long time. On Christmas Eve in Cuenca, Ecuador, when we all used to live there, we'd fill a whole church by ourselves. Now our motorcade is crawling through rush-hour traffic, and I can't wait to talk to them all at my cousin Rosalie's place.

Stan reaches over and turns on the radio.

"Mi khamokha baylim, Adonai?
Mi khamokha nedar bakodesh—"

Ah, New York, where you can get Jewish liturgy on WQXR on Friday evenings, live from Temple Emanu-El in Manhattan.

"It gets dark so quickly this time of year," I observe.

"Oh? You ready to start talking again?"

"Yeah."

"Good. 'Cause I was getting tired of staring into the blackness of death all by myself here."

"Sorry. Is it that bad? Am I being that difficult?"

"You tell me. Am I going to fit in at this thing?"

"You'll be fine."

"Because let me tell you, I've been to those Italian weddings where the bridesmaids are all chewing gum, smoking, and drinking long-neck beers with the other hand. And that's during the ceremony. You should see them at the party."

"Don't worry, we stopped subjecting outsiders to the cruel bloodletting rites several years ago."

"Ki sheyshet yamim asah Adonai
Et ha'shamayim v'et ha'erets—"

"This is a nice area," I say.

"Yeah, I just love passing through a neighborhood where people are throwing out stuff that's better than what we have in our apartment."

"Uvayom hashvi'i, uvayom hashvi'i,
Shabbes vayi-nafash."

"What is this, Stan? The antidote to all those hymns?"

"Let's just say that I'm not one of those people who associates the Gregorian Chants of medieval Christianity with boundless benevolence."

"Okay, bad example."

"Yeah, let's pick another century."

I stare out the window as we crawl onto the Long Island Expressway. We're doing about ten miles an hour when our headlights sweep past a sign that says:

LITTER REMOVAL NEXT MILE

BY

CHIPPENDALE'S

Ooh, now I'm psyched. I fully expect to see an exotic dancer picking up litter in full bowtie-and-beefcake regalia.

So where the hell is he?

My cousin Rosalie's apartment on Woodside Avenue has an unobstructed view of both the LIRR tracks and the elevated Number 7 train, and it was never meant to hold this many people. The Mendez cousins on my father's side are over by the food, the little ones with their straight black mop-tops and wooden-bowl haircuts, the adults having gone to great length to thicken and tease up their "Jivaro" hair. My cousin Ruthie is here with her crew, representing the Espinozas and waiting for the night to begin.

My Aunt Estrella—Ruthie's mom and the new matriarch of my mother's side of the family—comes around offering slabs of Ecuadorian cheese laid out on a tray like tiny oblong coffin lids.

"*Cómete algo*, Mena," she insists, leading us to the food-covered table of plenty.

"*Por supuesto. Gracias, tía.*"

"What is that stuff?" Stan whispers.

"Looks like fried chicken, fried rice and fried *yuca*," I tell him. "We were trying to think of a way to fry the salad, too, but the lettuce kept dissolving."

I spot my cousin Sergio over by the guacamole, busily chatting up his sister-in-law's kid sister, Paloma, and turn to avoid eye contact with the black sheep of the family. I know it's a cliché, but what else are you going to call a guy who steals from his own sisters, including Rosalie, a divorced mom with three kids? Every family's got one, right?

"Where is Uncle Mateo?" I ask.

"They wouldn't give him a visa," says Aunt Estrella.

"Wouldn't give him a visa? He's seventy-two years old! What do they think he's going to do, take jobs away from geriatric Americans?"

"I told him to call you," she says. "I told him you know how to fix things on a computer."

"I can use one to write him a letter of support for the INS, if that's what you mean, but I couldn't hack into their files and get away with it."

"What's this world coming to?" she laments. "Pretty soon you'll be able to get pictures of people having sex on your computer!"

"Uh, you already can—"

"Yes, I ask you, what's this world coming to?" she says, shaking her head and walking away.

I follow her into the bedroom to comfort her as best I can. We sit on the polyester bedspread, and I tell her how my teenage daughter, Antonia, is doing, and that, on the subject of computers, she once knew more about PCs than I did. I still remember her tiny four-year-old hands manipulating the mouse better than I could at the time. I don't tell her how Antonia's starting to prefer Stan's Reform temple to my church just because they have cushions on the seats, or how some of the white kids try to torment her by calling her "Pocahontas."

"It's okay to cry, *tía*."

"There used to be eight of us," she says.

"I know."

"Including your mother, God rest her soul."

"Yes. She was so young . . ."

"*Todo depende de Dios*." It all depends on God.

"*Sí. Es el único.*"

Then she gets off the bed and hobbles over to the dresser, where she has set up a makeshift shrine to her sister with two candles on either side of a yellowing photo of Aunt Celia when she was a strong, handsome woman, back in the 1950s. She opens a big box of kitchen matches and takes out a thick wooden match. Fingers shaking, she strikes twice before getting a spark, then raises the sputtering flame to light the twin candles. She blows out the match, lays it aside smoking and covers her eyes with her palms. I draw near, ready to put my hands on her shoulders to steady her, when her palms fall away from her dry eyes and she turns to go, leaving the candles lit.

Stan steps aside to let her pass.

"Has she ever done that before?" he asks.

"Done what?"

"Lit a pair of candles on Friday night."

"Oh. I guess so. I haven't lived with the Espinozas since I was a kid."

"Well, it's just that that's a Jewish ritual, lighting the *shabbes* candles."

"What do you mean?"

"I mean—well, it depends. Is she doing it because it's your aunt's wake, or does she do this every Friday night?"

"I guess I remember her doing it back in the old days, now that I think of it. But she never made a big deal out of it or anything."

"Hmm."

"Hmm—what?"

"Have you ever heard of the Marranos?"

"The word sounds familiar. What about it? Give it to me straight, doctor."

"Okay." He leans against the vanity, his back to the mirror, and addresses me as if I were a group of med students. "In 1492, the same year everyone else celebrates as a year of discovery, Ferdinand and Isabella gave the Jews in Spain three choices: convert, be expelled from the country, or die. A lot of them converted and started going to Mass every Sunday, while secretly continuing to practice their religion. They were known as crypto-Jews, or Marranos. A bunch of them emigrated to South America seeking a little freedom from religious persecution—fat chance—and where, over the centuries, they forgot who they were."

"Wait a minute. You're saying I'm Jewish?"

"Well, part-Jewish, anyway. Where do you think you got that frizzy hair from? Your cousins on your dad's side all have that straight Inca hair."

"I always thought it was a bit of Black Africa in the blood, by way of the Caribbean coastline."

"That too, yeah. I've met your extended family in Guayaquil. Damn, Filomena—you embody the Diaspora all by yourself."

"Hot damn. Open the Champagne."

"But I've got to tell you, Espinoza is just Spanish for Spinoza, and as philosophers go, he was as Jewish as they come."

"Yo, Fil, Koppelman's lawyer called to say the video's not enough to demonstrate liability for his client's cancer," Chip tells me. "I need you to go back and get an air sample."

"Could be a problem with that. Most air samplers are tripod-mounted canisters that need to run for a few days, and the smaller ones are designed to indicate the presence of volatile organics, not passive cigarette smoke. Unless you want me to dress up as a cleaning woman and go in there with the sampler disguised as a vacuum cleaner—"

"We could probably sneak you onto the custodial staff at Bloomingdale's, but not a tiny shop like that." He scratches his chin. "So now what?"

"We could try tracking down some of the former employees of Czernowitz Jewelers and find out if any of them have developed similar symptoms."

He snaps his fingers and shoots his index at me: "Get right on it."

"You want me to have his lawyer subpoena the employment records?"

"Nah. That'd only put him wise to our game plan, and he'd shred the stuff before we ever saw it. We need the goods on this guy by Monday. You better head back to 47th Street and get me some answers the old-fashioned way."

"I can't. It's Saturday."

He looks at me.

"All the shops are owned by Orthodox Jews. They're closed on Saturday."

"They open Sunday?"

"Yeah, but—" I don't like where this is going.

"So do it tomorrow."

I open my mouth to protest.

"Half day," he says, walking back to his office.

Great. Working on *both* Sabbaths. If I'm really Catholic and part Jewish, then I'm sure getting the worst of both worlds here. But if Chip's going to make me log the hours, I'm going to do some investigating for myself. First I need to get some business out of the way. I make some calls trying to dig up character witnesses for a harmless old loon who was dragged in by the cops after he downed a fifth of Rumple Minze and tried to hijack the Eighth Avenue local to Cuba. In the current climate, fear of terrorism could inflate that into a federal crime, and we're trying to get it dropped to a simple case of drunk and disorderly.

Then I call Aunt Estrella, who tells me that the women in the family have been lighting candles on Friday night for as long as she can remember, but she doesn't know how the tradition got started, or anything else about it. I call the rest of my relatives on the Espinoza side, with the same results. I spend over an hour investigating my own genealogy on the Internet, trying to find out who I really am and what I'm made of, with no luck. Did I really expect to find reliable or accurate records dating back five hundred years in cyberspace?

Time to go to a *real* source.

"This explains why some kids didn't talk to me, and the dirty looks we got even in my home town. They knew something was different about us. Why didn't anybody tell me? What does it mean?"

"It means they almost succeeded in erasing your history," the rabbi answers.

Rabbi Kushner is a healthy fifty-five, with a closely trimmed beard and a few gray hairs to show his age and wisdom. He's Reform, of course.

"And it all comes down to frizzy hair?"

"This generation doesn't do it as much anymore, but the struggle for assimilation used to include nose jobs, ironing your hair, losing the accent, and changing your name from Weinstein to Winston."

"And all those cut-off parts are probably waiting for us when we get to heaven."

"I wouldn't know about that," he says, with a good-natured smile.

I look around his office at the diplomas, awards, and commemorative plaques, many in parallel text English and Hebrew, including two terra cotta tablets of the Ten Commandments hanging above his Macintosh computer.

My turn to joke: "'Thou shalt *not* kill?' Oh. Why didn't anyone tell me? Too bad you guys aren't authorized to hear confessions."

He chuckles. "Actually, I've got my own confession to make."

"What's that?"

He checks his watch, and leans forward.

"Just between us, I used to envy the Catholic sacrament of penance. The idea that by openly confessing your sins and saying a few quick penitential prayers you could walk away free and clear was very appealing to me as a young man."

"Don't Jews have a similar ritual during the High Holy Days?"

"Sure, once a year. Our Catholic brethren perform that service any day of the week."

"Redemption-on-demand: that's our specialty, all right."

"But I once heard Rabbi Fisher at Temple Isaiah give a sermon about how for Jews, the idea of sin and redemption is a lot more complicated than it is for most Christians."

"Imagine that. What a shocker."

"He said our souls are like diamonds, and sin is like a scratch on the diamond. You can't erase it and go back to a pristine state. But you can take that scratch and turn it into something else, make a pretty pattern out of it, something that isn't an obvious flaw. More of a reminder that you can redesign yourself and resolve to do better in the future. But you can never wipe the flaws in the diamond completely clean."

"You know, I really feel an affinity for that way of thinking," I say, nodding.

"Welcome to the wonderful world of moral ambiguity."

"Just one more question, Rabbi."

"Sure."

"What the heck is *Tu B'Shevat*?"

It's bright and chilly on this strange Sunday, the streets eerily quiet, and I'm out here staring at Menorah-shaped pendants, wondering if I should be wearing one—at least one day a week, anyway—instead of my cross of Ecuadorian gold. But it's time to get down to business.

I've been asking around the diamond shops, figuring that it's a small enough enclave, and that people probably have a pretty good idea who's been working for who. I walk into the ninth place so far today, ready to flash my private investigator's license and lay out the scam that I am trying to trace a distant relative about a matter regarding an inheritance—which is kind of true, in a twisted way.

But for some reason I keep being drawn to the menorah-shaped pendants.

"See something you like?" says the man behind the counter. He's young and pale, with a wispy beard and sidelocks.

"Yes, I really like the Tree of Life motif, the ones with the seven branches symbolizing the days of creation."

He examines me from head to foot. I'm not Hadassah Cardozo today.

"Yes, that is a popular one," he says tonelessly.

I lean over for a closer look at them, marveling at the undulating bark and the divinely intermingling branches. As good an image as any of God's creation. I kneel down to look at the array of golden trees on the bottom shelf. Then I see a pint-sized metal box with a tiny indicator screen behind the display. It's not a humidity meter.

"Is that a motion detector?" I ask.

"No, it's a Mo*town* detector. It can detect Motown music within a five hundred-yard radius."

It takes a second, then a giggle bubbles up my throat like a can of soda that somebody shook before opening.

"What's the matter, you didn't think I had a sense of humor?" he says.

"No. I would never think that."

His dark eyes roll up to the ceiling.

"Well, maybe a little—" I admit.

"It's just slow on Sundays. I get bored with the same old routine."

"Seriously?"

"Seriously."

"Okay. So what's with the box?"

His eyes flit from wall to wall. I've got a sudden urge to reach for the bug spray.

"Hey, you said it was a slow day. Come on, tell me."

"Well, some people say it's an urban legend," he begins. "About some gold that was stolen from a hospital upstate back in the mid-thirties, and it never turned up."

I wait a moment. "So what about it?"

"Well, some people say it did turn up, in Buffalo, mostly in high school class rings during the 1940s."

Another moment. "And?"

"And—well—the thieves didn't know. If you're not trained, you have no idea what you're dealing with."

Shorter moment. "So what were they dealing with? And don't say *well* again."

"Wel—I mean, that it wasn't an ordinary shipment of gold. It was a box of radium-tipped needles for surgical use. You know, for treating cancer."

"Did they do that back in the thirties?"

"I guess so. Anyway, the thing is that the gold is supposed to be radioactive. So some especially cautious jewelry shop owners like to keep a Geiger counter around, just in case a bit of it ever comes back to bite us."

"You mean that thing's on right now?"

"Yes, ma'am."

"Has it ever picked up anything?"

"Not on my shift."

"I see. Thanks."

"Don't mention it."

And I walk out of there, my mind aswirl.

I make some calls. By miracle, I find the right people. My friend Gina at the EPA is spending this glorious Sunday morning at home with her two toddlers. She shares some frantic working-mother moments with me, then connects me to a medical caseworker, who calls another caseworker, who hooks me up with a woman who has just survived a piece of radioactive gold jewelry.

"It's no legend," she says. "I lost two fingers on account of that ring. The tumor's going to be active on my corpse. Come on over, I'll show it to you."

"No, I've got to do something else right now."

I hear that Herodotus bemoaned the invention of iron, seeing nothing in the shimmering, molten metal but a way to make swords and arrowheads that much deadlier. As with any invention, the opportunities for charity and depravity exist side by side.

Take radium needles, for example.

Needles are supposed to inoculate you against diseases by giving you a small, ineffective dose of the nasty things so that you can build up your immunity to them. But what if you get infected with the disease of money fever? Because we've all been inoculated with various strains of that old sickness, and we all know that some people will get addicted to that golden needle and catch a *serious* case of the fever.

Lou Koppelman said it started in his mother's throat.

I head back to the crime scene and wait until Mr. Czernowitz is alone. Then I walk in and ask him,

"So how was your *Tu b'Shevat*?"

"Fine," he says. "And yours—?" He glances up at me, registers a Spanish face, starts to go back to his jewels, then his eyes meet mine.

I tell him, "You know, I just learned that means the 'Fifteenth of Shevat.' Kind of an Israeli Arbor Day—you know, thanking God for the successful regeneration of patches of desert by planting green fields and forests. You're supposed to celebrate by eating almonds and dates and other delicacies from Israel. I love the way every Jewish holiday ultimately revolves around food."

He eyes me the way a groundskeeper watches a cloudy sky.

"But you prefer to smoke," I say.

And the clouds are darkening.

"I've been smoking for fifty-one years and it hasn't killed me yet," he says, with a stale chuckle.

"No, but it sure clouded your thinking."

His eyes narrow, the lids shielding the whites.

"What are you talking about?"

"I'm talking about radioactive jewelry, Mr. Czernowitz. Specifically, the radioactive necklace that you gave to Laura Koppelman."

There's a microsecond of genuine shock, probably a defensive reflex, then the shell hardens and he says, "Get out of my store or I'll call the cops."

"Good. Then we can all go out to Cedar Grove Cemetery and dig up the corpse and hold a Geiger counter up to it. It's not going anywhere—that stuff has a half-life of sixteen hundred years. Hell, I bet we could get a reading right through six feet of clay."

"I said get out—!"

"Look, you're not fooling me, Mr. Czernowitz. I just have the nasty habit of blurting out the truth when nobody wants to hear it. I must have gotten it from my mother."

The arc of his anger fizzles and his face and shoulders collapse.

They don't always crumble this easily, believe me.

"You *knew*," I say.

Yes, he knew. And that's not the worst part.

He tells me that he owed her a huge retirement and a piece of the business. And that it was cheaper this way.

He asks me if he'll have to go to a federal prison.

I tell him, "No, that's where they send all the crooked corporate accountants. They send all the small-time dirtbags to the state pen."

It's a lonely place where greed lives, and I don't like it there. I want to go home to my daughter and my boyfriend and feel human for an hour, luxuriating in their warm touches, and convince my child not to waste her life watching television.

My job is investigating other people's screw-ups, but I suspect that I'll never learn much about my own predecessors, and what strands of DNA were knitted together to make me, or discover precisely how hatred sliced away at my people, and how we managed to dodge the blade at every turn.

As the cops take Mr. Czernowitz on the perp walk down 47th Street, I turn to walk away, and someone in the crowd asks, "Who was that? What did he do?"

What did he do? He switched gods, baby.

He became Americanized.

He betrayed his people.

And it comes to me, like a line I've heard on a million TV shows. "He was one mighty scratched diamond."

ABOUT THE AUTHORS

Kenneth Wishnia was born in Hanover, NH, to a roving band of traveling academics. He earned a B.A. from Brown University (1982) and a Ph.D. in comparative literature from SUNY Stony Brook (1996). He teaches writing, literature, and other deviant forms of thought at Suffolk Community College in Brentwood, Long Island, where he is a professor of English.

Ken's novels have been nominated for the Edgar, Anthony, and Macavity Awards, and have made Best Mystery of the Year lists at *Booklist*, *Library Journal*, the *Jewish Press*, and the *Washington Post*. His short stories have appeared in *Ellery Queen's Mystery Magazine*, *Alfred Hitchcock's Mystery Magazine*, *Murder in Vegas*, *Long Island Noir*, *Queens Noir*, *Politics Noir*, *Send My Love and a Molotov Cocktail*, and elsewhere.

His most recent novel, *The Fifth Servant*, was an Indie Notable selection, one of the "Best Jewish Books of 2010" according to the Association of Jewish Libraries, a finalist for the Sue Feder Memorial Historical Mystery Award, and winner of a Premio Letterario ADEI-WIZO, a literary prize awarded by the Associazione Donne Ebree d'Italia, the Italian branch of the Women's International Zionist Organization.

He is married to a wonderful Catholic woman from Ecuador, and they have two children who are completely insane.

For more information, go to www.kennethwishnia.com.

Alison Gaylin's debut novel, *Hide Your Eyes*, was nominated for an Edgar Award in the Best First Novel category. Her 2012 novel, *And She Was*, the first in a new series featuring private investigator Brenna Spector, was a *USA Today* bestseller and recently won the Shamus Award for Best Paperback Original.

ABOUT PM PRESS

PM Press was founded at the end of 2007 by a small collection of folks with decades of publishing, media, and organizing experience. PM Press co-conspirators have published and distributed hundreds of books, pamphlets, CDs, and DVDs. Members of PM have founded enduring book fairs, spearheaded victorious tenant organizing campaigns, and worked closely with bookstores, academic conferences, and even rock bands to deliver political and challenging ideas to all walks of life. We're old enough to know what we're doing and young enough to know what's at stake. PM Press is always on the lookout for talented and skilled volunteers, artists, activists and writers to work with. If you have a great idea for a project or can contribute in some way, please get in touch.

PM Press, PO Box 23912, Oakland, CA 94623 www.pmpress.org

FRIENDS OF PM PRESS

These are indisputably momentous times—the financial system is melting down globally and the Empire is stumbling. Now more than ever there is a vital need for radical ideas. *Friends of PM* allows you to directly help impact, amplify, and revitalize the discourse and actions of radical writers, filmmakers, and artists. It provides us with a stable foundation from which we can build upon our early successes and provides a much-needed subsidy for the materials that can't necessarily pay their own way. You can help make that happen—and receive every new title automatically delivered to your door once a month—by joining as a Friend of PM Press. And, we'll throw in a free T-shirt when you sign up.

Here are your options:

- **$30 a month** Get all books and pamphlets plus 50% discount on all webstore purchases

- **$40 a month** Get all PM Press releases (including CDs and DVDs) plus 50% discount on all webstore purchases

- **$100 a month** Superstar—Everything plus PM merchandise, free downloads, and 50% discount on all webstore purchases

For those who can't afford $30 or more a month, we're introducing **Sustainer Rates** at $15, $10 and $5. Sustainers get a free PM Press T-shirt and a 50% discount on all purchases from our website.

Your Visa or Mastercard will be billed once a month, until you tell us to stop. Or until our efforts succeed in bringing the revolution around. Or the financial meltdown of Capital makes plastic redundant. Whichever comes first.

23 Shades of Black
Kenneth Wishnia
with an introduction by Barbara D'Amato
ISBN: 978-1-60486-587-5 $17.95   300 pages

As one of the first *latinas* on the NYPD, Filomena
Buscarsela is not just a woman in a man's world, she
is a woman of color in a white man's world. And it's
hell. Mistreated and betrayed by her fellow officers,
Filomena pursues a case independently. *23 Shades
of Black* is a kick-ass novel that was nominated for the Edgar and the
Anthony Awards, and made Booklist's Best First Mysteries of the Year.

Soft Money
Kenneth Wishnia
with an introduction by Gary Phillips
ISBN: 978-1-60486-680-3 $16.95   288 pages

Even the best cops burn out. *23 Shades of Black*'s
Filomena Buscarsela returns, having traded in her
uniform for the trials of single motherhood. She may
have left the department, but when the owner of her
neighborhood *bodega* is murdered, Filomena doesn't
need much prodding from the dead man's grieving sister to step in.

The Glass Factory
Kenneth Wishnia
with an introduction by Reed Farrel Coleman
ISBN: 978-1-60486-762-6 $16.95   256 pages

Ex-NYPD cop Filomena Buscarsela—the irrepressible
urban crime fighter of *23 Shades of Black* and *Soft
Money*—is back. This time, the tough-talking, street-
smart *latina* heroine sets her sights on seemingly
idyllic suburbia, where an endless sea of green lawns
hides a toxic trail of money . . . and murder.

Send My Love and a Molotov Cocktail:
Stories of Crime, Love and Rebellion
Edited by Gary Phillips and Andrea Gibbons
ISBN: 978-1-60486-096-2 $19.95   368 pages

An incendiary mixture of genres and voices, this
collection of short stories compiles a unique set
of work that revolves around riots, revolts, and
revolution. Ideal for any fan of noir, science fiction,
and revolution and mayhem, this collection includes works from
Kenneth Wishnia, Paco Ignacio Taibo II, Cory Doctorow, Kim Stanley
Robinson, and Summer Brenner.